BLACKBLOOD

KREE SULLIVAN

*actual size

Copyright © 2025 Kree Sullivan

www.tinyghostpress.com

ISBN:
E-book 978-1-915585-23-3
Paperback 978-1-915585-24-0
Hardcover 978-1-915585-25-7

Cover Art by: Alexa Sharpe

For Dad. May the story never end.

BLACKBLOOD

The Wanderer was a small man, and to his name he had his magic and his horse.

The world for him was a vast and untold story, one he and his horse together could write. They travelled mountains and deserts and oceans, to all corners of the gods' creation. They sought out every speck of knowledge, every inch of dirt, and they were never satisfied.

But their lives were infinite and their world of sand and rock too small. After many centuries of travel, the Wanderer and his horse found there was nothing left to discover. They rested upon the all-too-familiar ground and wondered what came next. What was the point of a wanderer who had seen all there was to see and met all there were to meet?

As the Wanderer stared into the blood-black sky, he asked his horse, "What do you think is up there?"

She lifted her nose to the heavens and replied, "The gods, I suppose."

"You're the fastest horse in the world. Do you think you could reach them?"

She tossed her mane and snorted. "Of course."

The Wanderer laughed as he climbed upon her back. "What's left but to try? I want to see more."

They cantered across the sweeping sands—fast, fast, faster.

"What if we can never come back?" the horse asked.

"I cannot wait to find out."

—Excerpt from a Y'ashtrian fable, *"The Mare and the Wanderer"*.

1

ARMINA

The Rabbit's Day festivities haven't wound down an inch despite the fact it's hotter than a cook pan under the desert sun. Noisy children rush past where Valaina and I parked the semi half up on the curb, and I jam a finger in the ear not pressed against the pay phone's receiver so I can hear the voice on the other end.

"I ain't entering Wallton for shit," the man says. He has a squawk like an old fox, the kind that got half its voice box ripped out in a game of chicken with a coyote. "The artifact's not worth the traffic."

I flip my messy ponytail over my shoulder and scowl despite the fact that the man can't see it. I hope he feels it as I respond, "So you'd rather *us* brave the traffic and drive . . . where, exactly? Last I checked, the *Blackblood* was doing you a favor."

"I'm less than fifty miles from the city, outside the Wrendrop Community. There's a rest station with a tavern called The Skeletal Mare. Can't miss it—'s got a horse skull dangling out front."

I run a hand over my face, wiping away my irritation along with the noontime sweat. "Fine. Today, evening, Skeletal Mare outside of Wrendrop."

The man hangs up without a goodbye.

As I return the phone to its cradle, something warm slaps into my free hand. A greasy square of waxed paper full of twisted cinnamon bread heats my palm almost unbearably, and I wince as molten sugar drips onto the base of my thumb.

Valaina stands above me, her own hunk of bread hanging out her mouth, her sunglasses shielding her brown eyes from the sun. She looks pretty today, with her sugar-stained mouth and the wind tugging at her curly black hair. If the sight of her didn't make me want to start a fight for no reason, I might even feel inclined to kiss her. Rabbit's Day is for romance, after all, and we used to be—

"Any luck?" She leans against our semitruck's scrubbed-metal side. *My* truck. The *Blackblood.*

Averard's truck.

"Depends on what you define as luck." I rip a chunk out of the bread. It hurts my teeth how sweet it is, but I haven't eaten since yesterday morning, so any food's a welcome comfort. "Do we have an offer? Yes. Do I know if it's of any merit?" I shrug and crumple the waxed paper between my fingers. "The man seemed ready enough to be rid of his artifact, so I think we'll get a good price."

Valaina raises her eyebrows and tilts her head so I can see her eyes beneath her sunglasses. Can't say I blame her for any skepticism. The pair of us've been an awful mess since Averard died. He was the captain of our little three-man brigade, our "pirate ship without an ocean", as he'd call it. When he went and got himself murdered, he left us with nothing more than the truck, a battered pistol, and an old black coat. Valaina kept the pistol, and I kept the coat, and neither of us talk about how we picked them off his corpse before we ran.

Keepsakes of a dead man are not instructions, and they're certainly not a business plan. They won't put food in our stomachs or keep the Huntsmen away. Smuggling magical artifacts is dangerous enough if you know what you're doing, but despite me turning nineteen at the beginning of this year and Valaina being two years older, Averard always insisted we were too young to help him yet with the more particular aspects of the job. Val and I know the trade; we know how to sell. But acquisitions? Not under our purview.

I tug open the *Blackblood's* door, reaching high up its frame to pull myself inside. Valaina watches me struggle before stepping around the truck's low-bellied trailer and throwing open the passenger-side door. She hops inside and wipes her sticky hands on her pants, then lifts her long legs and tucks them between the dashboard and the windshield. "Guess your seller's not meeting us in Wallton," she says.

I snort in response and start the engine. It rumbles to life beneath us—not anything that'd be mistaken for a purr like some of those fancy new flatbeds, or even the hum of a family's personal car. The *Blackblood* sounds like a call to adventure. Like the rush of power through veins.

"I get it, to be honest," Valaina continues as I ease off the curb with a faint *thu-thump*. Families scatter as the *Blackblood* mounts the street. "Don't know how anyone can stand to live this close to the Tidal Wall."

I peer out my side mirrors at the object in question. I wouldn't say that Wallton's built *close* to the Wall, but the black stone expanse rises hazy like a mountain across the whole horizon. It's a barricade of sorts, one that divides our Arachnida Federation from the country of Tempestor. Far as I know, it was erected not twenty years back, when the Huntsmen attempted a hostile takeover of Tempestor. When their coup failed, Tempestor built that wall to keep the rest of us out.

The Huntsmen trying to take Tempestor was peak foolishness, even though it must've made sense to their blood-addled minds. Tempestor's a country of mages. Run by 'em. Can't imagine any Huntsman'd stand to see such a place exist unopposed.

The Arachnida Federation doesn't have anything like a central government—too many little towns with too much space between them, connected by nothing but sand and sky—so the Huntsmen Order's the closest thing we've got to an authority. Ostensibly, they uphold any laws agreed upon between settlements and keep the desert roads safe. But the truth is, the Huntsmen exist primarily to hunt what few free mages are left.

Your average person tends to get shot if they approach too close to the Tidal Wall. Huntsmen tend to disappear without more than a bloodstain on the desert sand.

Val and I came out to Wallton after Averard died, hoping it might prove a good place to lie low a while, take stock of what artifacts we've got in the trailer, and figure out a gameplan to keep business moving. But we can't stay here forever. There's too big a risk of getting comfortable.

I cleave my attention to the road, trying not to get stray kids or dogs stuck under my front wheels. Red and pink streamers twist from the telephone wires above, and the *clickity-clack* of rabbit skulls sounds from strings on every brightly colored food stall. I stop for a parade of pedestrians tied together with a golden streamer around their waists, but as I rest my hand on my chin, my eyes meet those of a man across the crowd.

Black eyes. Pitch black.

He watches me with bored disdain, and I try not to sink in my seat. Huntsmen aren't supposed to show their faces all the way out in Wallton. Have they forgotten how to fear the Tidal Wall? Or are they preparing for something?

Valaina doesn't notice him. Instead, she rummages in the space between her seat and her door, extracting a beat-up, dog-eared romance novel. She draws Averard's pistol from her belt and deposits it on the seat between us, a more solid barrier than the Tidal Wall ever was. Been a month since Averard died, and near as long since Valaina and I've talked about anything other than business. I'm trying to navigate what it means to be captain of an enterprise I was never taught to lead, what it means to have lost the only parental figure I've ever known. I don't have time to figure out what it means to be someone's ex-girlfriend.

"Huntsmen must be bored." I nod toward the man as he slips past our window. "Not enough free mages left for them to hunt."

Valaina returns to her book with little more than a glance at the Huntsman. Her shoulders shift as she tugs her long-sleeve shirt a little closer at the throat. "Dunno," she says. "Still plenty out there."

We overcome the pedestrian traffic and drive through the city's gates into the desert proper. The sun reflects off my truck's hood and makes the world shine, and a breeze scatters sand across my windshield. But even as I concentrate on the long drive ahead of us, an unease rises in my chest.

I've known Valaina more than half my life, and I've known her different than everyone else. She's not empathetic or gentle, and she has an angry streak wider than the Federation itself. I've heard her called a liar and a snake, and I've seen her act like both, but she's always willing to speak her truths if you know how to listen.

Still plenty out there, she says, but I hear what she really means.

Still too many for me.

2

ARMINA

The old man on the phone was right about one thing: The Skeletal Mare's not easy to miss. A sign creaks above the tavern's ramshackle porch—an ancient horse skull, its rictus grin beaming out at the desert's yellow sands. The name's faded to the point of being almost illegible, painted on the bone in dripping ink.

The Skeletal Mare's a death goddess from some ancient Y'ashtrian religion, although I don't think anyone in the southern country still practices it. The Mare's a lot like the Scarred Rabbit in that regard, even though the Rabbit has its own namesake holiday celebrated even this far north. Averard's told me all the stories, so I know the whole pantheon—from the Crooked Viper, the trickster god, to the Fleetfoot Deer, the goddess of seasons. They've all got their own constellations, and Averard made sure Val and I could pick out each and every one in the freckled sky.

The Skeletal Mare and her rider, the Wanderer, supposedly ferry souls to the afterlife, but in all likelihood, that's lullaby bullshit. Still, it brought me a bit of comfort in the days after Averard died, thinking the Mare and the Wanderer carried him far, far away. Over the stars.

After I park the truck, I slide out the door and stretch until all my joints pop. Valaina hops out her side and crosses in front of the grille. She tucks her hands into her jeans pockets, her mirrored sunglasses reflecting the tavern's creaky sign. I nudge her shoulder, and she tilts her chin, not quite ignoring me but barely acknowledging my presence.

"Can you refuel while I go talk to this guy?" I ask, jutting my thumb toward the single run-down gas pump.

Val makes a noncommittal grunt, but she strides toward the pump without being asked again.

I set my sights on that porch and try to force my soul to occupy a bit of the space Averard's left behind.

I tried to look my best today, despite general road weariness making it seem like I've never met a hairbrush or an ironing board. My ponytail is the neatest it's ever been, and I even shined my boots as best I could despite their permanent scuffs. I've got my own revolver at my hip and Averard's black coat on my shoulders. It doesn't fit, of course, since Averard was a good seven or so inches taller. It may not be a coat to grow into, and sure, it's still got some of his blood on the collar, but it helps me keep my head high. I need that today.

An old man sits on the tavern's porch, elbows resting on a rickety table. His scrubby yellow beard looks dirty in the overhang's half shade, as do his broad-brimmed hat and shabby clothes. He keeps his gaze pinned to the tankard in his hand.

I walk up and slam my foot on the porch boards, which makes the old man huff. "You Baker?"

He swirls his drink and takes a long sip. The shadows on his face from his hat and the overhang make it difficult to pinpoint his expression, but the turn of his mouth makes me think it's somewhere between bored and disdainful.

I step fully onto the boards and get closer. I know people like him—cheaters and cads, all thinking they can pull one over on me 'cause they're older or bigger. I watched Averard at this game plenty growing up. Sometimes it's about who does the better job keeping their cool.

"Cut the bullshit," I say. "If you don't want my help, I'm happy to get back in my truck and move along."

He places his tankard down and tugs the brim of his hat lower, like a card player afraid to give away his hand. He tosses one arm carelessly over the back of his chair. "Listen here, miss—"

"Captain."

"Miss Captain. You can talk all you want about me needing you more than you need me, but if that were the case, you'd've given up whatever artifact I possess as a loss a long while ago." He reaches into his pocket and withdraws something, clenches it between his filthy fingers.

It's a sphere. Matte black and perfectly smooth. He drops it onto the table's wooden surface, where it wobbles and pitches before coming to a rest. It doesn't gleam or sparkle under the sun—instead, it absorbs all that light like a hole punched directly into the daytime.

Well, it's certainly magic. Don't get that color on much else.

"What's it do?" I ask.

"Great question." Baker tilts the table with his foot, and the sphere rolls in a slow, perfect curve. It reaches the edge, hesitates, and then dips over, plummeting toward the ground.

I lurch forward, hand out to catch it, but before it touches the floor planks, the sphere flickers, disappears, and reappears stock-still at the center of the table.

"It does that," Baker says.

My fingers itch. Averard would've loved this thing, would've loved examining it and tinkering with it, figuring out how the magic works. Magic, as far as I know, is all about the intent of the caster, so the sphere can only do what the mage enchanted it to do. What purpose could a teleporting ball have? I'd love to fiddle with it too.

I swallow the notion and rock back on my heels, which makes the porch squeak. Interesting as it is, if all this sphere does is teleport itself from one place to another, it's of little use to the *Blackblood*. "Neat trick. Does it do anything else?"

Baker grunts and rolls the ball back toward his palm. "Viper's veins, I've no damn idea. It's magic, and I'm not looking to get on the Order's bad side by tampering with the wrong thing. That's why I called you." He holds out the orb to me. "You're the expert in getting rid of this stuff. Are you gonna buy it or not, smuggler?"

I hesitate. Can't imagine there's a ton of buyers for a self-teleporting orb. But it's a fascinating bit of magic, and knowing Averard would've loved it, knowing that I need to do something to kickstart myself in carrying on his legacy, makes the choice easier.

"Fine," I say, extending my hand to pick up the sphere. "But it'll be a hard sell for me, so I can't offer more than thirteen—"

Baker snatches my wrist. He drops the sphere, which teleports itself onto the table, rolls off, and teleports back again.

He stands, his grip inhumanly strong. His hat tips back, and for the first time, his eyes bore into mine. In his free hand, he's produced a sword from near enough nowhere, the blade of which is as black as his eyes.

Black as the blood of the mages they hunt. Black as the blood they drink.

I've never seen a Huntsman this close before. Across busy streets, sure, or lurking in dusty shadows and roaming the scattered settlements like wolf packs. Averard never let us stray too near, said some things even a smuggler ought not to get involved with.

"I'm meant to arrest you"—Baker's grip tightens, and he draws me close enough that I smell his teeth—"for trafficking in restricted magical goods and paraphernalia. But seeing as

I've got more important things to deal with right now than a novice artifact smuggler, I'll have to take a different approach." His blade lifts, and the edge catches between the lapel of Averard's coat and the skin of my throat. "I'll tell the Huntsmaster you put up a fight."

That's the funny thing, really. Averard taught me next to nothing about finding buyers and sellers, but he sure did teach me how to put up a fight.

I whip out the revolver at my hip, place it against Baker's chest, and fire a shot. A second. The bullets sink into the meat of him, and he bleeds red.

A normal person would've been obliterated by point-blank shots like that. They would've at least been knocked on their ass, unconscious and bleeding out, until someone took pity or mercy on them. But Huntsmen drink mage blood, and drinking mage blood makes everything *more*. Doubles human strength and speed. Sharpens all five senses. Drink as much blood as the Huntsmen do and you become near enough magic yourself.

The bullets only jolt him, but it's enough to make him release my wrist. He runs his hand over the divots in his chest as if shocked he's capable of bleeding. I take full advantage of this momentary respite to turn tail and run.

The truck is far. It's too damn far, and Valaina's nowhere in sight. I hear the Huntsman's pounding footsteps on the dirt behind me, and I push myself to run faster. My leg quakes in protest of the extra strain.

The truck grows from a hazy smudge into its beautiful boxy form. Its trailer gleams under the harsh sun, and as I scream Valaina's name, she appears around the grille. Her attention slides to the Huntsman at my back, and she jumps about a foot in the air before throwing open the driver's door and hauling herself inside.

My hands hit the truck's rusted paint as Valaina starts the engine. I scramble through the open door and slam it shut, then crowd Valaina out of my way and into the passenger seat. My door rattles as the Huntsman throws himself against it. Valaina squawks when the Huntsman's sword pommel crashes against my window. It crashes again and this time breaks through with a spray of glass and blood. I duck to avoid the rain of shards and dodge the pommel slamming toward my face as I yank the gear shift and stomp on the accelerator.

"Shit," Valaina declares, which really does sum up the situation.

Our truck picks up speed. The Huntsman's fist and pommel jab at my face while his other hand grips the window frame. His boots clunk and scrabble against the door.

Valaina pushes up in her seat and clambers across me. I strain to see the road over her back as she grabs the pommel, pulls Averard's pistol off her belt, points it through the busted window, and unloads her clip at the Huntsman. His grip on his sword breaks by the third shot, and I hear him scrape down the side of the truck and hit the ground. The truck gives a satisfying *thump*. Then the Huntsman's behind us.

Valaina returns to her seat, black-bladed sword now clutched in her fist.

This wasn't supposed to happen. This was supposed to be easy. We've spent the last month lying low, and in a single stupid half hour, I've managed to make all our care and caution moot.

Valaina settles down after replacing her clip with the spares we keep under the seat. Her arms remain taut and tense, and she taps Averard's pistol on her knee, thumb on the hammer and index finger tight against the trigger guard. She doesn't calm as evening passes into night, as oncoming traffic dissipates and only the *Blackblood's* headlights remain to illuminate the road.

There're no settlements in this direction—nothing around for miles, in fact, but dunes and asphalt and stars. Constellations blur through the windshield, and among them, it's easy to spot the real Skeletal Mare. A dozen stars outline her body and the Wanderer astride it as together they canter across the cosmos.

My hands keep to the wheel and my feet the gas pedal for another few hours. Valaina continues to thumb her pistol's hammer, glaring a hole into the dash all the while.

I clear my throat to break the silence, and she releases her torrent.

"Brother's Blood, Armina!" she snaps, and it takes all my well-honed strength of character not to bash my head on the steering wheel. "Not a month in charge and the Huntsmen're up our ass! Always knew Averard coddled you, but I didn't expect—"

Instead of driving us head-first into the nearest dune, I pull onto the shoulder as calmly as possible and round on Valaina.

Even with her expression twisted by snarling disappointment, I miss her. I miss her laugh; I miss her conversation. Miss the way her hand would twine in mine at the end of a long drive. I kissed her smile a thousand times in better days, and if her stubborn, pig-headed self-absorption didn't make me want to chew her eyes out, I'd kiss it a thousand more.

"Are you listening to me?" she demands.

I tilt my head against the headrest and close my eyes. I can't look at her anymore.

"What happened back there?"

"Seems our Mr. Baker is a Huntsman."

Valaina makes a noise like a hissing snake. "That'd imply that the Huntsmen are still after us."

I open my eyes and stare out the windshield into the desert. Slowly, I shake my head. "Impossible. It was probably just—"

"How are you staying so calm? A run-in with the Huntsmen after everything? Coincidences like that don't happen! Fuck!" She shoves back into her seat and runs a hand through her hair. "This is all Averard's fault."

My nails dig into the upholstery beneath me. "How could any of this be his fault?"

He didn't let us interact with Huntsmen; he kept us on the move; he tugged on my hand as a child whenever I got too close. The Huntsmen don't bother the *Blackblood*. They don't know we exist. I try not to remember the blood; I try not to remember the knife—

"What, do you think we went to the Tidal Wall for fun?" Valaina asks. "You think I suggested hiding in Wallton because the food in the city's real good?"

"Averard was too careful to—"

"Averard's *dead*."

I want to kick her from the cab and drive my truck until it falls off the end of the world, until the Skeletal Mare and the Wanderer carry *me* over the horizon. Everything's still as fresh as an open sore. It's still festering.

Valaina's voice lowers, and one of her hands finds mine. Her fingers squeeze. "We haven't had much time to grieve, but Averard's gone. It's time we really think about whether this life's the right one for us without him."

I tug my hand from hers. "Of course it's right for us. The *Blackblood* is a smuggler's truck; it doesn't know how to do anything else. We're Averard's crew, and this is his truck, and—"

"It's not his anymore, Armina!" Valaina leans toward me in her seat, her hands in the air in front of her like she plans to grab and shake me. "The *Blackblood* is yours. It's ours. I won't see you throw our lives away over the sensibilities of a dead man!"

It's too much. It's been too much for weeks, but this time, I can't even find the words to argue about it. I grab the sword Valaina stole from the Huntsman and kick open my door.

"I'm putting this in storage," I snarl before swinging into the night. I slam the door shut, cutting off Valaina's protests.

The stars glitter down, and I allow myself to get lost in their glare. My first memories are of Averard pointing toward them, holding my small hand in his large one as he listed the celestial bodies and told me their secrets. *That's the Crooked Viper—he ripped the magic from half of mankind to hoard for himself. That's the Resplendent Fox—she gave her enchanted flute to the one human lucky enough to catch her. Those are the Twins—the Brother and Sister who created the world and everything in it.* Even now, I can recount the tales as easily as I can count the stars.

When the pinpricks of light begin to blur and my thoughts to muddle, I give up on my search of the heavens and haul myself inside the *Blackblood's* trailer. It's darker than pitch in here, and I fumble for the flashlight hooked somewhere on the wall. Once found, I flick it on, and its dusty beam illuminates the silhouettes of our artifacts.

Averard, Valaina, and I always slept outside unless the nights got too cold, in which case Averard would wrap us kids in blankets and send us to find an open spot in the trailer to sleep while he took the cab. Valaina and I never minded—I was already halfway in love with her the moment she joined us, and she was accustomed to far less comfortable conditions. We'd make space between the hills of furniture and crates and fall asleep surrounded by the strange hum of magic.

Magic's got a tangible presence: it weighs down the room and bites up the sinuses. It's a bit like the pressure before a sneeze, gathering at the corners of your eyes. Still, I'd rather sleep here tonight than in the cab with Val. I'd camp out under the sky, but something tells me it's safer to be inside and out of sight. Besides, I've got to find a home for this sword.

I've heard Averard call them mageblades, though we've never had one onboard. And with good reason—only Huntsmen can legally wield them, and if we were caught with one, we'd be way worse off than a smuggling charge. I don't even know what they do, really. It's definitely enchanted, judging from the color of the blade, but there are a lot of possibilities in an enchanted sword.

I push through a dozen blackened tapestries toward the back of the truck. Valaina keeps a better mental inventory than I do, but there must be somewhere I can hide this thing. I push aside a bag full of black gloves that only let themselves be removed at certain temperatures and a telescope that homes in on the creator's favorite stars. As I shimmy past a wardrobe that contains a portal to a sheer cliff face, my boot lands in something slick.

I point my flashlight at the ground.

A dark liquid splatter shines on the floor. A second. A third. I follow the glistening trail, wondering if one of our oil cans sprang a leak, or if there are mice messing with some liquid artifact I'm not aware we have. The beam of my light catches on a blanket pile, each fold of which is stained with the same inky liquid.

Then I notice the spill of pale limbs.

A person lies splayed beneath the topmost blanket, lips parted. Their eyes flick behind thin lids. Their choppy dark hair curls about their face, a few pieces crushed beneath their cheek.

But what stands out most to me are the black veins that crawl up their throat, stark against the paleness of their skin.

That and the black blood they're dripping onto the truck's aluminum floor.

3

CANTO

I'm dreaming of my mother again. Before she was taken, and before my arrest.

We're lying in our bed as we did when I was a child. Her hands run through my hair, combing the day's bad memories away, while she tells stories about her grandfather. He was free, she says. The magistrate of a whole city, a city of mages. Her voice grows hushed as she describes the buildings—towers of black glass and stone, grown with magic and built to suit our needs, our pleasures. Cradled and protected by walls as high as those of the Community, but we could leave whenever we wanted. The world was ours to explore.

She speaks like she's seen such buildings with her own eyes, though the Huntsmen make sure we know that mages have been confined to the Communities for centuries, long before her grandfather was born. But I love my mother's stories—that pretty myth of freedom.

A myth soon shattered by the banging of Huntsmen fists on our door.

A light shines in my face.

I stir, shying away from the light as I shake away the last wisps of the dream. I must have slept through the morning alarm. Last time I was stupid enough to do that, I ended up with finger-shaped bruises on my arm that didn't fade for weeks. It isn't an experience I'd like to repeat, but still, I curl into a tighter ball around my blanket to delay the inevitable. When the light persists, I swat at it.

"I'm awake," I grumble.

I expect the Huntsman to rip me out of bed for my defiant swipe, but instead, I hear a manic bark of laughter. My eyes shoot open.

The truck—the ugly, rusty disaster I climbed aboard earlier, hoping to escape certain death. Blood still slicks my hands from where I cut them, staining the blankets beneath me. I sit bolt upright as the memories return.

I was being escorted to Perishing—the Huntsmen headquarters and last stop for all mages who've invited their wrath. They put me in the car with Huntsman Baker, a pathetic excuse for a human being, and told him to make the drive miserable. Not a difficult challenge for a person like him who's prone to grumbling all the lovely ways he wishes he could tear a mage apart.

At Perishing, I'm sure, he would've had his wish. That was where they took my mother weeks ago, and she hadn't even broken any of their nebulous rules and regulations. They dragged her away from me in the middle of the night, all vicious smiles and dark laughter. Telling me to behave, or they'd take me to Perishing to share her fate.

Somehow, despite all logic and reason, I know she's still alive. If anyone could survive being a captive in that place, it's her. But I don't have her fortitude or sense of self-preservation. If they'd taken me there, I would have struggled and fussed and made myself such a nuisance that I wouldn't have survived a day.

I had to escape. In their custody, I probably would have died before I even saw Perishing's black spires. On my own, maybe I can make a plan to save her.

Now, beneath me, the truck is still as death. I study the woman blinding me with her flashlight, looking for evidence of her rank within the Huntsmen. She's shorter than me, although part of how small she looks may be blamed on her coat, which is easily three sizes too big. Her skin is sun-reddened and freckly, and her brown hair hangs at the back of her head in a frizzy tail.

In the hand not pointing the flashlight, she clutches a mageblade.

I lunge toward a rack of ratty cloth, magic pooling in the tips of my fingers. This may be a truck full of garbage, but it's an enchanter's dream. Anything here could be made into a weapon with the right intent.

Before my hand touches a single thing, the woman hisses, "Don't move."

The blade in her grip glints black, and my limbs still. Maybe escaping while Baker was distracted and boarding this truck was the wrong move. If I've somehow wandered from the custody of one Huntsman to another, it won't even my odds for survival if I indiscriminately attack. I'm surprised she hasn't grabbed me yet, muted my magic and slit my—

She lifts her flashlight higher, and the beam reveals the soft brown color of her eyes.

"I said don't move," she repeats.

Magic tingles in my palms, and her eyes flick around the trailer, and her grip on the mageblade tightens, and . . . oh. She's *afraid*.

No one has ever feared me before, not even on that night after Mother was taken, when I snuck into the Huntsmen's barracks. They laughed as they grabbed me and knocked the makeshift knife from my hands. As they dragged me to the bloodletting room.

I worry about the bubble of joy threatening to burst within me in the face of her fear.

The woman retreats a step, and the back of her thighs hit a crate behind her. She winces.

"I'm not going to hurt you," I say. Brown eyes mean she's not a Huntsman and therefore not a threat. I settle back onto the pile of blankets.

She watches me in the intense beam of her flashlight before throwing it down onto the crate. She tosses the mageblade aside in favor of placing a hand on the gun at her hip.

I'm so used to Huntsmen treating their blades like extensions of their arms that when she throws it, my body jerks as if to catch it. I know how much blood is used to forge one. Perhaps she doesn't.

"Those are very expensive," I say.

The woman fixes me with a glare sharper than any blade. Her thumbnail picks at her leather holster. "I know how valuable they are."

"I didn't mean how much money they're worth." I glance around the room, my eyes landing on the piles of objects. "You have quite a collection."

"How'd you get on my truck?" she demands.

"The trailer wasn't locked. I slid it open and walked inside."

"Are you the reason that Huntsman attacked me?" Her coat slips down her shoulder, and she pulls it up without dropping my gaze. "Did he think I was smuggling you, or—"

"I haven't been here long. The Huntsmen are after you, too?" Maybe this truck isn't as safe as I hoped.

"I guess so!" She tosses her hands in the air and starts pacing. "Brother's Blood, could this night get any worse?"

This is my first time meeting someone who isn't a Huntsman or a mage. She has a slight unevenness to her gait, and as she mumbles to herself, I marvel at her accent. All the mages I know speak in a clear, direct tone, each word a deliberate choice for fear of the Huntsmen misunderstanding. Those same Huntsmen just growl. This woman speaks so quickly that she's blurring half her words into a curdled mess.

"Why're *you* running?" she asks, snapping me back to attention. Her hand returns to her gun. "Did you organize a mage rebellion? Destroy a Community? Slaughter Huntsmen in their sleep?"

My breath catches. I remember the knife in my hands and the thrill in my gut, the pleasure of Huntsman throats yielding beneath my fury. My fingers tighten on the blankets beneath me.

Her pacing stops. "You've got to be joking."

I don't answer. I can't. Any sane person would turn their truck around and deliver me straight to the nearest Community.

We keep things in cages for a reason, after all.

"Are you listening?" The woman crosses the space between us and grabs my shoulder.

I snatch her wrist. She yanks back, but my grip tightens until my own fingers ache. I scramble on my blankets, press myself against the wall and the shadows until I could melt into them. Only then do I shove her away with enough force that she stumbles.

Apart from my mother, no one has ever gotten that close unless they intended me harm. And since I no longer live in a Community, no one will ever harm me again.

She grasps her wrist. Her brown eyes study my face, and her shoulders slump. "Let's start over, all right? I'm Armina."

I ease off the wall. Introductions I can handle. Whenever a new Huntsman arrives at Wrendrop, we stand in a line and introduce ourselves. They don't remember our names, but they like the ceremony of it. "Canto."

"Welcome to the *Blackblood*, Canto. I'm this truck's captain." Her hand falls away from her gun at last. "We're in the magical artifacts trade, but we don't smuggle mages. I'm sorry, but you can't stay here."

It's a kinder admission than I'd expected—she's at least a good enough liar to sound apologetic. But if I cannot stay on the truck, then what can I do? I'm accustomed to regimented sleep, regimented exercise, regimented *piss breaks*. What am I supposed to do with a vast, empty future?

I fumble my fingers into my boot and withdraw the only thing I was able to spirit away from the Community: a pendant, or part of one—the clasp broke a long time ago, before my mother gave it to me. The metal is black as blood now, and the spines of it branch out like veins. At its center is a gem that may have once been precious but is now as tarnished with magic as the rest.

The pendant is layered over with centuries of enchantments, each so melded into it that one has become indistinguishable from the next. My mother said it belonged to her grandfather, and his grandmother, and hers, going back further than memory. Before the knife and the barracks and the blood, I enchanted it to conceal itself from the Huntsmen—one more layer over the top.

Now, faced with open uncertainty, I hold it to my chest as I did before escaping Baker and boarding the truck. The ancient magic washes over me in crests and valleys, a comforting ebb and flow from the past. I close my eyes and squeeze my hand until the metal bites my palm again, until the afternoon's scabs peel open and more black blood flows out.

Armina grunts and sits on the floor, one leg folded against her chest and the other stretched out straight. In the brightness of the flashlight, I see her rub her knuckles on her thigh. "I don't feel right dumping you in the middle of nowhere," she says.

"The nearest settlement's too far to make the trip on foot. I can take you someplace, but I need a destination."

I've never needed to know the names of cities outside Wrendrop's walls. I've read some things about oceans and mountains and forests in books, the pictures worn through by years of mages running wistful fingers over them. My knowledge of the settled world could fit into a single volume, tattered at the binding and falling apart.

But as I sit in the shadows cast by thousands of enchanted objects, as the pendant pricks my palm and the magic and desires of the mages who cast it bolster me, I know where I want to go.

"I have to find my mother," I say. The Huntsmen don't have me anymore; they don't know where I am. They can't keep their black eyes on me, their swords at my throat and my blood on their teeth. I'll get her back. I have to.

"Where is she?"

I glare down at my hands and pry my palm open, wincing as the metal edges of the pendant pull from my flesh. It's an even darker black than it was before and slick now with blood.

I don't know if Armina's a friend, but I watched her toss that mageblade aside.

"They took her to their headquarters," I say. "To Perishing."

4

ARMINA

Perishing.

Everyone knows the onyx city built into the mountains way out west. Its matte-black spires stand tall enough to see from miles and miles away, the Order's answer to the Tidal Wall. It's where the Huntsmaster lives. It's where good Huntsmen retire and bad mages die.

I mean, that's the reputation. It's not a place us normal folk go, not even to pass through. The *Blackblood* obviously can't sell there, and Averard's always steered clear of it. Best to keep your truck out of the shadow of Perishing, he'd say. Nothing up there for a smuggler anyway.

At the mere mention of the place, I wish I could put Canto out in the sand. I wish I could just, I don't know, turn off morality for a minute and think about the health of the *Blackblood*.

Valaina would do it. I could ask her to. She'd take one look at this mage and—after she'd stopped laughing at the insanity of the situation—kick them off without a single thought.

But I've got too much Averard in me.

"We don't smuggle mages," he used to say, crouching to my level to grip my shoulders and meet my eye. "It's too dangerous, and we can't afford to attract any attention." But I knew him. He would've sworn up a storm, torn half his hair out, and then asked Canto how he could help.

Still, I'm trying to get *away* from the Huntsmen; driving the truck up to their stronghold's front gate would be no better than putting a bullet between my eyes. I don't want to end up like Averard.

Canto sits on their blanket pile, their long fingers tucked between their knees. Their blood all over my floor.

They look like death. Their eyes—a pretty color, almost gold—focus solidly on the ground. When they ask me to take them to Perishing, they're not asking me to save them—they're asking me to drive us to our graves. For what? If that's where their mother was taken, chances are, she's dead by now.

That thought makes me remember lifeless blue eyes and rich red blood splattered everywhere. A black-bladed knife in the throat. A person's memory dwindled down to the coat they used to wear and the pistol they once carried.

Canto's mother might still be alive. It's not their fault my captain isn't.

"Right. Okay. Well, I've a lot to think on, so let me leave you to rest. I'll be back in a bit to get you some food, and maybe some towels to clean up all that." I gesture to the blood.

Canto glances down at their hands as if noticing the mess for the first time. They swallow.

"You're not going to take me to Perishing, are you?" they ask.

I pick up the mageblade and shove it through my belt. "No. I'm not."

Canto's black veins stand out in the harsh glow of the flashlight like a roadmap on their skin. Their gray-tinged lips tighten.

I leave them in the truck and to their thoughts and close the hatch behind me.

I don't know what my next step is. If Canto had wandered aboard my truck at any other time, I'd have driven them out to the Tidal Wall and dropped them there. Maybe a mage could find a safe way across to Tempestor. We can't turn back now, though. Baker knows we came from Wallton, and if he thinks we somehow have his mage, that's probably the first place he'd look. Which means we have to go somewhere else. Which means, regardless of my intentions, I'm putting the *Blackblood* at risk. Valaina's life. My own.

I pull Averard's coat closer and try to absorb some of the knowledge I wish he'd left behind.

The night he died, we were driving along the Y'ashtrian border to the south, through the Vulpesh Forest. Valaina slept in the passenger seat, and I sat between her and Averard as he kept the wheel steady. The shadows of the trees bent around us, but between the veins of their branches, I could still see all those stars. Averard told me story after story in his low, gravelly voice, still full of childlike wonder.

At some point, we parked, ate around a hastily built campfire. Averard always said there were too many places to hide in the woods for his liking, so we doused our light quickly and said our good nights. Averard told us to sleep in the cab because he wanted to stay up a bit longer. When I offered him company, he shooed me away with a smile.

I woke in the middle of the night to the usual sounds—creatures shuffling in the brush, the truck pinging and settling around us, chirping insects. But something in the air made me sit up straight. A feeling, like the pop of static. Valaina slept in the seat beside me, her legs tucked to her chest, her breathing soft and even. I slid quietly out of the cab so as not to wake her.

The stars above flamed and glittered, but none as brightly as the Crooked Viper's tail.

And when I stepped around the trailer and found Averard's body, I knew we needed to run.

Feels like I've been running ever since. My legs are always stiff, but this is a new kind of tension. Whenever I stop moving long enough to breathe, I end up crying. And since I'm sick of crying, I don't stop moving anymore.

Valaina hasn't left the cab tonight—I see her curled-up silhouette through my shattered window. I climb inside, and she startles from her doze. Her hand flies to Averard's pistol, and when she sees it's only me, her shoulders don't relax; if anything, they stiffen. Her eyes flick to the mageblade I'm still carrying.

"I thought you were storing that," she says.

I pull it out of my belt. Truth is, I didn't want to leave it with Canto. Not sure whether to protect them or the sword, but I sensed it was, overall, a bad idea. The metal's warm in my grip, and unnaturally heavy in a way that makes my stomach sour.

I slide it under the seat so I don't need to look at it anymore. "Decided it was better to keep it where we can see it."

Valaina doesn't respond.

I fold my hands in my lap and take a deep breath.

"I've been thinking," I say, even as my brain tries to slam on the brakes before it's too late, "about what you said earlier."

Her eyes narrow, as if she senses she isn't about to get her way. "Go on."

"I don't want to give up on this business."

Valaina's cheeks go pink, and she opens her mouth to retort.

"Let me finish," I snap. "I love our job more than anything, and so did Averard. This life"—I gesture toward the dunes, the open sky, the whorls of sand blotting out the faded asphalt—"is all I've ever known."

I grew up on the *Blackblood,* playing with the steering wheel while Averard guided my hands. I wasn't born here, and I don't know who my parents are, but Averard brought me aboard and made me family. A decade and change later, he brought on

Valaina. It's always been the three of us and the truck and the desert.

"If you want out of this business," I continue, "I get it. I can't keep you."

Valaina's hands grip the seat's old upholstery. "Of course I don't want to leave you or the *Blackblood*. I just never thought . . . I didn't expect the Huntsmen to come for us. I assumed they wanted Averard dead and then we'd be left alone."

It's the first time either of us have stated it so plainly: that the Huntsmen killed Averard. We've thought it, and we've danced around it, but both of us know. The black knife we found in his throat couldn't've been anything but a Huntsman weapon. The color was too deep. Too perfect.

Now that Valaina's laid it bare, I still don't know if I'm ready to say it. But as I sit there and digest what we're facing, an idea crawls into my mind. A small spark of hope.

"Let's go to Crotalus City."

Crotalus is the biggest settlement in the whole Federation, clear across the country from Wallton. Its huge population means lots of trade, lots of people to hide among, and far less Huntsman authority despite its proximity to Perishing. It also has—

"Are we going to see Georgian?" Valaina sits up straighter in her seat.

Georgian was one of Averard's best customers, and probably the closest thing Val and I have to family outside the truck. She's the greatest hub of connections in the whole of Arachnida; she has uncountable threads tied around her fingers. If anyone can point us in the right direction, it's Georgian, and even if she can't, at least she's a comfortable shoulder to cry on.

"We're going to see Georgian," I confirm.

Valaina pulls her legs up to her chest and rests her chin on them. "Okay . . . okay. I guess Crotalus is a good place to start if we really want to make this work."

Whether it works or not, I have too much to do to dwell on it. Right now, I've got to start plotting our course and start working out what I want to say to Georgian. I need to get food and more comfortable blankets to Canto without Valaina noticing.

Valaina can't find out about Canto.

"You take the cab tonight." I kick my door open and slide out. "I'm gonna be up late thinking a whole bunch, and I don't want to wake you."

She nods to me without meeting my eyes and lies down across the seats.

I shut the door with a very final *thump*.

Above me, painted against the endless darkness, I see the curving pattern of the Viper's back. Its gleaming tail points ever westward.

Somewhere in that direction is Perishing—all the onyx spires of it. Maybe there are answers there. Maybe someone's mother. I hope the road never leads either me or Canto to find out.

5

ARMINA

The sky's finally tinging pink at the edges now that the longest night of my life's over. After my chat with Valaina, I went into the trailer and showed Canto the icebox where we keep our food. They seemed out of their depth looking at our meager selection, so I picked them a bag of snowy pears to start. They'd never seen them before, and I spent a good half hour peeling away the prickly green skin to reveal the white fruit. Canto accepted it with curiosity and not a small amount of hesitation, but it was worth the few spines I got stuck in my fingers to see their expression when they bit down for the first time.

I left them to rest and spent the night pacing in the sand at the side of the road. Whenever headlights flashed in the darkness, I dove into my trench, terrified of being seen by the wrong people. But far as I could tell, nothing came looking for us.

Now, I told Valaina we'd go to Crotalus City, but it's clear across the Federation. The longer I keep Canto aboard the *Blackblood*, the more likely Valaina is to find out about them. She's suspicious by nature—she'll only be convinced to stay in the cab for so long once she sniffs out my lies. We just need to make it to Crotalus. Just need to make it to Georgian.

The whip crack of the cab's door opening shakes me out of my thoughts, and Valaina slides onto the road. She stretches her arms high above her head, and I note that at some point, she took her long-sleeve shirt off and tied it around her waist, leaving her in only her undershirt. The sun catches on her dark skin, making the impossibly black scars running from her palms to her collar stand out stark.

She turns her head and catches me watching. Her arms lower.

"Morning," she says. She unties her shirt and pulls it back over her head. "Did you sleep at all?"

"No." I wrap Averard's coat tighter around my chest. There's still some of that nighttime cold clinging to everything, but it won't last much longer. "Did you?"

She lifts a hand to wave me over. She pulls a rolled-up piece of paper out of her back pocket and smooths it over the truck's hood.

"Spent most of the night figuring out what route we should take to Crotalus." She places her hand along the southern Vulpesh forest to cover the roads winding through. "Thought you might want to avoid the Y'ashtrian border. I know the drive would be shorter, but given what happened with Averard . . ." She pauses, then shakes her head. "That aside, I've a feeling the Huntsmen've beefed up their presence there if they've got their sights set on a smuggling operation as small as ours."

Her finger trails instead along the crescent curve of the Ashern mountains, a range that cuts the desert in half. "I figure we should pass through the Asherns. A more difficult route for a truck this size, and I doubt the Huntsmen'd think us bold enough to take it." She flips her map over and shows off a long list written in red pen. "I've got the route all planned out here. I think on day three, we should make a slightly longer stop in Hive. We need to replenish our food supplies, and I want to withdraw some money in case the Huntsmen try to get access to our account." She rerolls her map and sighs. "Bit of a roundabout path, and it'll turn a two-day drive into a five-day one, but I think the caution's worth it."

"It's a good plan," I say, my mind already drifting from the map to Canto. "Once we get to Crotalus, Georgian'll be able to point us in the right direction, or at least help us lay low."

"We could always flee to Y'ashtria," Valaina says with a yawn. "Or smuggle ourselves across the Wall to Tempestor."

I lean my cheek against the *Blackblood's* warm hood. "You'd hate that," I say.

Valaina rubs her arms, then turns and opens the truck's door. "I really would. Now, I'm going to nap a bit longer, and I recommend you do, too. Much as I relish the thrill of driving on no sleep, it'll be better if we don't rip the transmission out traveling through the Asherns."

Once Valaina disappears, I turn back toward the trailer's hatch. When I throw it open, morning light pours through, but our magic-blackened artifacts absorb it, making the truck resemble a dark alley.

The moment I jump inside and ease the hatch closed, I hear Canto slither out from wherever they're hiding. I fumble for the flashlight, but before I find it, a light flares on. Canto appears in the center of the trailer, holding a shadeless lamp. Despite the blackened bulb and complete lack of electricity, the room shines with an eerie gray light.

"Good morning." Canto's golden eyes peel me apart.

"Morning." I shove my hands into the pockets of Averard's coat. "Sleep well?"

"Better than expected." They lead me to their blanket nest where I see they've squirreled away a container of baked oat squares, the kind that Averard used to love and that Valaina and I haven't been able to convince ourselves to eat again. Canto's black veins stand out even in the low light as they pull out a square and crunch. "I've been awake for a few hours now. Usually, we're woken by the Community's alarm, but I guess my body can keep time without the sound."

I take a seat on a crate that contains magicked books, most of which have been with us for some time. They're incredibly valuable to the right collectors, but it can take a while to find a buyer. Enchanted books're dangerous because you don't know what they'll do until you read them.

Canto lowers themself onto the ground. "When do you need me to leave?"

I frown, momentarily confused before I realize that I never actually gave them any of the information that was churning through my skull. "Not for a few days yet. I'm gonna drive you out to Crotalus City."

I wait for their reaction, but it doesn't come.

"You know," I continue. "Biggest city in the Federation? Few hundred thousand people live there?"

Canto shakes their head. "I'm afraid I don't know much about your cities." They pause, fingers crumbling an oat square. "Is it close to Perishing?"

In Canto's face, behind their thinned lips and black veins, I see a strange mix of hunger and terror.

"Canto," I begin, surprised at how well my voice takes on Averard's "stern-warning" tone, "I know you said they have your mother there, but it wouldn't sit right with me if I let you waltz up to the Huntsmen's headquarters. Croatlus's a much safer place for you."

Canto's golden eyes follow the movement of my mouth like they're trying to decipher a foreign language. "I'm going to get my mother out of Perishing." They fold their hands around their knees, long fingers crisscrossed. "Now that I'm not under Huntsmen supervision, it should be easier. If I leave her there, she'll die."

"What do you plan to do, walk right in and pluck her out of their prisons?" I shake my head. "Whatever reason they took her must've been important to the Huntsmen. Interrupt their dealings and you'll get yourself dead, too."

Canto turns their eyes away from mine. "Maybe."

"Listen." I shift on the crate and tap my knuckles against my thigh. "I can't take you to Perishing, but I *can* set you up with one of the *Blackblood's* contacts. Her name's Georgian, and she's . . . equipped to handle someone like you."

"What does that mean?"

"She has mage friends. Free ones."

I thought Canto might gasp. Show some kind of delight or surprise. But instead, they stare back at me, their face unchanged.

"There are no free mages," they say.

My palms are sweating. In the dull light of the enchanted lamp, dust motes float between us. "I don't know the particulars. I've never met any mages, but we do a lot of trade with her, and there's no way she could keep her stock without a mage helping."

"What does she sell?"

I weigh my answer. "Medical supplies."

"Why would you need mages for medical supplies? You're not taking me to some sort of black market to harvest my blood, are you?" Canto's lips quirk as if they've said something funny instead of something profoundly horrifying.

"Of course not." I slide off my box and sit across from them on the floor. It's about as close as I dare get after last night, and still they lean away. "I know we're not going to be together long, but I'd like if you could trust me."

Canto blinks, their eyelashes brushing their cheek a moment too long. "That's asking a lot."

I push off my box and stand. "I'm afraid I can't give you much more than my word. But on my honor as captain of the *Blackblood*, I won't let the Huntsmen near you while you're under my protection. You're one of us for now, and we don't take threats to our own kindly. Now, feel free to help yourself to anything in here you might need. Once we're on the road, it'll be difficult for me to come see you."

"Is it just us on the truck?"

I hadn't expected that question, and I fail to hide my grimace. Canto's eyes study the expression, and I feel them forming a conclusion about it. "No, I've got another crewmate, but she's . . . not the biggest fan of mages. Best if we keep you a secret for now."

It feels stupid to say that—cruel, almost. Even though I know what Val's been through, none of that's Canto's fault.

Canto nods as if this makes all the sense in the world.

I turn to leave. Something about our interaction makes me uncomfortable in ways I can't describe. Whether that's the aura mages give off or something in my own self, I don't have time to dwell on it right now.

As I approach the hatch, however, Canto clears their throat. They stand, and their hands settle on the edge of the crate I'd been perched on a moment ago.

"Would you mind if I read some of these?" They pull out a book, its thick black cover interrupted only by embossed lettering that might've once been gold but is now oil-slick green.

I tuck my hands into my pockets and lean against the closed hatch. "It isn't that I'd mind so much as I don't know what those enchantments do. I'd worry that you'd read it and set the truck on fire or launch us into space."

Canto's impassive face breaks into a smile. Just a small one, but it's enough to light them up like the sun.

"No need to worry." They crack the book open and flip through a few pages. "Enchanting an object is limited by its original purpose. For example, you can enchant shoes that make you run faster, but not ones that will cook you dinner.

Same thing with books. They can only be enchanted to tell their stories." They run their fingers down the paper, and as they do, a trail of poppies crops up in their wake, crowding one another in their effort to grow off the pages. "Don't get me wrong: a mage *could* enchant a book to be very dangerous. But I'll try my best to avoid those."

I must be gawking at them because they close the book with a *snap* and tuck it against their chest. Petals flutter to the floor. "My mother taught me that."

I shake my head to clear the cobwebs. "Feel free to read whatever you'd like. In fact, if I bring you some paper, would you be willing to inventory them for me? We were always worried they'd explode; might find more buyers if we know what they do."

Canto's eyes flick away, and the blood rushing to their cheeks tinges them gray. "Of course."

6

RENN

Books and dust muffle all sound in the library. Today, the only thing that interrupts the perpetual quiet is paper shuffling as I dig a stack out of the intake box and flip through it. Before Pierce became Huntsmaster, I'd have a few files a day to sort through. Now, however, I'm lucky if I have time to eat lunch around the piles of paperwork.

The archive—the little scoop of Perishing I carved out for myself—waits for me to sit down and get to work. Court records won't alphabetize themselves, and duty rosters won't magically come into existence, and if I don't do it, no one will. But it's all right. I have the memory for this kind of work, the required focus. At least, that's what my father said when he named me the Huntsmen Order's head archivist.

Another thing from before Pierce became Huntsmaster.

I shove out the chair at my preferred table and flick on the lamp. Today's intake is lighter than usual: only a single exsanguination, a handful of new recruits, and a request from a Community in the south for a few more Huntsmen. I order them into neat piles, making my own notes in the margins.

The last piece I come to is a manilla file folder. I flip it open, expecting another potential recruit, but instead, the only thing inside is a sheet of paper with a handwritten paragraph and a single photo. An intake form. We usually receive a few of these a week, and my job is to register the mage in question and assign them a house in Perishing's attached Community. Then

I hand that file to the appropriate person, and they get the mage settled in their new home.

But this intake form has barely any information. The mage's picture is there, sure, as well as her name. She stares up at me out of brown eyes, her mouth twisted into a surprisingly genial smile. But the attached paragraph only mentions that she's being transferred from her Community and that she's highly dangerous.

Then I notice, scrawled in a tidy handwriting I recognize as Headmaster Pierce's, a note that mentions the mage has been detained in isolation.

Well, that's one less thing for me to do, I guess.

A sharp rap on my desk startles me. Iva Iverson, Pierce's second in command, stands there with her arms crossed. Her short curls stick out everywhere, and there's a flush to her brown, freckled cheeks. She's trying to control her breathing, but the tremor in her shoulders gives her away.

"Do you know how long it took me to find you?" she demands.

Longer than it should have. "I'm always here, sir."

"Pierce told me you'd be in the library. I didn't even know we *had* a library."

I stand and set my paperwork aside. "I suppose he wishes to see me now?"

Iverson scowls up at me. "I didn't run through every damn hall in Perishing because he wants to see you tomorrow." She points a sharp finger toward the door. "I swear, Mason, I'm going to ask Pierce to put a bell around your neck. You're always hiding somewhere."

Iverson's the type you need to watch out for. I may be head and shoulders taller than her, but she's unparalleled with a sword. That's probably why Pierce picked her as his second, although I'd wager it's also because she's well liked around the barracks. Huntsmen flock to power and confidence, and Iverson's got that in spades. She'd kill you with a grin, I think, before you could even ask her why.

I ease around her and exit the disrupted sanctuary of the library. She follows along behind.

"I don't need an escort," I say.

"You think I'm going to leave you alone so you can go off and find a new hole to hide in? I'm taking you to Pierce's office myself."

It's not like I can deny an order from the Huntsmaster, and I definitely won't get lost even without her trailing me around. I grew up in Perishing; it was mine. The onyx halls were my only playmate, but I couldn't imagine a better one. The Huntsmen in Perishing are organized, and the work is linear, but the building is far less so. It's an unending maze of rooms and staircases, a dozen floors waiting to be mapped out. You could spend years exploring it and every day discover something new.

I used to run through Perishing's halls as a child to hear the echo my shoes made on the obsidian flooring. Walking through them now, I hear noises coming from the other side of the walls: the laughing, the howling, and the screaming. Beside me, Iverson tilts her head, a smile on her lips as if enjoying her favorite song.

"Why do you wall yourself up in that stuffy room, anyway?" she asks. "Don't you ever want to do rotations with the rest of us? Play with the mages a bit?"

Her eyes follow a pair of Huntsmen prodding a mage in the direction of the Community. The mage has a thin trail of blood dripping from the crook of his arm.

The sight draws a grimace to my face. One of the reasons I'm glad to be head archivist is that I don't have to work with mages. They're far too intense for my liking. "Communities exist for the mages to lead productive, safe lives. We shouldn't interfere with those lives more than necessary."

Iverson's eyes find mine, and the corner of her mouth curls. "I haven't heard that kind of sentiment in a while. You really are like your father."

I decide to take it as a compliment.

When my father was Huntsmaster—before Pierce, before everything—he instilled within me the Order's virtues, each lesson taught with careful precision whenever he could make time in his busy schedule. The Order was founded on the belief that every being has the right to a life of safety and prosperity. Normal humans should be free to go about their days without the threat of dangerous magic. Mages should have lives of structure so they do not give in to their more violent tendencies. Huntsmen exist to preserve that careful balance.

I thought I would be Huntsmaster myself when the time came. I was the youngest recruit ever to drink the blood; I remember the way my father's eyes shone as he handed me the vial the moment they'd finished drawing it from the mage. It was so hot it burned my throat raw.

The eyes don't go full black until you've consumed several liters, but it's been long enough now that I can't remember the exact color mine used to be.

The door to the Huntsmaster's office looms in front of us. I knock, then step away and fold my hands behind my back. I must look less presentable than I should. My short blond hair is a mess, and I'm wearing the shirt I slept in. I've had dark circles under my eyes for weeks that no amount of sleep seems to cure.

If Pierce hasn't seen fit to exsanguinate me by now, a rumpled shirt likely won't send him over the edge.

I hear him bid me enter, and Iverson pushes the door open. She smirks at me, eyebrow raised. "Good luck with all that sentiment, Mason," she says as I step inside. She doesn't follow when the door swings closed behind me.

The Huntsmaster's office was once a familiar, comforting place. Visiting my father here was always a treat: he'd let me play under his desk and read his books, steal candy from the dish he hid in the bottommost drawer of his file cabinet. Pierce doesn't even keep a file cabinet—one of the first things he did upon taking over was move it into the library.

My father used to keep plants on the overflowing bookshelves. He had a lounging couch in one corner and a Federation map on the wall stuck with pins for all the places he'd visited. The map is the only thing that remains of my father's decor. Even the pins are gone.

Pierce sits behind his polished desk, hands folded atop its cleared center. My father's desk never had a square inch of space, but Pierce keeps things neat. His salt-and-pepper hair is shaved close, his tanned skin blemish-free, with only fine lines at the corners of his eyes and mouth to show his progression past middle age. His nails are cut so exactly I assume he must use a ruler, and his clothes look as if they've never known a wrinkle. His eyes are, of course, the blackest pitch.

Sitting before him, in a rickety chair someone must have dragged in because it certainly doesn't belong in this empty room, is Huntsman Baker. Baker is an older Huntsman stationed at a Community to the east—closest to the Tidal Wall, so it's not what I'd call anyone's favorite assignment. He's been sniffing after retirement for months now—which I know because I've had to file each of his requests—and he was finally approved for placement in Perishing not a week ago.

He's covered in dirt and blood, and his leg twists in a way that is probably irreparable. No clue what happened, but I suppose he has to make his report before he can visit the medic.

I tear my eyes away from him and stand at attention. "You asked to see me, sir?"

"Renn Mason. I take it you know Baker?" Pierce asks.

"By reputation."

"I suspect you'll get to know him far better soon. His most recent fuckup is going to generate a mountain of paperwork to rival Perishing in scope."

Baker sinks lower in his chair, and his face contorts with pain. Huntsmen do not whimper or beg, but his gritted teeth make it look like he's close.

"What did you do?" I ask.

He snarls at me, his cracked teeth bared and flecked with black and red blood.

Pierce clears his throat. "In truth, I called you here so we might avoid all the unnecessary work Baker has foisted upon us. I'm hoping we can put your skills to the test in a more . . . practical way."

Oh no. I don't really *do* practical.

"How much do you know about the illegal artifacts trade?" Pierce asks.

"The basics," I respond. "Smugglers getting ahold of artifacts and selling them off to independent buyers or taking them south through the Vulpesh Forest to trade across the Y'ashtrian border. My only direct contact with that sort of thing is dealing with the paperwork after we make arrests—detailing what artifacts we confiscated and keeping records of their distribution or destruction, as the case may be."

Pierce stands and strides away from his desk, toward my father's map. His walk is strong and purposeful; the Huntsmaster has no room for doubt. "We've been tracking a group of smugglers." He jabs at the map on a point in the Vulpesh Forest. He trails his finger upward, past the crescent curve of the Ashern Mountains and into the desert. "They've been in operation for decades, but we lost their trail some years ago. The previous Huntsmaster refused to see how great a threat they pose, but since I've taken command, we've found them once more."

My father did tend to take a more lenient stance in terms of what non-magical society could do with artifacts. If people want to ruin their lives by buying magic, he reasoned, the Huntsmen will be there to scrape up the pieces when it goes awry.

"We've already disposed of their former captain, so I need you to track down whoever remains and arrest them," Pierce continues. "We must take a stand, as a new administration, against any who so openly flout the Order's authority. We must keep the people safe."

So dawns the era of Huntsmaster Pierce.

"I agree with you on that account, sir, but I'm not sure I'm the best man for this." There are plenty who would lick the Huntsmaster's shoes for this opportunity, but I already have a job: making sure the legacy my father built doesn't crumble. I'm too busy—and, frankly, too important—to run across the continent looking for smugglers.

"I think the youngest Huntsman to ever drink the blood— the second in command to the previous Huntsmaster—is more than capable of capturing a few criminals," Pierce says.

"Of course I'm capable, but certainly, there are other Huntsmen who have more time to dedicate to doing this properly. In fact, I can go through the roster for you and make suggestions of—"

"I'll be blunt. After the incident with Huntsmaster Mason, the others whisper about your loyalties. Some call for your blood. Would you have me risk the ire of your fellow Huntsmen over one man's life?"

"No, sir, but—"

"A show of loyalty from you might build some goodwill."

I'm surprised the Huntsmen haven't already demanded my execution considering the severity of my father's alleged crimes. I'm unsure that arresting a single artifacts dealer will absolve my sin of being born to the wrong person, but the Huntsmaster has been generous enough to let me live. If I'm quick about his task, maybe my paperwork won't grow too out of control.

"What are the details?" I ask.

Pierce gestures to Baker. "Report."

Baker grunts and pushes himself higher in his chair. His twisted foot scrapes the ground and leaves a thin trail of blood. "I set up a meeting with the new captain at a rest stop a half-day's drive from the Wrendrop Community. Thought I'd nip them right up, but I was caught by surprise." He gestures to a red stain on his chest, which I hadn't even noticed juxtaposed with his mangled leg.

Huntsmen can sustain more damage than your average person, but less than some might think. I'm not fully convinced Baker isn't subsisting on pure spite at this point.

"And the leg?" I ask.

His scowl deepens. "None of your damned business, magefucker."

I won't rip his throat out; I won't rip his throat out; I won't—

"So," Pierce interjects, "you'll pick up where Baker left off. Arrest the captain and bring her here. I'd like this done soon." Pierce returns to his desk and folds his hands on its top once more.

"How should I find these smugglers?" I ask.

Pierce reaches into the front pocket of his jacket. He withdraws a glass vial and places it on the desk with a soft *tap*. The red-brown liquid inside shifts sluggishly.

"There was one saving grace in this disaster," Pierce says. "The new captain managed to confiscate Baker's mageblade."

Baker no longer meets our eyes, glaring instead at the floor tile.

I pick the vial up off the table, and my stomach churns.

A mageblade isn't just a weapon—of course not. A revolver is more efficient than a blade, and a Huntsman's base strength and endurance means we can kill with our bare hands if necessary. A mageblade is a precious symbol of our commitment to the cause, our identities as Huntsmen.

It's also a potent tracking device.

"Last time Baker saw them, they were a few hours' drive from Wallton." Pierce watches my fingers clutching the vial. "We can assume they're heading west to avoid retracing their steps. Drink that and it will lead you directly to them."

"Yes, sir. I'll collect my things and—"

"Drink it now."

At this point, Baker does glance in my direction. His scowl is permanently plastered to his face, and it somehow becomes uglier as I uncork the vial.

Trying to hold back a shudder of revulsion, I close my eyes and tilt Baker's blood into my mouth. It tastes like rotting copper, cold and starting to coagulate. Not nearly as nice as mage blood.

After a few moments, an incessant tug stirs in the pit of my stomach, faint now but certain to grow stronger as I get closer to the blade the blood is resonating with. It should lead me within a mile of my target, and from there, I can handle the rest.

I set the empty vial back on Pierce's desk. The red residue at the bottom reminds me how long it's been since I've had any mage blood.

"You'll leave immediately." Pierce swipes the vial off his desk and tucks it back into his pocket. "Before you do, head to the bloodletting room. Give a vial in case we need to track you, too."

I try not to grimace as I nod.

"Very well. Dismissed."

Before I turn to go, Baker shifts in his chair and clears his throat. "Aren't you going to tell him about the mage?"

Huntsmen know how to be still—instinct, maybe, a predator skill inherited through the blood. So when I say Pierce goes stiller than a corpse, I really do mean every muscle in his body freezes taut.

"Mage?" I ask.

Pierce breathes out through his nose in one long huff. "Baker was also transporting a criminal from Wrendrop to Perishing for exsanguination. Seems he allowed his charge to slip his grasp."

I think I may vomit up my heart, it's beating so fast. A lost mage. An escaped criminal. "You want me to get them back?"

Pierce shakes his head. Light from his desk lamp glints across the flat black surface of his eyes. "No. I want you to kill them."

7

ARMINA

The rumble of the *Blackblood's* engine keeps me focused as the road disappears beneath us. We drive through the day and well into the night, stopping only to swap places or to eat. I feel massively guilty that I can't bring Canto any of the hot food Valaina and I make, but when I check on them after we've pulled off the road to sleep, I find them surrounded by books and snowy pear peels.

When Valaina's not driving, she alternates between dozing, going over the map loudly to herself, and reading me excerpts from her latest paperback. I don't ever respond, but Valaina likes an audience, not a consultation. When I drive, I get lost in the sameness of the landscape. Dunes rise and fall like breaths, and sweeping serpents of sand drift across the road.

I worry. I worry about Canto stuck in the back of the truck, about what will happen to them once we part ways in Crotalus. I worry about the *Blackblood*, about what's waiting for us at the end of the long drive. Even when I doze off at night, I dream of black eyes and snarling human faces and a spectral horse carrying Averard away, away.

By the afternoon of our second day, we've settled into a rhythm. Having a goal makes things so much easier to navigate, and Valaina and I haven't argued once since the driving started. She's curled up like a cat against her door, watching the sand roll by where it's beginning to turn into rough rock. The Ashern mountain pass grows tall up ahead, and our road has narrowed considerably. We haven't seen another vehicle all day, and the soothing quiet makes our surroundings somehow more beautiful. The wind howls through my still-empty window, bringing with it distant smells: water, dirt, pine. A bird wheels overhead, a black blot on the otherwise pristine sky.

When I hear the roar of another engine, it takes me a moment to react.

"Fuck is that?" Valaina mumbles. She tilts her head to gaze into the truck's side-view mirror. "Uh, Mina?"

"Mmm?"

"A motorcyclist's behind us. He's tailgating pretty close."

There's a loud, shrieking wail of metal grinding metal. Valaina screams, which makes me jerk the wheel, causing the truck to list dangerously toward the rocky walls that rise around us. I glare at her from the corner of my eye, but she's kneeling in her seat and rolling down her window.

"Shit!" she hollers, arms and torso half outside, the wind turning her head into a tornado of dark curls.

"What's happening?" I demand.

Valaina turns to me, eyes wide and lips parted. "The crazy bastard jumped from his bike onto the *Blackblood*. He's climbing the hatch like a fucking squirrel."

My first thought is of Canto, hiding in the deep dark trailer among the artifacts. I don't need to spare a second thought for what kind of man could launch himself from a motorcycle at speed.

"Take the wheel," I say.

"What?" Valaina draws back inside the cab.

"I said take the damn wheel!"

To her credit, she doesn't question me again. Her hands fall on the wheel as mine leave it to grip the open window.

"You've got to be joking!" she shouts, but I barely hear her over the wind and the pulse pounding in my ears. As I ease off the gas and pull myself out the window, Valaina slides into my spot. Our pace continues uninterrupted.

The exit is awkward. My legs aren't that strong, and I have to shimmy out to maintain my grip on the window frame. We aren't driving at breakneck speed, but it's fast enough that the wind makes my eyes water.

Once I'm fully through the window, clutching the frame for dear life, I look back into the cab. Valaina stares at me, her hands tight on the wheel.

"Eyes on the road!" I shout. "I need you driving your best because I'm about to knock that bastard into the dirt."

I don't wait for her response. I steady my knees on either side of the window and clamber onto the top of the cab.

The marker lights twist under my weight as I use them to pull myself up. Once I'm on the roof, I let my sleeves cover my hands and cling to one of the exhaust pipes. Even through the leather of Averard's coat, the heat from the pipe is scorching.

The man's still scaling the *Blackblood's* trailer, and the moment he clears the roof, any shred of hope that he isn't a Huntsman dies. He crouches to maintain balance, but otherwise, his body remains steady. He's enormous, clearing six feet by a mile, and his eyes are so black I can see them a full truck away.

They don't look like eyes, really—they look like holes. If you stare too long, you might fall in and drown.

He shouts something at me that the wind swallows. I pull my revolver out of my belt and fire a shot, but it goes too wide. I try again, but the truck bucks beneath me, and I stumble and cling to the exhaust pipe.

I shove my revolver back into its holster. That's not gonna work.

There's a gap between the cab and trailer, but it's small enough that I'm able to maneuver over it on my hands and knees. Once across, I glance up, only to realize the Huntsman's not three feet away. Even crouched, he towers over me, and I realize there's no way I'm knocking him off this truck. Not unless I take him with me.

"You must be the captain." He's close enough now that I make out his words. "If you could tell your driver to stop, we can get this over with. Less paperwork if you come without a fight."

I launch myself at him.

I get the slim satisfaction of seeing surprise filter over his face before I hit him—all right, it isn't so much a hit as a collision as the truck's momentum throws me forward. I'd hoped he'd lose his balance, but instead, I find myself clinging to him for dear life, my arms wrapped around his chest as my feet slip on the roof.

"I . . . hmm," he says as I try to knock him over. It's like trying to topple the *Blackblood* with my bare hands. "This isn't quite how I expected this would go."

He reaches behind his back with one arm, grabs the collar of Averard's coat, and pulls me over his shoulder. I slam against the roof of the trailer, and suddenly, his considerable weight is on me.

I punch him, but I swear, it hurts my fist more than it does his face.

"You're under arrest," he says. "I'll be taking you back to Perishing for trial—after I search your truck. We've got ourselves a missing mage." He leans in, his nose an inch from mine. I can't escape those eyes anymore. "Only, the Huntsmaster didn't tell me it was you."

"I'm not a mage!" I snarl, shoving his shoulders. There's a sinking sensation in my gut, terror pulling me down. Tears from a mix of fury and frustration spill from the corners of my eyes. What would Averard do? Does it even matter now?

Then I realize that the sinking sensation isn't in my gut—I'm literally sinking into the roof of the truck.

The Huntsman makes a noise in his throat when he notices the black liquid pooling around his wrists and sucking him downward. "How are you doing this?" he demands.

I'm about to tell him to fuck off, but I'm already up to my mouth in the goo, and I'm trying not to inhale whatever the roof has become. My body dangles into the truck below, then all at once, both the Huntsman and I crash through.

He lands on my leg. It crumples beneath his weight.

Canto stands on a crate, their hand pressed to the roof. They jump down and drag me away from the Huntsman before he regains his bearings. They clutch a book to their chest.

The Huntsman shakes his head like a dog flicking away water. He rises to his feet, but Canto clears their throat.

"Stay back," they snap and lift the book higher.

The Huntsman's black gaze follows the lines of Canto's veins from the tips of their fingers to their golden eyes.

"The Huntsmaster didn't say anything about two mages," he spits.

8

CANTO

The Wrendrop Community had a library: two worn bookshelves shoved under the overhang of the main office. We were permitted to borrow books during daytime hours provided we had completed our assigned work. Over the last eighteen years, I've read every book on that shelf cover to cover a dozen times each.

It would take another eighteen years to read all the books on Armina's truck.

There are geography books, cookbooks, novels. Children's picture books, how-to books, books overflowing with art. I didn't know there were this many subjects in the world, this many things to learn or see or do. I hardly slept last night after finding a book about continents on the other side of the world, when I realized how impossibly big an ocean dividing one place from another could be.

Being alone among all these books may well turn me spoiled.

When I hear pounding on the truck's roof, hear Armina's noises of anger and pain, I tuck the book I'd been perusing closer to my chest, as if I can protect it from what's coming. I know what's up there. It's inescapable, and I've been waiting for it.

So I climb the crate. I place my hand on the roof.

They fall into the truck and thud to the ground in a tangle. Armina gasps, a sound more like shock than pain, but when she doesn't spring up, I drag her toward me, put myself between her and the monster.

She grabs her leg. I didn't even know a leg could twist like that.

The book's paper tears in my shaking hands as I fumble it open. Little poems and pretty pictures pass across my vision as I try to find something useful. I haven't had enough time to read much of this book; what if there's nothing useful in it? What if I—

The Huntsman lunges. His hand wraps around my upper arm, and I almost drop the book as my fingertips numb. My skin tingles like when you fall asleep in an awkward position only to wake up in pain. The Huntsman forces my magic deep inside my chest—too deep to access.

"That's it." The Huntsman's voice hums. I am trapped beneath that black-eyed stare, my boots pinned to the ground. "Be a good mage and set the book down."

My arms lower. My blood will make them stronger. My mother will die.

A gunshot strips the air clean, so close that my ears ring with its report. A curl of smoke twines from the end of the gun Armina holds aloft. The bullet has torn through the truck's wall, leaving a blackened puncture. Wind whistles through it like a scream.

She missed the Huntsman, but I am awake now.

Huntsmen can stop a mage from doing magic, but they can't do anything about an object that's already enchanted. The book's power tugs at my fingers, and I meet the Huntsman's eyes with my own glare. His brow furrows as his power shoves harder at my magic, but it's too late. I begin to read.

"Sleep now, my baby, need never fear. I will protect you; I am right here."

The Huntsman's grip tightens, but doubt seeps into his blackened stare.

"I'll never leave you, so please be strong."

The Huntsman gathers himself enough to grasp the book with his free hand, his fingers crumpling the page. But the words remain in glittering black ink. He hasn't destroyed them enough to stop me.

"Rest for me, darling, till comes the dawn."

He crashes to the floor. His grip breaks, and my magic floods back.

Armina swears. I whip around to see her clinging to one of the storage crates, all her weight on her right leg. The knee of the left twists inward, and her ankle crumples somewhere in the vicinity of her thigh.

I become aware that I'm staring when she says, "You all right?"

I blink. "What?"

"Are you okay?" She sits on the crate, and her eyes land on my sweaty, trembling hands still clutching the book in a death grip. "That must've been scary."

I laugh. I can't help it. It was scary, it *was*, but—

"Are *you* okay?" I ask. "Your *leg*."

The question seems to catch her off guard. She scowls down at her limb, then tightens her fingers around her ankle and, with a crunch, wrenches it more or less in the correct direction. Then she lifts the hem of her trousers.

She doesn't have a leg.

Or rather, she has one, but it isn't a flesh-and-bone leg: it's an intricate weave of mangled pitch-black metal. Some of the fibers in it have been severed and are poking out at odd angles.

"Lost it as a baby, and before you ask, I don't remember how. As for this thing . . ." She knocks her knuckles against her prosthesis. "Remember Georgian, the medical supplier I mentioned? She makes them. Been going to her ever since I was a kid. Grow a few inches? Get a new leg."

My eyes slide across her knee. "How far up does it go?"

In the silence that ensues, I realize I've asked something rude.

As I'm contemplating what it will be like traveling to Crotalus on foot, Armina laughs.

"Mid-thigh." She taps her leg at what I assume is the spot. She lowers her cuff and leans her elbows on her knees. "More important: how long've we got before our new friend wakes up?"

The Huntsman whimpers in his sleep. His lips part, and his hair flutters as he breathes. He looks soft and gentle like this. I almost retch.

"Dawn, if I had to guess?"

"Fifteen hours then, round about. That gives us time to figure out what to do with him."

I place my boot on his shoulder to kick him over, but he's heavy, and I barely make him shift. I tilt his chin with my toe instead. "Got a knife?"

"You're not slitting his throat in the middle of my truck."

"We could leave him on the side of the road."

"He'll come after us again."

"We can slit his throat after leaving him on the side of the road."

Armina tosses her hair over her shoulder, her leg still hanging crooked above the floor. "He was sent here for a reason. We set him free? He'll return to the Order and track us down again. We kill him, and they find the body? I don't think *that'll* help lessen whatever sentence they have cooked up for us back at Perishing."

I lower my foot from his face. "I know what sentence they have planned. For *both* of us. Do you think exsanguinations are reserved for mages?"

Her mouth tenses. "Exsanguinations?"

"You don't know." I toss my book back onto its pile. "Did you buy into the whole 'it's called a Community; how quaint'?"

"Well, I didn't think it was paradise, but—"

"Let me tell you something, Captain. Living in a Community is like putting on an act. Every day, you wake up, and you follow the script the Huntsmen provide. If you fail, you're punished. And that script changes every day. The Huntsmen will always find an excuse. And exsanguination is their number one punishment." Thinking about it makes my pulse stutter. "They bleed you dry."

Armina's hands clench so tight that I wouldn't be surprised if her bones cracked. "I didn't know that; I . . . Of course you're in your rights to kill him. But, if possible, could you give me a little time? Truth is, I need to find out what he knows."

"What could he possibly know?"

She shifts on her crate, wincing as her leg gives another unpleasant groan. She pulls that too-big coat around her shoulders like a blanket. "I wasn't always captain of the *Blackblood.* It really belongs to a man named Averard. He was the type who always knew what to say, knew what to do. Whenever there was trouble, Averard was right there to talk you through it. He would've gone to Perishing. He would've saved your mother." She lowers her head into her hands. "The Huntsmen killed him."

She shakes her head slowly side to side, her whole body moving with the momentum. "I found his body," she mutters. "He was sitting by the fire where I left him, black blade sticking through his throat." She tugs on the lapel of her coat, and now that I'm properly looking, I see dried blood flaking off it.

No wonder it doesn't fit.

"Are you certain?" I ask. "A Huntsman would never leave their mageblade behind."

Mageblades are pure magic—made entirely of blood. After new Huntsman initiates take their first sip, the rest of that mage's blood is used to forge the blade. It's mingled with the blood of its wielder to become a perfect, personalized tool. A life becomes a weapon.

That type of magic is difficult to perform. Difficult to find any mage *willing* to perform. Most would rather die than enchant such a corruption.

"This wasn't a normal mageblade," Armina says. "It was more like a mageknife or something? It was small."

"Do you still have it?"

"My crewmate and I buried him in the woods; we were panicking so much we must've left it behind."

"That does sound odd," I admit. "But I doubt it was the Huntsmen. If they wanted your father dead, I imagine they would have surrounded him in broad daylight and ripped him apart with their bare hands. They don't keep secrets." I shrug. "Why should they?"

Armina grimaces. "He wasn't my father."

"Then why do you care if we catch his killer?"

"Because I need to *know*. I need to know who to direct this great, rotting fury at." She presses her hands against her chest and squeezes her lapels between them. "I'm mad; I'm confused; I'm . . . directionless. And I wanna know who did it so no one ever, *ever* hurts me like this again."

Oh.

I understand that. I understand that so well that it burns.

Distantly, I feel the truck come to a stop beneath us, but the look on Armina's face distracts me. She's around my age, and the determined, angry set of her jaw makes me think that if she had been born a mage, we could have been friends.

"Very well," I say. "This Huntsman can live a little longer." As a peace offering, I gesture toward her leg. "Do you want me to fix that?"

She rubs her knee. "Can you?"

I kneel on the floor and lift her ankle, twisting it this way and that. The metal creaks; something inside rattles. "You'll still want to visit your medical supplier, but I can straighten it out and reinforce it so you can walk."

"All yours, then."

The metal is cold and unfamiliar beneath my fingers. The enchantment in it thrums like a weak heartbeat; even if I knew the will of the caster, it's too damaged at this point to revive.

I reach into my pocket and press the spines of my mother's pendant into my thumb, then run the resultant blood up Armina's calf. It's easier to enchant over something if there's a little blood involved.

I don't even think Armina notices—she's too fixated on the way the broken fibers realign themselves beneath my palm.

Once finished, I double check that the prosthesis is straight, then release her. "How's that?"

She eases off the box and takes a tentative step forward, then another. I know immediately that something is wrong: she's rotating her hip rather than bending at the knee, making her gait stiff and jerky.

"It'll get me to Crotalus." When she stops and stands still, there is no discernable difference from before. "Thanks."

"I didn't do it right."

"You're not a master craftsperson. This isn't the first time it's been damaged. I'll deal." She glares down at the slumbering Huntsman. "Still, replacements aren't cheap. Wish I could make him pay for it."

"He will." It's my turn to perch on the box. "Speaking of, if we don't want him to slaughter us immediately upon waking, we need to restrain him."

The scrape and grind of metal rents the air. Armina swivels so fast that she loses her precarious balance.

Someone steps through the truck's hatch.

A person stands backlit against the sinking desert sun. They point a gun into the dark trailer with one hand, and the other clutches a mageblade.

Have more Huntsmen found us? It's a miracle we managed to subdue one; we stand little chance against another.

I leap from my crate and grab my book again, but Armina lets out a shaky laugh.

"Okay, Val, don't freak out."

The person at the hatch steps further inside. It's a tall woman with mirrored glasses pushed into her hair. She inspects the Huntsman at our feet, but when she glances up and spots me, her brown eyes widen. She pivots and trains her gun at my forehead.

"Valaina." Armina limps toward her.

"What in the Magistrate's bloody Branches is going on?" Valaina lurches forward, boot landing hard on the Huntsman's fingers. She doesn't appear to notice. "Hands where I can see them, mage."

I raise an eyebrow at Armina and slowly lift my hands into the air.

Armina makes a weird croaking noise. "Valaina, I'm sorry; I—"

"You're sorry? What're you sorry for?" Valaina's eyes find mine again, and her teeth bare. "Did you know it was in here?"

"Yes," Armina says. "Please, put your pistol down so we can talk. Canto means you no harm."

"Doesn't matter what it means. It does harm just existing." She jabs her pistol at the Huntsman on the ground. "Brought him around, didn't it? Aren't we in enough danger, Armina? Did you think it'd be fun to spice things up and add a little more?" Valaina's weapon returns to me, though pointed at my throat now instead of my head. "Where did you even get it?"

"I can speak for myself," I say, which earns me an almost inhuman snarl from Valaina. I remain seated, afraid to move too much lest I scare her into pulling the trigger.

"I escaped from the Huntsmen several days ago and sought refuge aboard this truck. Armina learned of my existence after the fact. This Huntsman must have tracked the truck down to get me back."

Valaina rounds on Armina, her eyes blazing. "Did you not think I had a right to know you were smuggling a mage in the truck where we keep our artifacts?"

"I thought—"

"You thought you could solve all our problems like how Averard did when we were kids. How we'd go to sleep, and the next morning, everything would be better again. This is serious, Armina. Mages are dangerous, and we're supposed to be a team. You know how I feel about this."

The hand holding her pistol drops to the side, and the fury drops from her gaze. Instead, her eyes fill with something heavier—something afraid. The fingers of her free hand claw into her sleeve.

"Please, Val. I couldn't leave them in the middle of the desert," Armina says.

"Why not?"

"Because I'm not in the habit of leaving innocent people to die."

"*Innocent*," Valaina spits. Her teeth grit, then she shoves her pistol back into its holster. She stomps over to the Huntsman.

"I've seen you do some crazy shit in your life, but having a secret pet mage has to be the most mind-numbingly stupid thing you've ever done."

"I'm not a pet," I say.

"I didn't ask you."

"Valaina," Armina snaps.

Valaina ignores her and crouches beside the Huntsman. She nudges her fingers against his neck, checking for a pulse.

Armina's nostrils flare, and she limps toward Valaina. She grabs Valaina's arm and tugs her upward. "*Hey.*"

Valaina shoves Armina away. They're chest to chest; Valaina has several inches of height on Armina, but neither flinch.

"Oh? Did you have something you wanted to tell me?" Valaina demands. "Bit late for that, don't you think?"

Armina pushes her shoulder—not hard enough to make her fall, but hard enough to make her sway. "What would've happened If I'd told you about Canto immediately?" Armina jabs her finger in my direction, and I do my best to appear delicate and unthreatening.

"We would've had this conversation sooner—"

"No, this isn't a conversation. You would've thrown this *fit* sooner. I was hoping to get to Crotalus and get Canto off the *Blackblood* with you none the wiser. You think I want to hurt you, Valaina?"

"Yeah, I think you'd *love* to—"

"I know how you feel about mages! You've been a part of my family for almost a decade." Armina sighs and rubs her temples. "It's a few more days. The plan is to drop Canto off with Georgian, and then this'll all be behind us. And I promise, next time I decide to do something 'mind-numbingly stupid', I'll run it by you first."

Valaina's eyes rove from Armina's face to mine. Her glare is fierce, defiant, and if I hadn't seen similar expressions every day on the faces of the Huntsmen, I might feel compelled to quail beneath it.

Then Armina's hand lands on Valaina's wrist, and some of the tension eases from her clenched jaw.

"Fine." Valaina pulls her hand away and crosses her arms. "We take the mage to Crotalus, then we never have to see or think about it ever again. But I don't want it in the trailer with our artifacts. I want it in the cab where I can watch it." She scowls and glares down at the Huntsman. Her eyebrows furrow. "Maybe . . . maybe once we're rid of it, that'll be the end of our Huntsmen troubles. They've got no reason to hunt us if we don't have their mage, yeah?"

"Right," Armina agrees. "Valaina, I *am* sorry. Let's just . . . find a means to restrain the Huntsman for now, yeah? One thing at a time?"

"Yeah, yeah, okay." The venom seems to drop out of Valaina as quickly as it rose, and she circles the Huntsman like a curious vulture. "Where to begin?" She glances up at me with a sneer. "Can the mage paralyze him with magic or something? Bet it would love that."

"I prefer 'they', please." I slide off my box and cautiously approach the Huntsman. Valaina stiffens but doesn't retreat. "Technically, I could paralyze him," I say. "But I won't."

"You won't?" Valaina's mouth twists at the corners, as if she's amused.

"No. Mages don't . . . we aren't supposed to enchant people. I used the power of a book to put him to sleep for a while, but that isn't the same thing as enchanting his body directly. Enchanted objects take on the will of their creator and strive toward the purpose for which they were created. Same thing with enchanted people. But since people have wills of their own, the resultant enchantment is volatile. Torn between obeying his own will and mine, he could become destructive, hurt himself or others, the enchantment warring against his own nature." I frown at his peaceful face. "And the enchantment will always win."

"What do you propose, then? We chain him up?"

"Well, yes. That could work. The chains would need to be metal, though—he'd be able to break rope."

"We've got chains," Armina says. "They're being used to keep some of the heavier merchandise steady, but if we rearrange a few things, we can spare them. Valaina, if you'd gather those for us, Canto and I will find the best place to restrain our guest."

Valaina looks like she might protest again, might restart the fight with renewed zeal. But instead, her shoulders sag, and she turns away from us. "Whatever you say, Captain."

She wanders deeper into the trailer, hands balled into fists at her sides. We hear the scrape and clank of metal dragging toward the front of the truck.

Armina places a hand on her forehead and sighs. "I'm sorry."

"For what?"

"I didn't want any of this to happen. I wanted you to stay a secret."

Mages are too hard a secret to keep, I almost say. Instead, I watch the shadows around us loom, aided by the dim lamp light and the brightness of evening shining through the open hatch. My trailer's quiet is broken by the sounds of chains and footsteps and Huntsman snores.

This isn't like my house in the Community with its one room, its thin mattress, its white walls. There is clutter and mess and noise. There is magic.

"I don't need you to apologize." I shift a crate to the side to clear a path through the furniture. "I need you to help me find something to tie the Huntsman down with.

9

RENN

I've never been a fan of sleeping. Feels like hours wasted that could be put to better use. This sleep, however, is so deep I want to stay pinned beneath it.

Like most nights, I dream of my father. Unlike most nights, I don't dream of watching his blood drip onto the stone floor of a bloodletting room.

Instead, we sit side by side on Perishing's wall, staring past the crumbled black mountain and into the swaying forest. Our legs dangle over the edge of the parapet, and the sun burns the horizon orange.

It's a familiar sight, one he and I indulged in whenever work slowed enough to allow it—a rare, precious respite. He was always so busy taking reports from Huntsmen and other Communities, and I had my library. But when time could be made, we made it, even if we spoke of nothing and just watched the small, small world below.

My father turns to me, his bearded face picking up the sun's golds and creams and browns, and he smiles without an ounce of fear or pain. A wonderful expression I wish I could paint over the last one I'd seen on him.

"It's yours," he says. *"All of it."*

I shake my head, the movement slowed through dream molasses. *"Perishing belongs to Pierce now."*

His black eyes crinkle at the corners, and he turns his gaze back to the horizon. *"I don't mean Perishing."*

The real world returns to me in patches: the low murmur of a voice, footsteps on metal, swaying lamp light.

I peel my eyes open. I'm surrounded on all sides by mountains of artifacts, and the oppressive magic makes my nose itch and my head ache. I groan and try to massage away the pain, but I can't move my hands.

"Good, you're awake."

The mage captain sits before me on a folding chair. She's still drowning in that black coat, hunched with her hands clasped and looking like she hasn't slept in weeks. The flame of magic burns through her, screaming louder than any artifact in the trailer. I lurch forward, intent to grab her and smother all that noise, but I jerk back. The strained whine of grinding metal pierces into my already throbbing head.

I'm chained to a piece of furniture, a wardrobe or something. I wrench against my bonds, and the wood creaks. Creaks but doesn't break, and I growl in frustration as I wrench again.

How long have I been out?

"You're only gonna hurt yourself," the captain says.

This cannot be happening. Huntsmen don't get captured by little mages in dirty trucks. I haven't lost. I cannot possibly lose at my first chance to prove that I am not my father—

"Have you calmed down yet, or do you need a minute?"

I lunge at her again. This time, the wardrobe drags a few centimeters.

"Come closer and you'll find I don't need my hands to kill you," I snarl.

She doesn't move from her seat, but she does fidget with the cuffs of her sleeves. "The only reason you aren't dead's because I thought you'd be useful. Don't make me regret it."

The Huntsmaster said the same thing a year ago. The sentiment loses its edge the second time around.

This mission should have been routine. I may be more accustomed to paperwork than fieldwork, but arresting and retrieving a few smugglers and their truck is the sort of grunt-work hunt I've assigned a million lesser Huntsmen in the past. If there is a failure here, it's that I wasn't briefed enough. Two mages. Pierce didn't think that relevant to mention?

The captain doesn't look like a mage. I can't see any veins on her skin, and her mouth and eyes have a normal reddish hue where a mage's are stained gray. But she feels like one: the headache pressure of magic.

"Where's the other mage?" I demand.

"Trust me, you don't want to meet them. I actually stopped them from killing you, so a 'thank you, Captain,' wouldn't go amiss."

"Why did you stop them?"

I don't even fear death anymore. Not like I used to, wide awake in my bed at the barracks, my father's pleading eyes still boring into my memory from his seat in the chair while the other Huntsmen held me back. Waiting for those same Huntsmen to strap *me* down and finish what they'd started.

The captain watches me. I wonder what she's looking for. "I have questions. Ones only a Huntsman can answer."

"And if I won't answer your questions?"

She pushes out of her chair and stands. I'm not sure whether this is meant to intimidate me, but if I were upright, she wouldn't reach my shoulder. She takes a step forward, and I note how her leg wobbles. A weakness. I tuck it away in my filing-cabinet memory.

"You'll want to," she says, "or I'll give the mage you *and* my dullest knife."

Someone clears their throat behind me, and I wrench the wardrobe another few pointless centimeters, trying to see.

"As fun as threatening our Huntsman is, I'm not sure it'll get us anywhere."

It's another female voice—young, full of exasperation. She steps into view, and I take in her curly hair, her almost amused expression so unlike the captain's.

"Don't lecture *me* about threatening people," the captain replies. "After what you did to Canto? And they hadn't even attacked anyone."

The new woman crosses her arms. "Yet."

Another weakness.

The captain shakes her head and turns back to me. "My name's Armina, and this is Valaina. What should we call you?"

What should they call me? Is this an interrogation or a job interview?

"Renn." I hope I don't sound as bewildered as I feel.

Armina sits back down and stretches her leg. The ankle tilts at an unnatural angle. Did she break it when we fell through the roof? Is she walking around on a *broken leg*? "Well, Renn, how did you find our truck?"

"Luck," I say. I don't see my mageblade on her, but I'm suddenly glad the Huntsmaster took a vial of my blood. "Do you know what they're going to do to you when I get you to Perishing?"

Her eyes are hard, her limbs stiff. Trying to keep all hints of emotion off her face.

"You're not the interrogator here," she says. "Besides, I've no idea why the Huntsmen'd want to do anything with me. I sell furniture that folds your clothes for you and instruments that play themselves. The few dangerous things I do have are more a hazard to the user than anyone else."

"Your fellow mage put me to sleep with a book."

"A book of lullabies meant for babies."

I lean back against my bonds. The rough metal chains bite into my skin, and blood wells on my wrists. "Even innocuous enchantments can kill if used by the wrong person, so they *all* must be contained. You sow discord for a profit and undermine the integrity of our organization by putting artifacts into the hands of possibly unstable individuals. You endanger every Federation citizen by not fully understanding the threat magic poses."

Armina looks like she wants to argue, but it's Valaina who steps toward me. She rolls up the sleeves of her shirt, exposing the skin of her arms. Blackened scars run across her flesh in haphazard strokes.

"I understand what happens when you press magic to the point where it snaps," she hisses. "Not everyone is strong enough to fight back."

Black scars. Only a blade dipped in mage blood could cause those kinds of wounds, and the only people with access to mage blood are Huntsmen and mages themselves. There would be no reason for a Huntsman to waste blood like that, so . . .

"Why are you here?" I ask. "Why would you voluntarily work with mages?"

Valaina falls back into place behind Armina. "I'm not working with them, and they'll be gone soon enough."

"I'm talking about your captain."

Armina and Valaina glance at one another. Valaina makes a small choking sound, turns away from me, and raises a fist to her mouth to cough. Her hand barely covers her smile.

Armina rolls her eyes and addresses me again. "Enough, enough. Back to my questions, if you don't mind." She leans her forearms on her knees. "Have you ever heard of a man named Averard?"

The mirth drops from Valaina's face, but Armina's gaze bores into me.

Averard? I rack my brain, running through ancient files and memorized documents. I remember something coming across my desk, not long before my father's fall from grace. A hunt request to track down a thief . . . . Unusual because the thief in question wasn't a mage, and rarely does a Huntsman *ask* for an assignment with run-of-the-mill lawbreakers. I forwarded the request to my father for perusal but didn't think about it further.

That thief may have been an Averard. The name sounds familiar, at least, and thievery and smuggling seem like they would go hand in hand.

"Is he important?" I want to know what he stole; the request hadn't been particularly detailed, which is probably why my father rejected it.

Armina changes the subject instead of replying. "I found a Huntsman artifact not long ago. Short knife with a black blade. What might something like that be used for?"

The question catches me by such surprise that it's my turn to laugh. "Where did you find one of those?" I shake my head. "They're weapons for field agents. Men and women looking to join the Order have to prove themselves first. Give them a blade, see what they can do with it. Usually it isn't much, but it's good to have contacts for grunt work."

Armina shrinks in her chair. "Grunt work," she says.

Valaina grips her shoulder.

Seems our captain didn't stumble across that knife by chance.

"Any more questions?" I ask. "Shall I give you a rundown of Perishing's cafeteria schedule? Our workout routine?"

Armina stands and folds her chair. She stacks it on top of a crate before limping toward the trailer hatch. Valaina follows.

"Captain," I call.

Armina pauses.

"What are you planning to do with me?"

She whips back around and strides toward me, stopping half a foot away. I lunge forward, but before I can do anything, she grabs my jaw and pushes my chin up to look at her.

"You're with me for now." Her fingernails are sharp on my skin. "Until you piss me off, or until I find some way to dump you so they'll never find the body. You stay in the chains. Valaina or I will help you with whatever daily bullshit you need to stay alive. If you threaten either of us, you lose that privilege."

Now that we're making contact, I push forward with the dredges of mage blood in my system and try to quell the roar of her magic. Nothing happens, and I glare up at her. "What kind of mage are you?"

Her grip tightens. "I've no idea how you got it into your head, but I'm not a mage. Don't cause a fuss aboard my truck and I won't bleed you out on my floor like you do the mages in your so-called Communities. Do you understand?"

My black eyes meet her brown ones. I'm not afraid of her. I'm trained to handle monsters.

"Loud and clear, Captain."

10

ARMINA

"We shouldn't leave him alone in there."

Canto stands by the *Blackblood's* back wheel as I close the cab door. They're wearing a coat Valaina and I dug up from storage, an unenchanted garment made of faded-red wool. We also found a Rabbit's Day mask hidden in some old decorations from our childhood. It covers most of Canto's face, although their gold eyes peek out from the rabbit's empty sockets. We had to cut holes in the coat hood for the tall rabbit ears, but the whole ensemble is effective enough at covering their prominent veins.

At Valaina's insistence, we're still making our pit stop in Hive. It's especially important, she said, now that we have a whole two extra mouths to feed.

"Not much of a choice," Valaina answers in my stead as she hops out of the passenger seat. "I trust a trussed-up Huntsman a bit more than I trust you, so let's have no more complaining and get this trip over with as fast as possible." She shoves her hands into her pants pockets and gives Canto a once-over. "You look like a kid. A stupidly tall kid."

"You don't want to know what you look like," Canto spits back.

I step between them before things escalate. "Let's keep on task. Valaina, you said you wanted to withdraw extra cash, so go ahead and do that. Canto, stay with me and we'll pick up supplies."

Valaina steps off without a word, toward the city proper.

Canto watches her go with narrowed eyes, then says, "Can we get more of those oat squares?"

The *Blackblood*'s parked right outside of Hive in a camper lot. Nothing about the truck marks it as particularly special—we've purposely kept the paint pocked and the wheel wells dirt-stained so it'll blend in with other suppliers on the road. Can't imagine the Huntsmen could track us from it alone, and we made sure that Renn is properly gagged, so he can't draw attention by screaming.

Hive looks hungover from the remnants of Rabbit's Day, red banners still waving and trash littering the street. Canto's blessedly not too out of place—I see a child or two still wearing similar masks. The streets're too narrow for a truck the *Blackblood*'s size: every few feet, we have to press against a building so we don't get flattened by a bicyclist hopped up on way too much caffeine and post-holiday cheer. The dirty buildings near blot out the cloudless sky, and I kick a paper cup out of the way as we venture toward the market stalls.

Most of them are still closed despite it being early afternoon, and the few that're open look half asleep, their awnings not even propped up to alert customers that they're ready for business. We stop at the bodega Averard used to take us to whenever we visited Hive, and I can't help the small twist of nostalgia. Averard, ushering us inside, letting me pick out ice cream and road snacks and books. Valaina coming with us for the first time, her eyes huge as she examined the sheer number of sweets to choose from. She made herself sick that night, but Averard said that everyone deserves to get sick from having too much good at least once in their life.

The nostalgia only doubles the moment Canto and I step through the door. They turn in an actual full circle to get the scope of the place, swinging so widely that the hem of their coat knocks a display of sunglasses onto the ground.

They freeze as the frames clatter to the floor, and their hands rise defensively to their chest.

The bodega owner, a sunburnt man with very little hair, glances up from the novel he's reading and wrinkles his nose. "Don't stand there all stunned. Pick 'em up." He waves his book at us before returning to it.

Canto's breath leaves them in a rush, and they crouch to gather the dropped glasses.

I stoop to help, and they whisper, "Why didn't he get mad?"

"I dunno, he seemed kind of annoyed to me."

I start aligning the glasses back on the display before I realize what Canto meant. The owner got annoyed, sure, but he didn't get *pissed*. He didn't hurt anyone.

I watch Canto scoop up glasses with the care of someone holding a baby for the first time.

When everything's fixed, the pair of us scan the aisles for what we want. Valaina drilled a list in my head of her particulars, so I make sure to grab those first as Canto becomes fascinated by the sheer number of soaps available for purchase.

"Pick whatever you like," I say as I grab my own favorite.

Canto's rabbit mask hides their expression from me, but their hands tremble as they choose a snowy pear scent from the shelves.

We unload our burden on the bodega counter, and the owner tallies us up. As he drops our purchases into a brown paper bag, his bodega cat leaps onto the counter and sniffs at us. She's been around as long as I can remember; I'm pretty sure she's part bobcat, judging by the tufted ears, but she's friendly enough. She watches us out of yellow eyes that oddly resemble Canto's before she reaches out a paw and baps them on the hand.

Canto pulls their hand back to their chest in surprise, and the bodega owner laughs. "She wants you to pet her. Go on, she don't bite if you're gentle."

Canto reaches out tentative fingers and rests them on the cat's head, flattening her ears to the sides. She gives Canto an almost withering glare before pressing against their palm and walking forward so it runs down her spine to her stumpy tail.

The owner guffaws as he passes me our shopping. "'S like you've never seen a cat before."

Canto shakes their head, withdrawing their hand. "No one had cats in my, um, city."

"The whole city? Where you from?"

I pick up our bags and shove one into Canto's chest. "They're adopted," I say. "And we're mostly on the road these days. Have a good one."

The owner seems perplexed, but he gives a friendly nod nonetheless. I usher out Canto, who keeps staring at the cat, who's now grooming her leg on top of the owner's book.

We step back out onto the street, and I adjust the bag in my arms. "You're terrible at this whole 'low profile' thing," I say.

"I'm sorry," Canto says, and they actually sound it. "I have . . . a particular set of rules I know how to follow. The outside world deviates from those rules entirely."

"I suppose that's true. How's it feel, being free?"

"I'm not free." They lower their head so I can't even see their eyes through the mask.

Since we entered the bodega, more and more stalls've opened for business outside. We pass a few, the owners still too tired to call out to us and hawk their wares. I know Valaina'll probably be a bit, so I slow my stroll, looking for anything interesting that Canto might've never seen before.

Further along, at the end of the street, a stall catches my eye. They're selling raw wool, mostly, with some processed skeins dyed with juniper berries or iron. Tethered to the table, a young goat investigates the ground around its feet, pulling up weeds with more curiosity than hunger.

A woman wearing a headscarf she must've made from the product sits behind the table, sipping from a hand-thrown mug. She smiles at me, then her eyes sweep down Averard's coat and across Canto, and her smile dissipates like the steam from her drink.

As we cross the street toward the stall, the woman's hand tightens around the mug. Then she relaxes and inclines her head toward us.

"How might I help you today?" she asks. Her Y'ashtrian accent—heavy in the back of her throat, then rounding as it falls off her tongue—is almost stern enough to feel scolding, though her face remains neutral. I'd guess she's closing in on middle age: her golden-brown skin creases at the eyes, and she's got flecks of white in her dark eyebrows. Her red nails clack on her mug, and she leans back in her chair, feigning nonchalance.

I glance at her wares, trying to spot what, exactly, has her so spooked. Canto crouches by the goat, hands curled on their knees as they watch it forage. It looks up at Canto, bleats, then headbutts their knee with its tiny horns. Canto snorts and bops its head with their knuckles.

The shopkeep watches them, clearly trying very hard not to look at me.

"Something wrong?" I ask.

"Nothing, nothing," she says, still not looking in my direction. "It is just your coat. Thought for a moment it was familiar."

I grasp my cuffs and squeeze the leather. "Do you know Averard?"

She startles hard enough that coffee spills on her hands, and she lets out a string of Y'ashtrian curses that make her goat scramble away from Canto to hide under the table.

"So it *is* his coat," the woman says as she mops up the mess with the hem of her shirt. "Where is he? Did he sell it to you?"

I pull Averard's coat tighter around my shoulders. "No, I . . . I'm borrowing it. We're coworkers." I leave it at that in case this woman doesn't know what we do, in case she's another danger in an already awful situation.

"Borrowing it, hmph." She waves a dismissive hand. "He must like you, then. Never saw him without the thing."

"How do you know him?" The question burns on my tongue, eager to get out. I've met dozens of Averard's contacts before, but I don't know this one. Not a lot of Y'ashtrians live this side of the border, so I imagine I'd remember her pretty well.

"Business associates." She produces a bolt of brown fabric from under her table. She reaches into its folds, and with a small tug, draws into view a few centimeters of black felt, so dark it looks like something's taken a chunk out of her palm.

Canto stands upright so fast their rabbit ears clip the corner of the table, knocking the mask askew. They straighten it as they lean over the cloth, plucking it up to run between their thumb and forefinger.

The woman tugs the cloth away again and shoots Canto a suspicious glare. "The inside of that coat's made of it," she says, "between the leather shell and the lining. Nothing special in the weave—just a bit more difficult to pierce." She smirks and sets down her coffee. "Someone purchased it as a gift for him, for the . . ." She seems to struggle with the word as she gestures to the air around her. "The *Áhvt na Krohpin*. After he saw how fine my product is, he would trade when we crossed paths, though I am so rarely in one spot."

"Where did you get it?" Canto asks. The woman and I both look up at them. Their voice trembles at the edges.

The woman shakes her head, lip curled and easy demeanor dropped. "I would say that I never give up my sources, but there are no sources left to give up, thanks to Averard." The wooden bangles on her wrists clack as she bends down and lifts the little goat into her lap. "His stunt made things more difficult for the rest of us in the trade, and he will find no friends in these parts." She scowls as she scratches the goat between its horns.

I open my mouth to press her further, to ask what Averard did, when I feel a tug at my elbow.

"Making friends?" Valaina asks, examining the woman through her mirrored sunglasses with her arms crossed. Whether or not it's supposed to be intimidating, the woman doesn't react, simply pets her goat and watches us.

"Not . . . not exactly," I say. "This is an associate of Averard's."

The woman's gaze lands on the pistol at Valaina's hip. Her eyebrows raise.

"Right, well. We'll send him your regards," Valaina says. She turns and marches back down the street toward Hive's exit.

I bob my head at the woman in goodbye and apology both, but Canto doesn't move.

"Where are the mages that enchanted that cloth?" Canto asks.

The woman sets her goat down and sighs. "I gave you as much of an answer as I am willing to give. Now leave space at my shop for paying customers. And call Averard a *Pohrüt* for me. He will understand this."

I tug Canto's sleeve before they argue any further, and they begrudgingly set off with me after Valaina.

When we're far enough from the woman's shop, I ask, "What was all that about?"

The sun hits Canto's mask, dyeing the plaster the yellow-white of bone. Canto's long fingers twist in their coat, as if trying to pluck away some unseen irritant. "The cloth was an artifact."

"Yeah, and? We have loads on the *Blackblood*."

"Not like those." Canto shakes their head and holds their hand out, the black scab from the other day's injury still solid in the creases of their palm. "The enchantments on your truck are old, some older than both of us combined. That cloth? Couldn't have been made more than a year ago." They clench their fist. "Are there . . . are there really free mages out there?"

Despite the day's dry, dry heat, a chill sweat breaks out on my forehead. That information might mean free mages to Canto, but to me, it means that whatever Averard did to upset that shopkeep, it must've been pretty recent. And way too close to when he died to be a coincidence.

11

ARMINA

The dark smear of Crotalus City looms ahead. I keep my foot steady on the gas, my eyes pinned to the place where the road meets the city's first squat building. Those buildings pop up like gravestones and way markers until we're surrounded. For the first time in hundreds of miles, the *Blackblood* sees some shade.

Valaina's in the passenger seat, slumped against the door like an aristocrat, proving once again she's perfect when she isn't talking. Canto sits between us, straight and rigid, their eyes burning a hole into the horizon.

The further we get into the city, the taller the buildings grow, and the more people crowd the streets. Trucks like ours are a common enough sight in Crotalus. Like Wallton in the east, it's the last stop before you hit a barrier—Perishing, in this case. Truckers come here to refuel or get a bite to eat or unload their wares before picking up more to deliver to settlements all across the Federation.

Other than its status as a final destination, Crotalus City and Wallton have little in common. Crotalus's population is five or six times the size, for one. For another, it's much older, one of the oldest settlements in the Federation. Its buildings are a hodgepodge of stone and brick and woodwork, each built at different times and at the whims of different people. The buildings' heights and widths vary like crooked teeth, and the few plants that grow in the dark spaces between are scraggly and reaching. Sand invades every corner, sweeping in from the desert until the sidewalks and roads are half dune themselves.

"What's the plan?" Valaina's inspecting her cuticles, one foot propped on the seat an inch from Canto's thigh. Despite her casual appearance, she's had Avarard's pistol sitting on her lap since she discovered Canto, finger resting on the trigger guard like a threat.

"Canto and I will visit Georgian about my leg and see if she can get Canto into hiding," I reply.

Canto glances in my direction. "What if I don't want to go into hiding?"

"If you still mean to infiltrate Perishing, then Georgian's better equipped than me to help you with that death wish."

Canto scoffs but returns their attention to the road.

"What am I supposed to do?" Valaina continues. When I don't respond, she lets out a long, fake sigh that turns into a little growl at the end. "Oh, come on. It's bad enough I've had to play babysitter for him on the road. Don't make me spend more time in his insufferable presence."

"Oh, he's insufferable now? Just yesterday you called him 'pleasantly chatty and weirdly pretty for a Huntsman.'" I swing the truck around a corner and onto Crotalus's main street. A few people scatter from the *Blackblood's* approach.

Canto turns their head to stare at Valaina. She rolls her eyes at their grimace. "Brother's Blood, I was joking. I actually think he's kind of sad. You two've been sticking to the cab, so you haven't interacted with him much, but he talks. A lot. Even if you don't respond. Sometimes he'll say something really bleak."

"Like what?" I ask.

"Like how there's no point in taking him hostage because no one will care if he dies."

"Ah, that's one thing he and I agree on," Canto interjects.

"Soon he won't be your problem anyway." I pull the truck into our destination. This lot's not much, just a bare strip of dirt between the marketplace and one of the more middle-class residential districts. It's mostly merchant parking, but today, the lot's surprisingly empty. Most've probably moved on after the holiday, but the sight of the uninterrupted mud spikes my already high anxiety.

"Valaina." I ease the truck to a stop. "If you really don't think you can handle him, we can work out something else, but—"

"Oh, please. Don't." Valaina kicks open her door and slides out.

Valaina's got Renn's mageblade strapped to her side, and I've got the one I stole from Baker almost a week ago. I jump out of the cab and offer Canto my hand to help them down, but they ignore me. Their exit isn't exactly graceful: they've got one foot up on the door frame and the other searching with frantic toes for the ground. Eventually, they give up on a soft landing and allow themself to drop, which makes their knees buckle.

"I don't understand how you do it." They glare at me as if my composure offends them. "You're barely tall enough to reach the door."

"Practice," I respond.

They grumble and pull their mask down around their neck to tuck their hair more easily beneath their hood. As they do, I notice something clutched in their fingers and a streak of black running down their wrist.

"You have to be more careful." I nod to their hand. There may be almost no one else in this lot, but things'll be different once we're in the city proper. "Veins we can hide, but blood'll be trickier."

Canto stretches open their palm. Clutched in it is a twisted shape, blackened with magic and now wet with blood. It might've once been a piece of jewelry, but it's so corroded it more resembles a metal spider. Canto doesn't even seem to feel the pain as the points pull out of their skin.

"What's that?" I ask.

"Nothing." They shove it into their coat pocket. "A trinket of my mother's."

"What's it do?"

They inspect their palm, thumb smearing the blood. "Again, nothing." When they look into my face, their eyes are sharp. "I want to see the Huntsman."

"You think that's a good idea? You wanted to slit his throat a few days ago."

Canto snorts. "I still want to slit his throat, but don't worry; I'll behave."

What's the worst that can happen? I think, and I immediately I realize that I could end up with a dead mage or a dead Huntsman or both, and the *Blackblood* would be in an even worse position than it is now. But the determination in Canto's glare weakens my resolve. They've been patient enough with my insistence that we don't kill Renn, a patience I don't think I'd share if I'd been through what they have. If a minute to confront a Huntsman is all they're gonna demand in return, then far be it from me to deny them.

"If I let you talk to him, you keep your voice down, all right? You don't provoke him."

Canto's only response is a short, tense nod.

The muddy ground sticks to my boots and licks up the ends of Averard's coat. I lead Canto around the *Blackblood* and slide open the hatch. I haul myself through, and Canto climbs in behind me, a bit more elegant than their earlier descent from the cab.

Renn remains as he was, chained to the wardrobe. His sandy hair is disheveled, sticking out at odd angles like cactus spines, and he sags against his bonds. He's probably exhausted just from hanging there, but I don't care much.

When we enter, his head lifts, revealing bruise-dark circles under his black eyes. His gaze falls on Canto, and his teeth bare. "Look who's finally come to say hello."

Canto's bloody fingers twitch at their sides as if reaching for a weapon that isn't there.

"It's impolite to stare," Renn snarls, his chin dipping lower. "I thought mages were supposed to be nice. Surely they taught you how to greet a Huntsman in your Community? Go on—fold your hands together, look at the ground, and—"

Canto lunges. Their hand blurs as they drive it forward and slap Renn across the face. A thick streak of black blood from Canto's cut palm smears across Renn's reddening cheek.

"I know how to greet a Huntsman," Canto spits.

Renn's jaw stretches, and when he looks up at Canto, his fury has dissipated into an expression that borders on bewildered. "Did . . . did you just hit me?"

"What a stupid question," Canto says. "Shall I do it again so you remember properly this time?"

"That's enough," I snap. "Canto, did you hear a word I said about provoking him?" I take a step closer. If I let this go on much longer, there probably *will* be a body in my truck.

"Wait, Captain." Renn's voice draws me to a halt. His eyes never leave Canto's face, and his chest heaves. "Let them do whatever they want. Consider it a gift." His chin tilts to offer Canto a clearer shot at his face. "They know they're living on borrowed time."

Canto's breath stutters, and they take a step back from Renn.

Renn's exhaustion and cold calm make him look like a monster out of a storybook, the kind that lurks in the deep dark of the Vulpesh woods.

Before I think about what I'm doing, I ask, "What do you mean?"

He exhales, and a small, almost apologetic smile rises on his face. "The Huntsmaster gave me orders to kill them. They were being transported to Perishing for exsanguination anyway; a death sentence is a death sentence." The smile drops off his face, replaced with something bitter. "I've never had to kill anyone before, but I've seen exsanguinations; I would have given you a far kinder end."

Canto's fists tighten. I think they're about to hit Renn again, but instead, they turn and flee the trailer. Their red coat swishes behind them when they jump into the cool evening air just as Valaina pulls herself through the hatch.

Renn still works his jaw, watching where Canto disappeared. "Your mage friend is a reactive sort." He eyes Valaina as she comes closer. "Hope for your own sake you've found a way to restrain them."

"You really must enjoy the sound of your own voice." Valaina crosses her arms and tilts her head toward me. "When'll you be back?"

I try to keep my response as vague as possible. Renn's eyes flick to me, and I suddenly feel like I'm being filed away somewhere. "Can't rightly say. Depends on my benefactor's mood."

"And you'll be returning without the mage, like we agreed?"

"If I decide that Canto's safe, then yes, I'll come back alone."

"The only place safe for a mage is a Community," Renn says.

"Shut up," I snap.

Valaina sighs and collapses into a folding chair we set up to watch over Renn. "As annoying as our Huntsman friend is, he's right."

He isn't. I know that, after listening to Canto. I knew it before, I think, even if Averard tried to keep the Huntsmen off our radar and out of our lives. Valaina's been through too much to stay objective, and I understand her fears, but Canto isn't the mages who hurt her.

I tug the second mageblade from my belt and press it into Valaina's grip. "Keep an eye on this, too, all right? I can't exactly traipse through the city with it. Tomorrow, things'll be back to normal."

"All right, all right. Hurry it up," Valaina says, waving me away.

Renn says nothing as I turn to leave, but I feel his eyes on my spine, watching me go.

When I hop down from the trailer and pull the hatch closed behind me, I spy Canto huddled against one of the truck's wheels with their face buried in their knees. I approach loud enough so I don't startle them, then crouch at their side.

Eventually, their muffled words reach me between the gaps in their arms.

"A week."

"What's that?"

Canto peeks up, their eyes liquid gold from tears they're holding back. "I've been out of the Community for almost a week now. It shouldn't hurt this bad anymore; it should . . ." They swallow and scrub the back of their sleeve over their face. They bare their teeth as they dig a fist into their temple. "When do I stop being *angry*?"

I wish I could tell them, but I'm still looking for that answer myself. "I dunno, but at least today's the last day you'll ever have to see him."

Canto watches the city where the evening sun wraps its harsh glow around the buildings. "I wish I could be as certain."

Slowly, they push themself onto their feet and brush the dirt off their coat. They pull the rabbit mask from around their neck back over their face and look down at me with hardened eyes.

"The other day, when you interrogated him, did you get your answers?"

"I suppose I did."

"Were they the answers you wanted?"

I stand. For some reason, I find it difficult to tell the truth.

"No."

Everything in the city excites Canto.

Oh, they're trying to hide it from me, with the hood pulled low over their mask and their hands crammed so far into their pockets I'm afraid the wool might tear. But each new thing gets a reaction, no matter how subtle. Their head follows a woman wearing an extravagant hat with beads and feathers and netting. They make a noise of shock and twitch away when one of those horse-drawn carriages for tourists ambles down the street. We pass a food vendor, and Canto turns around, walking backward to keep it in their sights.

I buy us something—a Y'ashtrian dish with meat and flatbread. Canto lifts the bottom of their mask to eat it with a grace I could never manage, somehow making street food look elegant even as I shove mine wholesale into my mouth.

We round the corner of a park and thread our way through a few side streets. We're getting further into the business district, where the buildings are newer and taller. There's more metal here than in the rest of the city, more glass. Sand buffets around our ankles in little whorls, and despite the desert heat still clinging to the daytime, the alley shadows are cool.

As I finish off the last bites of my flatbread, I realize I don't hear Canto's footsteps anymore.

My hand plunges toward my revolver. Have the city's Huntsmen found us? Have they plucked Canto away from me without a sound? I pull my revolver free and spin around, thumb on the hammer and finger alongside the trigger.

Canto stands a few paces away, their long fingers resting on a building's shopfront. The rabbit mask hangs around their neck once more. They lean closer to the window, and their breath fogs the glass.

"Hey." I lower my revolver, but Canto continues to stare into the window, a frown tugging at the corners of their lips.

I trot over and nudge their foot with my toe. "I know all this is new, but we can't be out on the streets too long."

To my surprise, Canto catches my sleeve and curls their fingers into the leather. I follow their gaze to the shop display.

I'm not sure what it's selling, to be honest. Flowers, maybe? There's a whole slew of them in the window in dainty bunches, draped about with gauzy swaths of fabric. Their petals are lush and multicolored. Difficult to grow these types this deep in the desert. Expensive, probably imported from a settlement in the mountains or closer to the border. They're not really my thing, though, so I don't understand what's captured Canto's focus until I see the oval mirror at the center of the display.

Their face is reflected in it, and their lips part. A gray flush creeps up their throat.

Canto's fingers tighten on my sleeve. "I look like my mother."

They whisper the words with awe, reverence. Like they've entered the home of a god and every part of them feels the urge to bow in prayer. Their free hand separates from the window to trace their jaw, and they watch the trail of their fingers through the glass.

"Have you never seen your face before?" I ask.

They shake their head, eyes catching on the way their hair follows the movement. "Distorted by water or metal, but never this clear." Their fingers follow the river of veins from their cheek down to the collar of their coat. "I'm . . . sharp. My mother's face is rounder. And her eyes are a different color." They tug at the corner of one of their eyes, revealing the gray flesh beneath. "The roots of her hair are starting to turn to white; she tells me to pluck out any silver strands. Says it's good luck." Canto presses their forehead against the glass. "It hasn't brought us any luck at all."

I can't help it. I twist my hand to capture their fingers, thread them together with mine. I understand this sort of misery. And maybe the pain of losing someone never goes away, and maybe it doesn't even lessen, but I think suffering together is much better than suffering alone.

"I hope you find her. I hope you get her out of Perishing somehow so you can both be free."

"Sounds impossible," Canto says. "But I'm happy to die trying."

To die trying. Have I ever held a conviction that strong in my life? Canto thinks they're destined for failure, and still, *still*, the attempt is worth it. They'd rather slam their fists against the zero percent chance of getting their mother back than ever give her up.

Did Averard die trying?

The city is growing dark, darker, and we can't stay here any longer. Canto allows me to lead them away, but they're quiet. They stick close, and their hand is warm in mine.

It doesn't take long to get to Georgian's workshop. It's a broke-down two-story building on the edge of the red-light district, where it isn't uncommon to see sex workers and their patrons mingling, smoking, chatting on porches and in alcoves. Discordant strains of music and laughter echo from the houses and the streets around us. Canto's eyes cling to a prostitute in a half-open dress shirt, whose client has her hand down his pants.

In this area of town, everyone assumes you're here for business, so they pay you no mind; they're distracted with their own matters anyway. Averard used to say that the best way to hide magic is in the misdirection: distract, distract, distract.

I drag Canto up Georgian's porch steps, and we stand beneath the single bare lightbulb. I release Canto's hand to knock, and they wipe their palm on their thigh.

When the door cracks, I nearly run into it, expecting Georgian's open arms. She's a big woman, over six feet, with dark skin and her hair in locs. She's always wearing a boiler suit freckled with burns and stains and with pockets full of screwdrivers and other little tools. She'll throw her door wide and grab your smaller hands between both her large ones, and her calluses will scrape your knuckles. She'll pull you into the house and sit you down, and she won't bring you coffee or tea, but she will ask after your health, and she'll care about your answer.

Georgian isn't the one who opens the door.

Instead, in the crack of the jamb stands a different woman, this one petite and slim. She wears an immaculate knee-length skirt with a tucked-in blouse. Her small hands clutch the door, and her blue eyes peek out beneath raised blonde eyebrows.

Still, the surprise of her appearance isn't enough to distract me from the black veins crawling up her cheeks.

12
CANTO

She can't be real, this woman standing in the dark mouth of a dilapidated house, thirty feet away from where two people are having loud sex on the street. She can't be blinking at Armina and me out of those blue eyes; her gray lips can't be tugging into that frown. Unscarred. Untraumatized.

There shouldn't be free mages. There can't be. If there are free mages, then what the fuck did my mother and I suffer for?

"Uh," Armina says, "is Georgian home?"

The woman's eyes slide from Armina's to mine and then widen. "Get inside." She holds back the door for us and disappears into the shadows of the house.

I push past Armina. We're in a hallway, dark because only one of three overhead bulbs works. The floor runner is black beneath our feet from the passage of too many shoes over too long a time, and the wallpaper is floral from water stains. This woman, clean and prim, doesn't belong here.

"That our food?" booms a voice from down the hall.

The mage's frown deepens. "Not quite." She heads off toward a square of light at the end of the hall, leaving Armina and me alone by the door.

"What is happening?" I hiss at Armina.

"Dunno. Like I said before, Georgian works with mages, but I've never seen one in the house."

I hear the mage's soft murmur from the other room but nothing of what she says.

There's a great guffaw. "Customers? A mage? Well, all right." The voice lifts. "Come on in, now. Let's get a look at you."

The invitation breaks the lock on my feet, and I throw myself down the hallway toward the voices. I still don't understand how a mage can be here, in this loud city of cars and music and red blood. Before I left the Community, I would have said that going to a city was equally as difficult as going to the stars.

I step across the room's threshold. While the *Blackblood* is an undeniable mess, this room makes it look pristine. A dozen orange light bulbs are strung along the ceiling, illuminating the jagged scrap piles that litter the space. Judging by the glue stains and tack marks, the bare floor may once have been carpeted but is now mostly pencil shavings and staples. Metal shelves screw directly into the old plaster walls. Those shelves are stacked high with unlabeled cans and boxes marked with words like "saw blades" and "sandpaper."

At the center of it all is a worktable that spans half the room, made of mismatched wood and standing on as many legs as the *Blackblood* has wheels. It's piled with papers, books, pencils. There's an architect's compass stabbed into the table beside a stained coffee mug and a curled strip of lead.

Behind the table sits a big woman hunched over what appears to be a metal human arm clamped to the surface. She has a pair of tweezers in one hand and some smoking metal tool in the other, and she's inspecting the arm's metal ligaments like a gardener pruning weeds.

She glances up at us, and her eyes are magnified double by thick safety goggles. She stands, tosses aside her tools, and strips off her gloves. "I'll be damned. If it isn't Averard's brat."

The woman crosses the room and scoops Armina into what might generously be described as a hug but might more accurately be described as a tackle. Armina grunts, and I think I hear the metal of her leg groan in protest as she's lifted off the ground.

"Been a bit." The woman returns Armina to the floor. "See you brought a new friend. Where're Val and the good captain?"

Armina's expression crumples, and the silence stretches into discomfort.

The mage has planted herself against the far wall, in the shadow of a standing toolbox, and I want to get the unpleasantries over with so I can understand what she's doing here.

"He's dead," I say.

Armina's breath catches.

The big woman's joyous face falls, and her sooty fingers fly to her mouth. "I'm sorry to hear that. He was a good customer. Good friend." She jerks her chin toward me. "What's your name?"

"Canto."

She trundles back to her worktable and drops her safety goggles beside the metal arm. "Georgian. Pleasure to make your acquaintance. That right there"—she points to the mage, who steps out of her shade—"is Kateryna, my wife and assistant."

"I didn't know you were married," Armina says.

Georgian waves a hand. "Recent thing. Didn't make the papers; might be clear why."

"Mages can't get married," I say. Everyone turns toward me, and under their stares, I feel like I could shrivel away to nothing. "I mean, we . . . we can have families, but the Huntsmen don't recognize—"

"Where did you get this one, Armina?" Georgian collapses into her chair and leans her chin on her knuckles. "Pull them straight out of Perishing?"

"That's . . ." Armina trails off, and her fingers twist into her overlong coat sleeves. "Georgian, I need your help."

"Well, that much is apparent." Georgian points sharply at Armina's leg. "Did you think you could hide that limp from me? Take a seat and let me inspect the damage."

Armina grimaces but plants herself on a bench that's been haphazardly shoved into one corner. I follow, but I perch lightly, ready to run if necessary. Kateryna sits cross-legged on the end of Georgian's worktable and watches us.

Armina puts her hands on her upper thigh, one on the outside and one on the inside. She grits her teeth and twists. There's the shifting sound of metal, and then Armina pulls her leg, boot and all, out of her pants. She hands it to Georgian like she's handing her a book.

Now that the prosthesis is uncovered, I see all the places my enchantment hasn't fixed it. There's a huge dent in the thigh, and the knee twists slightly outward. It rattles as Georgian peels the boot off and passes that back to Armina.

Georgian straightens the knee and holds the limb up to her face. "Fox and Fiddler, Armina, what did you do to it?"

"It wasn't exactly something I *did*. Although that's part of our problem." Armina recounts the story of the Huntsman tied up in her truck. I try not to think about his face, the arrogant tilt of his jaw. His void-black eyes.

"We think the Huntsmen are after us. If we're gonna keep the *Blackblood* in business, we're gonna need a way to keep them off our trail."

"And you thought I could help with that?" Georgian weighs the leg in her hands before hefting it over her shoulder and making her way toward her bench again. "Well, let's take care of our most pressing problem first. You'll have trouble running from any Huntsmen with only one leg."

Georgian lays the leg down a few feet away from the metal arm and sits. Kateryna turns to face her.

"You need to replace the joint," Kateryna says, "if not the entire casing."

"But you can re-enchant it?" Georgian pulls on her goggles.

Kateryna's grim expression splits into a smirk. "Can *I* re-enchant it? Please. Although I'll need to strip it first. Looks like someone's tried to place a hasty enchantment over the original." Her eyes flick toward me, then back to her work.

"Sorry it isn't perfect." My fingers curl on my knees. "I've never done anything like it before."

A strand of blonde hair sticks to Kateryna's cheek, following the curve of a vein. "I didn't assume you had."

A retort rises in my mouth, but I catch it between my teeth before it tumbles out.

Georgian doesn't even glance up as she says, "It's not a bad patch job for someone who's never seen our work. Besides"—she picks up a screwdriver and begins dismantling the shin—"kid looks like they've never seen the light of day outside a Community."

Kateryna's expression softens into a mangled mix of curiosity and pity. No, no, this isn't *fair*. None of it is, from the silver graphite stain on the heel of her hand to the way the toe of her shoe touches Georgian's fingers. The way she doesn't need to hide the veins on her skin under a red-wool hood and a stupid animal mask. I peel the latter from around my neck and drop it onto the bench beside me with a clatter.

"What's it like?" Kateryna holds out her palm without taking her eyes off me, and Georgian places a few screws in it.

The question sets me on edge. "What's what like?"

"Living in a Community. I was born outside, so I've never even seen one."

The magic inside me curls inward as my muscles tense. "What . . . what do you mean you were born outside?"

"Oh, I assumed most people were? My mother kept my brother and I well away from wandering Huntsmen, so we've never had too much of an issue. We had to rely on people like Georgian, but Crotalus City's more welcoming than most, from what I've heard. You were born in one, then?"

I grew up in a brick cage being poked and prodded, threatened and contained. My mother grew up like that, and this woman has the nerve, the *audacity*, to have never known it.

There's a loud knock from down the hall. Kateryna slides off the table and leaves the room.

"Finally," Georgian mumbles. "I'm starving." She leans back in her chair and pushes up her goggles. "Don't get too mad at Kat, kid. She's never met a Community mage, and sometimes, her excitement gets ahead of her brain."

"She must think I'm something to gawk at," I say. "A reminder of what she could have been if she were born to someone else."

"Aye, maybe. You can't fault her for that."

"Why shouldn't I?" Heat rises in my face, bringing with it the need to scream. I don't want to be stared at and pitied like an animal in a cage anymore. I want to leave that life a thousand miles behind. "Why do you let her answer the door?"

"I'm not letting her do anything. The door needs to get answered, and I'm busy."

"What if it's a Huntsman?"

"You grew up around the Huntsmen. Do you think they knock?"

Kateryna returns with a plastic bag full of something that smells like grease and salt. She divides the contents between herself and Georgian, opening containers and spreading them out. She holds a flat paper box with soggy corners toward me. "They gave us extra dumplings. Want some?"

"No."

"They're good," she promises with a smile.

"I'll take some," Armina says.

I push out of my seat and cross the room, tug the box from Kateryna's hand.

"All of Crotalus's food is good," she continues as I spin around and drop the box into Armina's palms. "And there are a million places to try. We can go together, if you like. Now that you're free."

"I'm not free." I sit back down beside Armina as she opens the container. "I have people waiting for me."

"Oh? Are we busting into your old Community?" She picks up her fork and delivers far too many noodles into her mouth in a single bite. "Doing a jailbreak?" she asks, words muffled around her food.

"*We're* not doing anything. *I* need to get my mother out of Perishing."

Kateryna sucks in a breath. "You can't go to Perishing."

"Were you planning to stop me?"

"Good luck," Armina says as she tears into a dumpling with her teeth.

"I can't . . . *we* can't let you." Kateryna half turns toward Georgian. "They're just a kid."

"They look old enough to make their own choices." Georgian peels the leg open like a tin can. Metal fibers stick out everywhere.

Kateryna returns her attention to me. "The Huntsmen will kill you."

"They'll kill me anyway," I snarl, the Huntsman's earlier words stabbing into my mind. "What else am I supposed to do, live in a run-down house and get married and fake being happy just because I'm surviving?"

Kateryna purses her lips. "I may not have first-hand experience with the Communities, but I know what they do to mages. I was already in my twenties when—"

"Sorry, but you haven't the first idea what they do to mages. The Huntsmen dragged my mother to Perishing, and I am going to get her out, or I am going to die."

"Your mother wouldn't want—"

"Just stop."

Kateryna grows quiet, but her face scrunches with the effort of holding back further argument.

I don't want to hear anyone talk about what my mother would want. No one knows what she'd want but me.

Georgian breaks the silence, her boisterous voice growing soft at the edges. "You remind me of someone I used to know, Canto." The air smells like burnt metal, and smoke streams from where her gloved fingers reconnect severed lines. "He did a lot of stupid shit too. Did it because he said it was the right thing. Even escaped from Perishing once."

"A mage?" I ask, focusing all my attention on Georgian's face, even though she barely acknowledges us. Maybe there's hope for my mother after all.

"Not a mage himself, but he helped a few mages get free with him. Brought them aboard his truck and drove them to me. At that point, I'd gathered a bit of a reputation as a go-to person for hiding magic. Guess he'd heard of my work."

"Are you talking about Averard?" Armina wraps an arm around her torso and picks a spot of dried blood off her collar with a thumbnail. "When did he escape Perishing? Why was he even there? He never mentioned anything about that."

Georgian's smirks. "Ah, well. He was a secretive man."

Armina fidgets. "I met another one of his former contacts the other day. In Hive. She didn't tell me her name, but she was Y'ashtrian. She said Averard did something to upset the smuggling trade, but she didn't elaborate. Must've happened recently, though. Do you know anything about that?"

Georgian sits back and removes her gloves, tilts her head toward the leg. Kateryna rounds the table to begin her enchantment. Her fingers probe between strands of metal, and the veins in her face stand out stark. Her magic warms the air, a sensation I would normally take comfort in if I weren't so on edge.

"I don't know what to tell you, kid," Georgian says.

"The truth, maybe."

"The truth's a lot of complex tangles, not all of which I understand. Dunno who this Y'ashtrian contact is, but in the past year, Averard hasn't been his usual self. Last time you were here, he and I had a chat. Seems he'd been doing something a bit counterintuitive to the trade." She leans her elbows heavily on the table. "Tracking down free mages and convincing them not to work with non-magical folk anymore."

"What?" Armina fumbles her dumplings. They fall to the floor with a wet *plap*.

If the mess bothers Georgian, she doesn't show it. Armina sheepishly retrieves the container as Georgian nods. "I thought it was strange too, but he said he realized they were getting taken advantage of. He wouldn't elaborate, but he did ask me to help some of them find homes in the city. Put a couple into hiding in one of the neighborhoods, and a few more I sent on to friendlier settlements out east. Nice folk, if rather tight-lipped about their circumstances."

I catch Armina's eye as she fidgets with her sleeves, dumpling mess entirely abandoned in the face of this new information. This Averard is starting to sound bigger than legend: traveled the country in a magic-smuggling truck, escaped Perishing, saved a number of mages. He could be a hero from one of the story books I read on the *Blackblood*—the Wanderer or the Fiddler or some similar nonsense. If that's the legacy Armina's been trying to live up to, I can see why she feels like she's falling behind.

Georgian sighs and stands from her chair. She approaches our bench and rests a solid hand on each of our shoulders. "Wish I could tell you more, but like I said, Averard kept his secrets close. If you don't know, Armina, then I certainly don't. You can rest assured he was a good man. Complicated, maybe, but good."

"I liked him!" Kateryna chimes in from the spot where she's still enchanting.

"As for how he escaped Perishing or why he was there in the first place, I assume the answer to that's probably locked up in some secret vault in Perishing itself."

Armina's breath hitches, and before I think better of it, I turn toward her and grasp her hands. It's weird to touch someone like this, and I don't fully like it, but her warmth is a comfort, even as her fingers tremble.

"Come with me to Perishing," I say. It's less a request this time. "We can get my mother out. We can discover whatever Averard was hiding."

"Canto." Armina looks a second away from breaking. "I—"

"And, done." Kateryna holds the leg aloft and inspects it beneath the lights; she must have replaced whole sections of the enchantment, as some parts are a deeper black than others. The dents and bends have disappeared, replaced with smooth, solid metal.

Georgian crosses back over to her workbench. "I can't recommend going to Perishing." She picks up the leg and flexes the joint before carrying it over to us. "But I suppose it depends how bold you're feeling. Now, let's adjust and fit this thing before we get ourselves more upset."

Armina grumbles but complies, her fingers fumbling with the buttons on her pants. I pin my eyes to the floor, where Georgian's and Kateryna's boots tap and pace.

"You should watch how we enchant it, Canto," comes Georgian's voice. "In case a few more Huntsmen decide to drop in on you on the road."

Armina clears her throat. "I was actually hoping Canto could stay here. That you could help them." *Like you helped Averard's mages*, we're probably both thinking.

"Then they'll especially need to see how this enchants, if they want to work for us."

"Work for you?" I ask, surprised. An image flashes through my mind of me sitting behind that workbench, enchanting legs and arms and who knows what else as I chat with Georgian and Kateryna over steaming boxes of food. Laughing, smiling, no longer afraid to wake up in the morning to see what fresh horrors the day might bring. Safe.

"If you'd like. We could always use another set of hands around the workshop, and after seeing what you did to Armina's prosthesis with no experience, I can't begin to imagine how good you'll be once you're trained up." She stands over us now, broad form casting a shadow across our laps.

I stuff down the temptation. Once I rescue my mother, she and I will come back. Mother would be an incredible asset to Georgian's workshop; she'd love it here.

I glance up to see that Armina has removed her pants and folded them on the bench beside her. She glares at her whole leg, the expanse of her skin uninterrupted save for a single gray sock.

The remainder of her other leg ends mid-thigh. Her coat covers her hips, but I see the metal socket where her prosthesis will connect. It's a ring around her thigh about a half foot above the scar tissue. I'm not sure how it works.

But I don't care about that.

From hip to socket, her skin is clear, with only the occasional hair or freckle.

From socket to scar tissue, her skin is black as blood.

Kateryna gasps and claps her hands over her mouth. Georgian says something to her, but I don't register its meaning. I slide off my bench to kneel on the floor before Armina. I touch her tarnished skin. She flinches away.

"What happened to you?" Kateryna whispers, as if saying the words softly will make this better. I want to scream them.

I remember the evening we captured the Huntsman, the moment we were deciding what to do with him.

Enchanted objects take on the will of their creator, I'd said. *They strive toward the purpose for which they were created.*

Same thing with enchanted people.

13

RENN

I've never been confined like this before. Even after my father's arrest, when I was secluded to my room, I'd at least had my books and papers. Something to focus my mind on so that my worries didn't eat me alive. Now? Chained against a piece of magic furniture in a dark truck with smugglers for company? If only they'd leave me alone, I'd at least be able to think.

The scarred smuggler—Valaina—sits about ten feet away on her folding chair with the mageblade the captain gave her across her lap. She's reading what appears to be an incredibly trashy romance novel, the kind you'd never find in Perishing's library. Her legs stretch out in front of her, and she licks her thumb before turning the page.

"Now that the captain is gone, why don't we talk?" I ask.

Her eyes scan the text of her book, flicking with deliberate slowness over each line. "No, thanks."

I relax against my chains. "Come now, it's just a chat between friends. Nothing you say leaves this room."

"I can't begin to explain how uninterested I am in talking to you."

"That's a shame. I miss a good conversation." I pretend to stretch, using the movement as an excuse to watch her face. "You'd be surprised how sorely lacking such a thing is at Perishing."

"I'm not even the slightest bit surprised."

"Really? You've never been to a Community, then, or been around many Huntsmen. Most of them never shut up—"

"So I've realized."

"—but I guess we didn't have much in common. I never had time for friends, growing up. Spent a lot of time reading or training with my father." I tilt my head back against the wardrobe. "What about you? What are your parents like?"

She claps her book closed and folds her arms over her chest, letting the paperback dangle loosely between her fingers. "Why do you care?"

"I'm bored. Wouldn't you be, strapped to a piece of furniture with nothing to do?"

She shrugs. "You get used to it after a while."

The smile drops from my face like she slapped it off. "What?"

Her brown eyes land on mine, and her expression doesn't change. She offers no further explanations, simply watches. It's a familiar intensity, one I myself am guilty of. Calculating people. Filing them away, ticking all the boxes to understand how best to pick them apart.

"Does it have to do with your scars?" I ask.

Her jaw tightens, and her expression curdles from curious to irritated. Seems I've checked the correct box, as she uncrosses her legs and plants her boots firmly on the floor. "Does it have to do with . . . *obviously*." Her fingers tighten on her long sleeves. "So stop whining about a few days of discomfort. I don't want to hear it until you've had a few years."

"What happened to you?" I don't mean to ask the question—it's probably in my best interest to shut up at this point, considering the tension in her shoulders. But curiosity makes the words slip out.

Valaina sneers. "Nothing that the Huntsmen care about."

"Those are blood scars," I protest.

I've never seen a case like this, but all Huntsmen are drilled and prepared for any possibility. Mage blood is full of magic, and just like drinking it makes a Huntsman more susceptible to enchantment, so would injecting it beneath the skin with a needle or even a thin blade. But Huntsmen drink so much blood that it gives them a sort of mastery over it, making them powerful enough that they can prevent unwanted enchantment by force. If a little less were used . . . an enchanter could push past the limitations of the human body. Make it the perfect, pliant host for a powerful enchantment.

"I know what they are," Valaina snarls.

"No, I mean . . . of course the Huntsmen care. Our entire work is dedicated to stopping such practices."

"They didn't care enough to rescue me. The only reason I'm here is because of Averard. And I don't think even he cared that much."

Averard. There's that name again. The thief. "Did he rescue you?"

Valaina laughs. It sounds hollow. "If you consider bartering a rescue effort, then sure, he rescued me."

"Bartering?"

"Like any other artifact aboard the *Blackblood*. I guess he went to my captors to do business, and when he spotted me, he traded wares with them to let him take me. Then we came here, and . . ." She gestures at the artifacts. "He was always adamant that the truck was a safe place, that I'd be able to grow into the person I was meant to become." She laughs. "Sentimental bullshit."

"How old were you?" I ask, suddenly uneasy.

"Twelve."

At that age, I was working toward induction into the Order—long hours of strength and mental training, long hours alone or crammed in the prison ward, surrounded by mages that glared at me out of dead eyes. Sometimes the days were painful, but they were always my choice.

What was this operation? How did the Huntsmen never hear of it? Surely those mages didn't stop their experimentation, so how had they escaped not only capture, but notice?

This conversation has opened a whole new world of work for me. Once I get out of these chains, I'll go back to Perishing, file a hunt request to track down anything that might remain. No, I'll take it directly to the Huntsmaster. Surely this is more critical than a truck smuggling magic knitting needles.

That's what my father would have said, at least. I'm not so sure about Pierce.

"Why did you stay?" I finally ask. "Why not get out of this trade if you hate magic so much?"

"You know"—Valaina slaps her book to the floor and pushes up on her knees to stand—"no one's ever asked me that before." She lifts the grip of the mageblade and twirls it in her hand. I watch the black arc of it as it carves through the air. "I suppose I wanted to see what happened. And I liked most of the company."

She swings the sword toward me. I shove my shoulders back against the wardrobe, as if I could move it far enough to save my head. However, the blade stops an inch from my neck.

In the low light of the truck's trailer, her brown eyes narrow, and a slim, irritated smile flicks onto her lips like a snake's tongue. "What are you doing here, Huntsman? Pierce promised this would all be over once Averard was dead."

The wardrobe creaks behind me as I push back harder against it. It takes a few seconds for my brain to bypass the blade at my throat long enough to focus on her words—absurd, confusing, impossible words. "You know the Huntsmaster?"

She snorts and tosses the mageblade onto her chair, only to reach into her jacket pocket and produce a sheathed knife. She pulls it out and holds the black blade up to my eyes. "You could say I know him." Above the blade's edge, her face looms before me like the sun on a dark horizon. "Signed on about a year and a half ago when I realized I couldn't play nice much longer. Pierce contacted me almost immediately. He seemed keen to make an offer."

A year and a half ago. Pierce wasn't even Huntsmaster yet.

How did he find her application? I certainly don't remember seeing it, and every speck of Perishing's paperwork goes through me. He must have stolen it at some point. But why?

"I don't understand." I say. "If you're in Pierce's pocket, why did he need me to take the truck?"

Her lip raises in a sneer as she pulls the blade away and resheathes it. "That's the question, isn't it? I'm a great asset to the Huntsmen. I don't want blood or money or power. I only asked him to give my little truck immunity from all the things that'd hurt it. Let us sell our wares and roam the countryside, happy and ignorant and unimpeded by the big bad Huntsmen. The lying bastard must've needed you to do something he knew I wouldn't."

"That can't be true." I wrench against my bonds. "I know Pierce. He would never work with smugglers."

"You think so?" Her smile widens. "All Pierce wanted was Averard dead. Once I did that, he promised the *Blackblood* would have free reign of the Federation. Armina and I would be left alone."

"No Huntsman would ever—"

"Oh, please. Pretend otherwise all you like, but the Huntsmen don't care about the people. The Huntsmen care about control."

My father cared. The Federation is a lawless place, but he pruned it into shape. Gave it the proper direction to grow. I thought Pierce cared, too. But if this is true, if Pierce would make any agreement with mage smugglers and artifacts traders, then he's as much a traitor as my father ever was.

I can barely concentrate on what Valaina is saying. It isn't until I hear the chains rattle and slump from my body that I even realize she's unlocking me.

"You need to leave." She steps back when all the chains are undone. I fall to my knees and glare up at her, rubbing my wrists as the blood comes pounding back. "I don't care where. Perishing, or somewhere in Crotalus, or you can die." She draws my mageblade from her belt and tosses it at my feet. I snatch it and cradle it to my chest.

She kicks the other blade toward me as well. "Take these. Armina might not know how they work, but I do. The sooner I get them off my truck, the better. Now, be a good Huntsman and go far, far away."

I could kill her. Maybe that would be a favor enough to Pierce that I'd get my spot, my esteem, back. His secret would be safe, and he could start trusting me like he trusts any Huntsman. Enough that the others wouldn't whisper threats and rumors about me in the halls. I could join them at mealtimes, wouldn't have to hide in the library. I could feel like I belong again.

I wish I knew what my father would do. I wish I could go to his office and ask. But this isn't my father's Order anymore. It belongs to Pierce, and whatever his motives now, whatever his change of plans, when he made this deal with Valaina, he broke his oath to protect the people from magic.

Valaina tilts her chin toward the open trailer hatch. "Run."

Outside, the sinking sun leaves Crotalus City in shadows upon shadows. The road stretches wide, empty and foreign. I have two mageblades in my hands and a world full of enemies waiting for me, with Perishing now forever at my back.

I stand. Without turning to look at her, without speaking, I jump out of the hatch and run.

14

RENN

The neon lights of Crotalus City blink a multitude of colors, and the air is hazy with cigarette smoke and diesel fumes. I race from the muddy lot and push into the crowded street. People scramble out of the way when they see me coming. A Huntsman, they must be reasoning, only runs for one thing: there's a chase to be had and magic to be crushed into the pavement.

But there are no mages to chase and crush. Only me, and I don't know what I'm running toward.

I can't go back to Perishing. Pierce—Huntsmaster, leader of the Order, the one we're meant to look to for guidance in times of trouble—has gone against his oath for unknown ends. Then he sent me to clean up the mess. Me—expendable, should-be-dead spawn of the previous Huntsmaster, who Pierce finally found a use for.

If I died, no one would mourn; no one would question. The paperwork would grow until it consumed the library, but I doubt any of the other Huntsmen even care about the archive. That was always *my* project. Only necessary in my eyes.

Everything I have ever wanted to be, my entire life, I've given to this cause. I just want to protect people.

My ears ring, and my eyes tear up from the assault of light and color and sound. It's even worse after three days crammed into the back of a truck. My muscles scream as they stretch for the first time, but I can't stop moving. I need to find somewhere safe to think.

I turn a corner, and the buildings change from new metal and stone to older brick, grime eating away the white mortar. I shove into an alley. The space between the buildings narrows until the walls scrape my arms. When I finally maneuver the last few feet, I stumble into the open night air.

A woman squeaks and jumps back as I emerge, clutching a paper shopping bag. "H-Huntsman," she stutters.

What must I look like? Bruises all over my body, mage blood from the earlier slap on my face, hair and clothes an utter wreck. I stand up straighter, but she shrinks away and hurries off.

Before I left Perishing on this doomed bullshit mission, I'd been to Crotalus City a handful of times. I used to follow my father's boots to the Order's local post, stalk the marketplace for interesting trinkets, people-watch while my father haggled with local officials. Visits, like all things in my life, were regimented. Regulated. I saw only what it was appropriate for a Huntsman recruit to see.

Here, the mouth of the alley opens into a concrete, chain-linked square. A ring of houses lines the perimeter, with brick facades and crumbling porches and weed-strewn yards. There's paint on the ground denoting children's games, and two trees grow through the cracked asphalt.

Magic vibrates in the air, making it sing.

Children chase one another under the dim house lights. A pair of dogs run, barking, bounding after them. Adults watch from doorways and porch steps, smiling. I don't see any veins, but I know a mage is close. More than one, probably. A family.

Valaina's story rings in the back of my mind.

A little neighborhood like this could hide all manner of secrets, but I don't have time to investigate. I don't even have the authority anymore. But there's magic on the wind, and this is what I was built to do. In the encroaching darkness, as the city's light pollution makes the sky a purple-brown smudge, I pause.

And though each of my senses tunes itself in the pursuit of magic, I still manage to catch the tire iron before it connects with my skull.

I adjust my grip on the metal rod that came inches from concussing me and turn toward my assailant. It's a man, smaller than me and several decades older. He wears pajamas—something more suited to lounging than walking the city streets at night. He isn't even wearing shoes.

"Leave," he snarls. He wrenches at the tire iron.

I yank my arm in, then down, breaking his grip on the weapon. I toss it into the darkness of the alley behind us. "Why did you attack me?"

I study his face, his evening stubble and bushy eyebrows. In the low light, his pale cheeks flush, and while veins are visible beneath the white hair on his arms, they're a normal blue.

"Get out now, before my wife comes back with the rifle," he says.

He swings at me bare-fisted. The punch connects, but it's too weak to hurt much, and he hisses and shakes his hand. After a moment's recuperation, he swings at me again, and this time, I catch his fist, spin him around, and pull his arm behind his back. He sucks in a pained breath.

I'm fighting an old man. Why am I fighting an old man? What made him step off the safety of his porch to attack someone a third his age and ten times his skill level? It only makes sense if he's incredibly intoxicated or if he's protecting something.

Protecting something.

A woman barrels from one of the houses, waving the long nose of her rifle. It's the woman I almost bumped into earlier, the one with the grocery bag. Around us, on all those creaky porches, parents clutch the shoulders of their children. Children crane their necks to get a better look. There's no more laughter in the dark square, and the music and growling of engines from streets away have faded into an inconsequential hum.

I release the man, and he falls. I back away until my shoulders hit the brick of the house behind me. The woman stops to comfort the man. Her rifle is lowered. Her eyes are off me.

These people have never been in a brawl before. They've never faced something that could kill them without trying. Except that within their midst, a mage hides, taking advantage. Letting sheep protect a wolf.

"What should we do?" the woman asks.

The man sits upright. "If we let him go now, he'll go back to his cohort."

I shake my head. "Stand down. I need—"

I barely manage to yank my head out of the way as a bullet embeds itself into the brick behind me. It grazes my ear, and all sound turns tinny as blood spatters down the side of my neck.

And once again, I'm running.

The next shot hits a wooden porch, exploding the step in a hail of splinters. The nearby occupants, still watching the encounter, gasp and usher their families into the relative safety of their houses. As another shot cracks the asphalt to my left, I dive into an alley between two of the homes.

No footsteps follow. A mistake on their part. Shooting me in the narrow alley would have been simple, even for someone unskilled with a gun. Too afraid to give chase, then. They're probably more worried about hiding their mages right now than killing me. I imagine hurried, hushed meetings, connections being contacted. Maybe the mages will be hidden aboard a truck like the *Blackblood* by a similarly well-meaning but stupid smuggler like Armina. Driven to the Tidal Wall or the Y'ashtrian border or some insignificant settlement in the middle of the desert. Their whole lives uprooted because one lost Huntsman stumbled out of the wrong alley.

I exit onto more-familiar streets, the dark canopies of the closed marketplace snapping in the wind. I catch echoes of my childhood—the stale smells of people and incense and food linger even after the shopping day has concluded. I used to wander here while waiting for my father to finish his meetings at the marble town hall. Its golden bell tower rises above the market's awnings.

My feet lead me down the street to another familiar spot: the old wooden bench where I used to sit and swing my legs and watch people go about their business. It was fun to make up stories for them—why was this man scowling; why was that woman so hurried? Who were they, and what did they want? Everyone wore their lives on their faces and in their gestures. No one lies while doing their shopping.

I fall onto that bench now, my feet planted on the ground, utterly alone.

If people here *want* to defend mages, want to keep them in their neighborhoods as part of their communities, then why do I exist? Why do any of the Huntsmen exist? I can't shake the animosity in the old man's eyes, the fear in the woman's. They weren't even mages, and they hated me.

Something cracks in my mind. Splinters. I think about Pierce breaking our rules as it suits him, think of my father's terrified face in the exsanguination chamber. Maybe there's a reason those people were so angry. A reason I've never allowed myself to contemplate, one I hid from beneath papers and ink and ignorance.

"Hey there."

Someone leans on the back of my bench. I snap around.

Huntsman Baker leers at me, appearing markedly better than he did the other day—clothes clean and leg splinted. His lopsided grin indicates they've overloaded him with blood. He looks deranged.

Beside him stands Carrie, one of the newer recruits—a hulking red-headed man a year younger than me, only a few months off his first drink of blood. His black eyes still have the slightest hint of green.

Iverson brings up the rear, a scowl on her face as she jogs to a halt. "Baker," she snaps. "You can't just—"

"Yeah, yeah. But look what I found."

I ease off the bench and onto my feet. Carrie glances nervously between the others, his already blotchy face getting redder. Iverson stops glaring at Baker and looks toward me, her eyebrows raised.

"The others're gonna piss themselves," Baker continues, attention returning to me. "The Huntsmaster let me drink *your* blood this time, Mason."

"Not exactly where we expected to find him, but I suppose the details are of little consequence." Iverson rolls her shoulders, and her hand falls to the hilt of her mageblade. "Renn Mason, you are to report back to Perishing immediately. For trial."

My head spins. "For what crime?"

"Same as your father," Baker spits. "Magefucking."

I lunge at him, but in one sweep, Iverson has her mageblade at my throat, the edge pressed beneath my jaw. I back up several paces, and she follows.

"For conspiring against the Huntsmaster," she says, "for planning insurrection, and for keeping company with mages and mage supporters."

"What proof do you have?" I demand.

"What proof do we need?" She removes her blade from my throat and slides it back into her scabbard. "The Huntsmaster sent you on a simple fetch-and-return mission, and here you are, walking around Crotalus City in the dead of night, having neither fetched nor returned. Pierce knows how persuasive those smugglers can be, and since you're head archivist, we can't let all that knowledge fall into the wrong hands."

"My archives? Iverson, with all due respect, you didn't even know my library *existed* until—"

"Is that my mageblade?" Baker interrupts with a snarl. He limps toward me, his leg still stiff and awkward. He's in no fit state to be on a hunt. For that matter, someone like Iverson would never stoop so low as to work such a routine mission. Finding one missing Huntsman? It's the type of job I'd assign to a new recruit like Carrie—have him drink the Huntsman's blood, let him traipse across the Federation alone. It's not the type of job for seasoned veterans, and certainly not for the Huntsmaster's second-in-command.

"Why are the three of you even here?" I lower myself into a more defensive crouch.

Iverson's lips quirk. "Let's just say we were trying to find the sword, not you."

Baker bares his teeth. "Give me my mageblade, Mason." He lurches toward me, but I sidestep him easily.

"Some party the Huntsmaster sent," I growl at Baker. "You're practically falling apart."

"A broken leg won't stop me killing you," he snaps. "Anyone can tell how weak you are. When's the last time you drank?"

Iverson laughs, showing all her sharp, white teeth. "Mason doesn't take blood with us. He's too busy fucking his file cabinets."

It's difficult to be present in this moment, to not fall into the instinctual need to fight, to defend myself. I am better than that. I *am*. No matter what they think of me or of what my father did—

"Lot of rumors going around about your dad," Baker continues. "Heard he tore apart half a squadron when they arrested him. That can't be right, though. Not with you for a son." He clicks his tongue. "If Pierce hadn't found all that evidence of his crimes, your father might've turned the whole Order just as weak."

I spring at Baker, and Iverson isn't fast enough to stop me this time. He's howling in laughter as my shoulder connects with his torso, and we sprawl to the ground. His laughter quickly turns to rage as his back hits the dirt, and he tries to shove me off. My hands find his throat, and my legs clamp down on his shins, and with a jolt of pleasure, I hear the snap as his leg refractures.

I tighten my hands, bear my weight down. Pierce's evidence. Of course; of *course*. The man at the heart of all my fucking problems, twisting and turning and ruining *everything*. I believed in the Order's cause, even when it cost me my family. Believed in protecting people from things they don't understand. I poured my soul into paperwork and files, into keeping quiet and tame and loyal. That loyalty has bought me nothing.

My father tainted his own legacy, but this is mine. And if he could take out half a squadron, then I can take out all of Perishing.

Arms loop under mine and yank me off Baker's battered body. He sits up, spitting blood and teeth into the dirt, while I struggle against my new captor. Carrie grunts in my ear as he grapples with me, and I realize that maybe Baker had a point. It's been far too long since I drank any blood, and now I'm facing the consequences.

I should have taken a vial before I left Perishing. I should have drunk some over the last few weeks like Huntsmen are supposed to.

Carrie may be as tall as me and full of mage blood, but he's not as big or nearly as experienced. I jerk forward and throw him over my shoulder, and he lands in the dirt beside Baker.

Iverson's mageblade whistles through the air, forcing me back before I attack Baker again. The tip of her sword drags through my shirt, tearing it open as I plunge my hand down to draw my own blade. *My* blade. I'll throw Baker's into the next body of water I come across.

Iverson slices forward, and I catch her blade with mine. She's smaller than me, and I push that advantage, shoving hard on her sword to get it to drop. But she follows through and brings her sword out from beneath, and once again, it's arcing toward my chest.

I block. She slides the strong part of her blade by the hilt toward the weaker tip of mine, and I'm forced to bend backward at an awkward angle to avoid having my face sliced off. Iverson is the superior swordswoman, and as my blade slips off hers once more, I know I can't defeat her this way.

I push hard away from her and back up. For the third time tonight, I need to run.

"*Stop him,*" Baker snarls at Carrie as he struggles to drag himself off the ground.

Carrie rounds on me, but Iverson halts him with a single sweep of her hand. The radio strapped to her chest is beeping in time with its flashing red light. Iverson tugs it from her lapel and holds it to her mouth. "Sir?"

A deep, familiar voice crackles through the receiver. I can't understand the words, but a grin creeps onto Iverson's face, and she sheathes her sword. "Of course, Huntsmaster. We'll return at once."

She clips the radio back onto her chest. Our eyes meet, and she tilts her head toward the dark stain of Crotalus's buildings. "Go ahead, Mason. Go ahead and run. You've done your bit; the Order doesn't need you anymore."

I've known that truth for the last year. Hearing it said out loud, however, dredges the pain all the way up to the surface. The Order doesn't need me anymore. Maybe it never did. A single scorpion is inconsequential in the scope of the whole desert.

So I do as Iverson says and follow that last command. I turn tail and run.

The moment I'm far enough away, the moment the shadows of the alley overtake me, I let my sword slip from my hand and try to collect myself. I am *exhausted*. Not just from days spent suspended against a wardrobe, but from a life spent working toward a future that was never meant to be mine.

I'm angry, confused. I have no outlet for these feelings, and the streets are an unsafe place to explore them. I have to find shelter; I have to find a direction; I—

I could try to find Armina.

She mentioned she was going to take the mage somewhere. A benefactor, I think she said? Implied the mage would be safe wherever they were going.

Maybe I could be safe too.

15
CANTO

The blackened enchantment on Armina's skin could burn a hole through my palm. Maybe it would have, but Georgian nudges me out of her way. I move stiffly to the bench as she kneels before Armina and slots her prosthesis back on. Once it's attached, Georgian tests the connection, pushing the knee back against Armina's chest.

I dig into my pocket for my mother's pendant, press its spines into my palm. "Who enchanted you? When?"

Georgian steps back, and Armina rises. She bounces up and down, then crouches a few times. "Dunno."

"What do you mean, you don't know? Why aren't you worried—"

"Why should I worry?" She runs her hands down the smooth metal of her leg, eyes glued to the joint. "It's never bothered me before."

Her disregard floors me. I grew up knowing that magic is broad, but magic has rules, and one of those rules is you never, ever enchant people. To bend someone else to your will, to mold them toward a purpose—it's vile. I saw those blackened scars on Valaina, but those were only the promises of an enchantment, not the finished product. Papercuts compared to a bullet wound.

Armina sits back down and pulls on her pants. All her actions up to this point—from allowing me to stay aboard the *Blackblood* to what she decided to have for breakfast this morning—could be dictated by this enchantment. Humans aren't like boots or books; they're malleable. You can enchant them to do basically anything with the right amount of power.

Georgian rubs her chin in her hand. "I don't know that it's cause for panic, but Canto may have a point. The enchantment's spread since the last time you were here."

"I know," Armina says. "I'm keeping an eye on it, and if it climbs any further, Valaina will help me cut it back."

"*What?*" I demand. "Have you just been hacking your leg apart as the enchantment gets stronger?"

"No." Armina crosses her arms. "Growing up, it was only blackened on the scar tissue. I assumed whoever enchanted my leg just took it, you know? That the leg was what they wanted, gross as that sounds. It only started spreading about a year back. Faster recently."

"Why doesn't this upset you?"

Armina expels air in a huff, then stands and rounds on me. "It does upset me, but what am I gonna do about it? It's my *body*. It's not going anywhere, and panicking every time I think about it won't solve anything."

"This could kill you!" The house is stifling, and impressing upon Armina how awful this situation is has become my number one priority. "Depending on the savvy of the caster, this enchantment could make you do anything, *feel* anything."

"And I guess for the last nineteen years it wanted me to be a boring kid growing into a boring adult?"

"Maybe! Whatever it wants from you could come later— trigger at a certain age, at a certain distance. It could command you to murder someone, to kill yourself, to commit any number of crimes. You could kill Valaina; you could've killed Aver—"

She grabs my shirtfront and jerks me down until our noses touch. Her brown eyes blaze into mine. "Do you really think the terrors you're imagining I haven't also thought a thousand times?" Her voice is ice; the frost of it blooms down my spine. "There's nothing I can do. There's nothing you can do either."

She shoves me away. My legs hit the bench, and I collapse onto it. She gives me one last look before turning back to Georgian. "Thanks for the tune up. I'll wire your fee as soon as I can."

Georgian crosses her arms and leans back against her worktable. "And what about that Huntsman problem you wanted help solving?"

Armina shakes her head. "We'll worry about it another time." She tips her chin to Kateryna and storms out of the room. I hear her footsteps all the way down the hall, followed by the *creak-bang* of the door opening and closing.

I stare after her in numb silence.

"That girl." Georgian makes her way around her table and settles into the chair. She picks up a delicate blade and slices some of the exterior wires on the arm she'd been maintaining before.

"How awful," Kateryna mumbles.

I turn toward her. For the first time since we met, I feel the connection, the kinship of magic. Kateryna doesn't understand the Communities, but she might understand this. "Armina is making a terrible mistake."

Kateryna grimaces, but it's Georgian who responds. "What mistake's that?"

"She isn't taking this seriously."

"I think she takes it plenty seriously."

"Georgian." I stomp up to the worktable. "Armina is enchanted."

"What do you propose she do about that?"

This roundabout interrogation makes me want to scream. Armina is enchanted, and that could kill her. It could kill her and everyone around her.

"She needs to *care*." The tide of panic rises in my gut, making me want to vomit. "There must be something we can do. Maybe I could override the enchantment with another one—"

"What if that makes things worse?"

"I don't know!" I slam my palm down on the table, and a few loose screws jitter away. "I don't know how to solve this, but I cannot sit around and do nothing. The first eighteen years of my life involved sitting around and doing nothing. The enchantment on Armina doesn't care if we ignore it or if we're blindly optimistic that it will leave her alone. It's a bomb waiting to explode, and if it does, she won't be Armina anymore."

Georgian sets down her tools. She pushes out of her chair and walks toward me. Her eyes sweep over my hair, the veins in my throat. "Listen, Canto, I don't want you to think I'm patronizing you or anything, but you're young. You're fresh out of the Community, and I doubt you've met anyone who isn't a mage or a Huntsman before. The world's a lot bigger than the place you grew up, and people come with all different sorts of traumas."

"This is magic, though. I understand magic—"

"But you don't understand Armina. You think she's spent the last two decades enjoying having that thing in her leg? No, she's done her time being scared shitless of it. You reach a limit where you realize you've spent so long being afraid of something that there's no point in it. It's always there; it's always going to exist, and worrying about it'll only make you miserable."

The problem is, I *do* understand that.

Surrounded every day by Huntsmen, you eventually learn to ignore them. Ignore them long enough, and they become part of the scenery. Days can go by without ever having to interact with them, without having to think of them at all.

Until they catch you feeling safe and decide to swallow you whole.

I clench my fists, turn around, and cross toward the door.

"Where're you going?" Georgian asks.

"There must be some way I can help."

Kateryna snags my sleeve as I pass. "Are you sure? We could always use an extra hand around the shop, and I'd love to give you a tour of the city once you've settled in. There are so many fun things to see." The smile slips off her face. "You'd be safe here."

When she says it, I almost believe her. I almost believe there's a safe place left in the world, and that it happens to be in a run-down prosthetics shop.

I tug my sleeve from her grip. "I have to save Armina. I have to save my mother. I have to destroy the Huntsmen. And if I stay here too long, I'll become too complacent to do what needs to be done."

Georgian sighs. "I'll walk you back."

But I'm already halfway out the door.

I exit the house into the cold air. Someone in the neighborhood has turned on a radio, and staticky music twines down the street. I throw myself off the porch steps and into the night, the road back to the *Blackblood* alive in my brain.

I don't spot Armina again until I've already passed the shopfront with its mirror, passed the spot where the food vendors had set up their carts. She comes into view with her hands crammed into her pockets, wind tossing the flyaway hairs she hasn't managed to capture in her ponytail. She pauses at the final street, the dirt lot and the *Blackblood* now in sight.

"You're pretty loud for someone so light," she says. She turns toward me, eyebrows raised. "Might want to work on that."

I slink out of the shadow of a building. "I managed to sneak aboard your truck."

"A miracle." She hugs her coat closer. "What do you want, then? Got one last jab about how I'm going to kill everyone I love?"

The ten-foot distance between us might as well be the whole desert. "That came out blunter than I intended. I was just . . ." I struggle for the right word, the right connotation. "Scared."

She remains perfectly still as she watches this confession, and for a moment, I wonder if she's going to send me away again. What do I really know about Armina, anyway? How much can you get to know someone over the course of a week?

Then she sighs and joins me by the building's reaching shade. "Me too," she says. "Petrified, really. Before Averard died, he told me he had my enchantment under control. But he never let me in on what that control was, and now I have nothing. Valaina likes to pretend it doesn't exist, and I know better than to bring it up in front of her."

I take a deep breath. "There might be answers in Perishing."

She frowns at me. "I'm starting to think there's a lot of things in Perishing."

"If your—if Averard could break out, then we know it's possible. Maybe there's a solution to your enchantment there, or an answer as to why Averard died. My mother is the smartest mage I know. She could help you find answers, too; I'm sure of it."

Hesitation washes over Armina's face. She draws her bottom lip into her mouth and glances back at the truck. As the breeze brings with it the smells of tire rubber and damp earth, my heart leaps knowing she's at least considering it.

Then comes the shout.

It's a masculine howl, somewhere between a scream and a belt of laughter, and it comes from the direction of the truck. Armina freezes, then uses her body to edge me deeper into the building's shadow. I can't make out much from this distance, but I see the silhouettes of people converging on the truck. Two dozen swarming shapes.

The howling grows louder.

Armina's eyes fix on the outline in the lot. There's another shout. Raucous laughter. Silence.

The silhouettes around the truck have stilled to a terribly familiar, unwavering poise. I remember the silence Huntsmen are capable of, remember this quivering dread in the pit of my stomach.

"Stay here." Armina takes a step toward the lot, but I grasp her hand and reel her back into the safety of my shadow.

"Please don't go." My voice sounds small to my ears, as if it belongs to someone else.

"That's my truck; I—it's a captain's duty to defend their ship. If I can't do that, I can't call myself the—"

"The Huntsmaster is with them."

Her shoulders stiffen. Her breaths come out in frightened little bursts. "How do you—"

"Did you hear the way it got quiet?" I ask. "Huntsmen like to make noise, like they want to prove they exist as much as possible. But when the Huntsmaster is around . . ." I trail off, letting the utter, dreadful silence speak for itself.

Armina pulls her sleeve out of my grip. "Valaina's in the *Blackblood*. I can't leave her."

"You will *die*."

"You want to go to Perishing to save your mother, even though it'll kill you." She steps out of the shadow. "Maybe this is where I'll die trying."

She begins to walk toward the dirt lot, and I chase after her, catching up in a few strides. "I'll come with you, then. Together, we might be able to—"

She turns on me, so fast that it makes me stumble. She places a palm on my shoulder and pushes me away. "You're staying here. Go back to Georgian and tell her what's happening."

"I can't let you—"

"For once, Canto!" she snarls, shoving me backward again. "For godsdamned *once*, don't argue with me."

My hands fall to my sides. It feels as if the ground has cracked under my feet and is sucking me below.

Armina's hands ball into fists, and I wouldn't be surprised if she stomped her foot like a child just to exhaust her frustration. "I said I'd get you to safety, and you're going to *stay* safe," she continues. "Go. Georgian will know what to do."

She turns, hair whipping with her momentum, and stalks toward the lot.

Before I can breathe again, Armina is gone.

The night is still as glass, and the Huntsman stay silent. Blood pounds in my head, a rapid beat similar to being punched over and over. Heat crawls up my face, and I clutch my chest, doubling over as I try to breathe. Armina is going to die; Armina is going to die; Armina is—

"Well, shit."

I spin around. My feet catch on one another, and I bang hard to my knees. The ground scrapes open the barely healed cuts on my palms.

Leaning against the building, arms crossed and eyes pinned to the surrounded truck, is a Huntsman. A Huntsman who is supposed to be chained tight inside the trailer of that truck.

He frowns, and when his lips pull down, I see he still has some of my blood on his face.

16

ARMINA

The lights of Crotalus City drown out most of the stars.

The Crooked Viper's still overhead, burning as bright as always through the reddish haze. Everything else is a faded gray or too dim to make out as more than a blur. As the pavement turns to dirt beneath my boots, my mind's full of fears and constellations.

Averard would've said that it's fine to be afraid, good even, as long as I use that fear to act. So as the silhouette of my surrounded truck looms larger into view, I swallow down the boiling-hot uncertainty and prepare to face it.

A loose fence surrounds the parking lot, a mix of iron and wooden posts. I press my back against a beam and peer inward. The Huntsmen form a half circle around the truck, and I count about twenty of them from where I'm hidden. They stand uncomfortably still, so much so that if I didn't know what they were, I'd assume someone had planted a bunch of statues in the lot.

The night cracks with the familiar scraping shudder of the hatch opening. None of the Huntsmen move.

I have to get in there. They're not looking in my direction, so maybe . . .

I rush forward. To my ears, my boots sound louder than the *Blackblood's* engine. I use the few other trucks in the lot as cover, sliding along their sides and glancing around their headlights. Through driver and passenger windows, other truckers gaze down at me. A few even jerk their heads as if inviting me to hide in their trucks until the danger passes. But I ignore them and pray they remain silent.

The Huntsmen don't appear to notice my unstealthy approach. Even as I draw closer, none of them turn or twitch. It's like they're mesmerized.

When I reach the *Blackblood's* grille, I cling to the familiar metal and try to stabilize my heartbeat. Brother's Blood, what am I doing? No plan, all thoughtless action. If I could only get into the truck's cab without them noticing me and drive it through their weird little statue party. A few more Huntsmen under my tires'd do the world some good.

They must be here to rescue Renn. I should've killed him when I realized he couldn't give me what I wanted, but Averard always said lives were more useful than that. Throwing them away might bring you satisfaction, but it won't get you anything else.

Now all it's gotten me is the attention of the Huntsmaster.

The trailer rattles as people walk through it. I hear a *thud* as someone jumps out the back, followed quickly by a second. Then Valaina's voice snarls, "What the fuck are you doing here?"

My heart leaps. I shouldn't've worried so much. Valaina'd never go down unless it was with fists swinging.

A smooth, masculine voice responds, speaking calmly and ignoring her blatant disrespect. "My lieutenant radioed to inform me that she encountered the Huntsman I sent after you wandering the streets."

"I let him go," Valaina says. "You think I wanted one of your men on my truck?"

I strain harder to listen. Maybe Valaina saw the Huntsmen coming and released Renn to avoid such incriminating evidence?

I'd say it was good thinking, but admitting it now only makes us look more guilty.

"Pity. I was hoping you'd kill him."

What?

"I don't do favors for free."

"Of course not." There's a pause, then the man asks, "Where is your captain?"

"Dead," Valaina snaps.

"Your *other* captain."

"Dunno; maybe she's dead too."

The *Blackblood* shakes as something slams against its metal side. Valaina lets out a coughing laugh. "So the Huntsmaster's word means shit," she snarls. "What about our bargain?"

All the blood drains from my face; all my bones turn to ash. *Bargain*? With the *Huntsmaster*?

"If she's dead"—the man's voice remains calm—"consider our 'bargain' null."

I'm a full truck's length away from them, but I still hear Valaina's harsh breathing, hear her boots struggling against the muddy ground. The ground that may well have given out under *me* for all I feel attached to it. How long's Val been in contact with the Huntsmaster, and what does that mean for us? Did she ever love me? Does she know who killed Averard? Was she . . .

I swallow the thought away, unable to bear thinking it. I already lost the roadmap of my life when Averard died, and after what Georgian said, it's starting to seem like I never had a proper grasp on it anyway. Now I'm wondering if I ever knew anything at all.

My fingers curl against the headlight. *Betrayal, betrayal, betrayal.*

Something lands heavily in the dirt, and Valaina gasps in pain.

The Huntsmen burst back to life. The truck shakes as people pour aboard it, and my stomach churns at the thought of the Huntsmen taking the *Blackblood*, of them picking through the precious contents of Averard's life. The door of the cab flies open, and I duck closer to the ground, heart hammering.

What would Averard do? He'd form a plan, one that would have these Huntsmen dead or turning tail. He'd lift me into the cab and jump into the driver's seat, and he'd howl with laughter as we drove our way out of Crotalus City. We'd go for hours until we reached the safety of the open road, then stop and have food around the fire while we told tales of our close-but-not-close call.

But there is no Averard anymore, and with Valaina's *bargain*, it's starting to look like there isn't much of the *Blackblood* left at all.

The truck rumbles to life against my cheek. Canto was right: I need to get to Perishing. If there's even a slim chance of something being there that explains all this, then I'd be a fool not to try to take it. Canto and I will save their mother, we'll scour the stronghold, and we'll escape just like Averard did.

My chest slams against the *Blackblood's* grille, knocking the wind from my lungs. The truck's growl reverberates in my rib cage, and a blade presses to my throat.

"Take her weapon," a feminine voice says, and a hand tugs my revolver from its holster at my hip.

I turn my head, but the blade follows.

"Not smart, moving about so much," the voice says. Then, "Grab her."

Another tug comes at my collar, and the ground slips out from beneath me.

I'm lifted into the air by Averard's coat, the seams digging into my underarms. A burly Huntsman holds me aloft, my toes not even touching the ground. The sword disappears from my throat, and now I see the person who wields it: a petite woman with curly hair and black eyes.

The Huntswoman sheathes her weapon and steps toward me. She's so close I can count the freckles on her face. "You must be our captain."

I swing my leg toward her, but she leans back quick enough that I catch only air.

"Look at you!" the woman says. "Biting at your betters. What do you think, Griffiths? Can the little rabbit break her snare?"

The Huntsman holding me laughs and shakes Averard's coat. The seams dig deeper.

"Pierce'll be pleased the hunt is over," the woman continues. "I'll go fetch him; you make sure she doesn't slip off."

The Huntswoman turns and disappears around the *Blackblood's* trailer.

I reach back and dig my nails into the hand holding me. Skin snaps beneath my fingers, and blood wets the space between our hands. The Huntsman hisses in pain and shakes me again, but I dig my fingers deeper into his new wounds.

Coming to the lot was a mistake. It was all a mistake, and I have to get free.

My heel catches the Huntsman's stomach, and he drops me with a grunt, but the second I regain my footing, he knees me in the chest, and I sprawl to the ground. I swallow a mouthful of dirt as he grabs my hair and yanks up.

"Huntsmaster wants you alive." He winds my ponytail around his fist. "Didn't say anything about needing you conscious."

He punches me in the face.

My head jerks back, taking some of my hair with it. Blood trickles down my scalp, and one of my teeth cuts clean through my lip. My skull reverberates with the impact, and a bolt like static electricity runs through my entire body. For some reason, it feels as if my leg is gonna fall off.

Once again, I'm thrown to the ground.

I lie there, stunned, muck seeping down my collar. The starless sky watches me, vast and smokey, and the ringing in my ears drowns out everything else. I taste dirt and blood and bile.

A pair of feet strides into view, and the voice I heard talking to Valaina earlier speaks over me. "Get her up."

Arms loop under my own and lift me high enough that only the toes of my boots scrape the ground. My eyes blur as I try to focus on the surrounding faces of the Huntsmen, but my attention falls on the one standing directly in front of me.

The Huntsmaster.

I don't know how I know it's him; he's just . . . different from the others. Even through the pain and confusion, he gives off the aura of someone who understands his own authority. His back is so straight. His black eyes are so certain.

He makes me want to throw up. He makes me want to hide.

"What happened here?" the Huntsmaster asks. He turns toward me. "What did you do to him?"

He gestures to the ground. The Huntsman who hit me lies on his back in the dirt.

I can't even formulate words around my split mouth and pounding temples, so I resort to shaking my head.

"Iverson." The Huntsmaster points toward the prone figure, and the Huntswoman from earlier snaps to attention and hastens to her fallen comrade's side. She bends over him, hands pressed against his chest as she inspects his face.

"Brother's Blood," she swears, rocking back on her heels.

The Huntsmaster's eyebrows quirk. "Interesting."

"What should we do with him?" Iverson's eyes meet mine, and she searches my face as if looking for answers.

My head spins, and I try not to vomit all over myself. I have no idea what just happened. Everything hurts.

"Leave him. We have places to be, and I'm sure he got no more than he deserved." The Huntsmaster walks off.

The Huntsman holding me upright scoops me into his arms and follows.

He isn't holding me nicely, but no matter how I push and protest, he doesn't give an inch. Blood drips down my throat, and a steady pain squeezes my scalp and jaw. We follow a few paces after the Huntsmaster, and I hear the slow dissipation of the Huntsmen we left behind.

The Huntsmaster crosses over to the *Blackblood's* cab, opens the driver's door, and climbs inside. The Huntsman carries me to the passenger side and tosses me unceremoniously onto the seat. He slams the door shut behind me.

I tug at the handle and shove against the door. It doesn't budge. The top of the other Huntsman's head is still visible through the window, like he's holding the door closed from the outside.

The Huntsmaster settles into the driver's seat and leans out the still-broken window to adjust the mirror. Then he revs the engine and shifts into drive. We ease our way through the lot, and a sense of deep wrongness settles over me. I'm bleeding, and my head aches, and there's a man other than Averard driving my truck.

The truck bumps along the road in a familiar way, but I feel like an outsider beside the Huntsmaster. I curl Averard's coat against my knees, knowing I'm getting my own bloodstains on the leather beside his. I could throw open the door right now, pitch myself onto the road. Maybe the back wheels would run me over. Maybe I'd live. I feel like Pierce would come for my body either way.

Once we're in the desert proper, once we leave the crooked buildings of Crotalus behind, the Huntsmaster glances my way. He's got an oddly blank look about him, even as he studies me. His gaze travels over my split lip, and his eyes settle on my leg.

"I'm Huntsmaster Pierce." He turns back toward the windshield as we enter the desert. "Not an easy hunt, finding you."

"What do you want?" I ask.

Pierce's eyes glint in the headlights. Darkness hides most of his expression, but I watch those eyes narrow. "Not much, Armina. Just taking back what's mine."

17

RENN

There's a reason I never worked with mages back in Perishing. I convinced myself I was too busy to waste time on such things, that it was better to leave mages to their own devices within the Community as much as possible. That other Huntsmen enjoyed the work more, so why rob them of the opportunity?

The truth is, mages scare me.

Even this mage on the ground, even as I grab their arm to help them to their feet and push their magic deep down where it cannot hurt me. It's not the power they possess that frightens me. Huntsmen are also powerful, but Huntsmen are straightforward. Mage blood boosts our strength, but that's all.

What scares me the most about mages is their great internal *unknown*. Sometimes, I'll make eye contact with one, and it's like staring into the vastness of the night sky. I feel stripped away beneath such a gaze, vulnerable in a way I have never allowed myself to be before. Like every mage who sees me knows me and knows everything I've ever done.

The mage in my grasp has wide golden eyes and black blood all over their hands. Why did Armina leave them here alone? I feel the judgment in their stare and try not to let my own fear show on my face.

We watch each other in silence until—

"Back off," they snap.

The command festers in my brain. I can't let a mage order me around. My pride, my reputation as a Huntsman demands that I stand steady against this defiance, insists it would be a stain on the Order to show them any leniency or comfort.

But what does reputation matter anymore in the face of everything that's happened tonight?

"Back. Off," they say again.

I crush my instinctual disdain, and beneath their peeling gaze, I acquiesce and loosen my grip a fraction. I hold their wrist like a friend rather than an authority. They're scared and alone and have just watched their only ally walk toward certain death. If there's anything I've learned over the years, it's that people who are scared and alone want control.

Right?

"Let go and give me my magic back." They wipe their bleeding hand on their red coat, leaving black handprints on their stomach and side.

"Forgive me for being cautious," I say. Releasing their magic would be foolish; all my training tells me so. An invitation for death. "I was hoping we might talk."

"I don't like chatty Huntsmen." Their voice wavers, but their eyes do not.

"I'll let go if you hear me out."

They laugh, a wild, animal sound that leaves my heart racing. "No. No bargains; no games. If you won't give me my magic back, then kill me."

They can't possibly mean that, but nothing in their expression gives away a bluff.

"What has you in a rush? Your friend Armina walking directly into the Order's waiting arms? There isn't anything you can do for her now."

"Kill me or leave."

I don't like the way their mouth sets, the way their fingers twitch. The way their voice steadies the more we talk. Their eyes are fire, and they burn.

"If you try to rescue her, someone will kill you," I continue. "There have to be two-dozen Huntsmen in that lot."

"No more talking."

They close the gap between us, and now I have to stop myself from stepping back. Heat pours off them, even with their magic suppressed. It always surprises me how warm mages are. It doesn't matter that their blood can scorch your tongue; looking at them, they're the sort of creatures you'd expect to have ice in their veins.

"What will it be?" they ask.

Given the choice between killing them or letting them go free, the answer should be obvious. To any Huntsman it would be obvious.

Killing this mage would give me my own opportunity to escape. I may not be the Order's target, as Iverson suggested, but that doesn't mean they'd be pleased to see me walk free. A person like me—the previous Huntsmaster's son who lived there for nearly twenty years and therefore has more insider knowledge than most—could be an excellent tool in the right hands. They'll be after me eventually, but if another Huntsman were to confront me while I was engorged on a whole person's worth of blood, they wouldn't stand a chance.

But blood doesn't last forever, and killing this mage wouldn't bring anyone safety or justice.

"I'll let go," I say. "Consider it a peace offering."

They continue to stare at me with those gold eyes.

Slowly, I relinquish my grip. A gray flush returns to their cheeks and lips as the power trickles back into their limbs. Their shoulders settle.

Then they slam their foot down on the pavement, and the world explodes.

Blackened shards of sidewalk fly everywhere—I feel the wetness of blood on my skin but not yet the pain of the wounds.

The ground beneath my feet warps, and I lose my balance, hitting the concrete. Pavement surges up my legs like an encroaching sandstorm. I claw and struggle and push, but by the time the concrete stops eating me alive, I've only managed to keep my head and one arm clear. The void-black stone engulfs my legs and half my torso, trapping them beneath the surface.

The mage crouches beside me and kneels on my free arm.

If I thought their eyes burned before, that was nothing compared to their scorch now—brighter than sunlight off the desert dunes. They place one hand on my shoulder and push it to the ground at an awkward, painful angle. Then they hold up their fist. In it they clutch a chunk of pavement, and I watch as it blackens and melts around their fingers. Now that we're touching again, I scramble to blot their magic, but it's too late: the enchantment takes root and sharpens the rock to claws.

A million ways to die, a thousand people who want to kill me, and I meet my end on a dirty city street because I thought it was worth it—just once—to let my guard down.

"Is this really what you want?" I ask. Beneath the concrete, pain flares in my injuries from the initial explosion.

The mage's fingers wrap around my neck. "More than anything."

My eyes flutter closed, and I concentrate on my heartbeat pounding in my wounds, on the warm places where the mage's skin touches mine. I don't want to die. Not while people like Pierce and Baker make the world worse by existing in it. Not when I still haven't figured out the point of everything that's happening around me.

My life has never been my own, but it is even less so now. It belongs to the mage whose fingers are slowly tightening around my throat.

"Tell me," I say.

They pause.

"Tell you what?"

My legs begin to go numb. "Why you want to kill me."

They press their weight down on my shoulder again, and I open my eyes. Their face hovers inches above mine, and I follow the trail of veins up their cheek, the branching map of them a distraction from their anger. I've never been this close to a mage before. Their fury is beautiful.

"Do you really not know?" they ask. "After everything the Huntsmen have done to me?"

"I've never done anything to you."

They laugh again, the sound almost begrudging in the way it pours from their mouth. "It's amazing how you can look me in the eye and lie through your teeth."

"I've never done anything to you *personally*."

"It's all personal."

The sky, muted gray and starless, frames their face. Their fingers on my throat make it hard to breathe.

I don't know what happens after we die. I've heard stories of Y'ashtrian horse goddesses and what might wait beyond this world, but no—in my opinion, death must be as empty as tonight's sky.

"Kill me or leave," I mutter.

The mage's hand tightens. "What did you say?"

My eyes drift down to meet theirs. "Despite everything you've said, I'm still alive. Why? You must think I'm worth something."

They smile. I thought I knew how terror felt before that smile, but it turns out that I was wrong. "Not at all. It's just that the last time I killed a Huntsman, I didn't get to savor it." Their clawed hand leaves my throat and drags down my collar toward my chest, leaving a hot stripe of pain in its wake. "I've been holding onto this fear for a very long time. I'd like to give some of it back to you."

Their finger digs deeper into my skin, and I stifle a gasp of pain. The sound comes through my gritted teeth as a whimper, which is undoubtedly worse. "How many Huntsmen have you killed?"

They spread their palm flat over my heart, then crook their fingers like a scorpion's legs. "I lost count after eight. Maybe they shouldn't have taken my mother from me."

The tips of their fingers drive into my chest, and adrenaline takes over. The arm not buried beneath the concrete swings up from under the mage's weight and shoves them far enough aside to loosen them from my chest. Their claws drag rivulets across my stomach, though not deep enough to have punctured anything other than skin. The mage lunges for my throat again, but I grab a fistful of their hair and pull them down beside me.

They scramble, trying to free themself from my grip, but I twist my arm and press them to the sidewalk with my forearm across their throat. Their clawed hand whips up to bite into my wrist. It's hard to concentrate on keeping their magic blunted through the pain, harder still while they thrash and snarl.

"Your mother. That's what this is about?" I demand. Huntsmen arrest mages for all manner of crimes, and I can't imagine that the mother of one this violent is any less so herself.

Still . . .

Still. *They shouldn't have taken my mother from me.* They shouldn't have taken my father from *me.* Somehow, Pierce convinced the world that the man I knew—diligent and serious but capable of insurmountable affection—would throw not only his mission but his son aside. For what?

I dug up the arrest records after all was said and done. Carefully annotated them with the trial's results and filed it in the appropriate place, next to his court transcripts, his order for exsanguination. They alleged that my father was responsible for the destruction of the Prickweed Pine Community, gone in the span of a single night, its Huntsmen massacred, its mages scattered. A message written on the walls over and over in red, red blood that read *The Wanderer Walks Free.*

Eager Huntsmen brought forward evidence of my father's involvement: visits he'd paid there over the past few years, conversations he'd had with the Huntsmen in charge, mages he'd spoken to. Every testimony, every witness, meticulously detailed in the court records.

Huntsmen don't *take* notes. They don't *have* the attention span for details.

His detractors claimed he'd become friends with this so-called Wanderer, a mage who had been imprisoned there for decades. That he destroyed both the Community and his reputation for their friendship. I never believed that. He loved the Order, and he loved me, not some unknown mage in some random Community.

Why did I ever accept those blatant lies? Why don't I have the guts to be as angry as this mage?

I feel that fury now, flushing my face alongside the exertion of keeping the mage pinned. Maybe Armina could have shown me to safety, but I don't want that anymore.

I look at the mage beside me, and an idea unfolds itself. An opportunity.

"I can help you find her," I say.

"You don't want to help me." Their voice comes out choked beneath the pressure on their windpipe. "You want to put me back in a cage."

"Listen, I was in charge of all Perishing's paperwork; I have an excellent memory for details. I can find your mother—"

"I don't believe you."

Huntsmen are strong, but it's been several weeks since I've drunk any blood, and I'm reaching the limit of that strength. With these injuries, I'm running on fumes.

"What's her name? Tell me that, and I'll tell you her entire file. Exactly why she's in Perishing. Where she is."

"So you can hurt her?"

"How am I supposed to do that? You have me buried in the street."

Their breaths come out haggard; if they're anything like the mages back at Perishing, they're unaccustomed to strenuous activity. They give me one final glare before their stone claws retract from my arm. Their shoulders slump against the pavement. "Calliope Keer."

An image flashes to mind, plucked out of the mental file where I keep every bit of information Perishing has given me over the years. A small, rectangular headshot of a woman with black hair and a single hand-written page in a nearly empty folder. No details of her crime.

Nothing about a child.

"She's being kept in isolation," I say, "beneath the city at the lowest level of the structure. The area itself isn't under heavy guard, but the areas leading up to it are."

Blood drips off my stomach. It patters on the cracked pavement. The mage's face is red from it, smeared on their neck and lips where I have my bleeding arm pressed to their throat.

The mage's eyes flick across my face. "What about Armina?"

"Assuming they don't kill her outright . . . most likely the general prison cells. More guards there, but also more consistent guard rotation. And trust me, after half a decade of handing out duty schedules, I know exactly who will be where and when."

The mage is silent a moment, then they whisper, "Why would you want to help me?"

I shrug as best I can. "The Order took something from me, too. Let's just say the other Huntsmen wouldn't be disappointed to see me dead."

Beneath my arm, the mage's pulse stutters.

I wonder how long we'll stay like this, seething in a miasma of mutual resentment. Until we starve to death, maybe. Until the Huntsmen or some other scavengers find us. I would probably deserve it after hiding my head under the dunes for so long. But I'm not going to die before I get my answers from Pierce.

I feel a weak shove against my arm.

"Let me up," the mage says.

"You'll kill me."

"Maybe. Do you want to lie here forever, or do you want to find out?"

They don't meet my gaze, just stare at the sky above us with their mouth screwed into a tight frown.

With a wince, I lift my arm off their throat.

They stand and stretch, then glare down at me. "You will never bind my magic again."

My hand, which had crept forward to grip the toe of their boot, retreats. I half prepare for a death blow, but instead, they keep speaking.

"You won't touch me. The moment we save my mother and Armina, you leave." They stoop and press their hand against the blackened concrete at my knees. "You'll give me your mageblade."

My heart freezes in my chest at the idea of losing it once more, but I nod. Trust is expensive, and giving up my blade is a small price to pay. If Iverson is to be believed, the Huntsmen won't need to track it any longer, and they don't have any more of my blood besides. If this mage wants to hold onto it, it should be safe enough to let them do so.

The concrete around my body squeezes sharply once, then recedes like the tide. Aching sensations flow back into my limbs, so I curl into a sitting position and rub my ankles. Small pools of thickening blood collect around me on the shattered ground, and my injuries, though not deep or of immediate concern, need to be cleaned and bandaged before they get infected.

"Your name is Renn, yes?" The mage watches me with their hands tucked into their coat pockets, making no effort to scrub my blood off their face.

"Renn Mason." I stand and test my balance. We need to start planning our way to Perishing. We could rent a car, but I'm not keen to show my face in better-traveled parts of the city. Something like a bus is out of the question, and—

"Canto Keer."

The mage isn't looking at me. Instead, they glare at where my shoe meets the split concrete. Baker's mageblade lies beside my boot, absorbing the light from the distant streetlamps.

"Right. Here." I draw my own mageblade out of my belt.

The mage flinches when I hold it out to them, but after a moment, they wrap their hand around the hilt. Their toe makes contact with the mageblade by our feet. It clatters against the stone. "What's this one?"

"Belongs to another Huntsman named Baker. I was going to—"

Canto's face scrunches, and the ground melts again. It seeps forward like an oil spill until it covers the other mageblade and sucks it beneath the surface. The concrete bubbles, then smooths out, black and still.

A shiver runs down my spine.

"I wish I could offer it a better burial, but we're running low on time," Canto says. "Now then—let's get started."

18

CANTO

I'm making a terrible, stupid mistake.

I didn't have the opportunity to make mistakes of this magnitude in the Community. Trust a Huntsman? Especially *this* Huntsman, with an expression like he's trying to calm a frightened animal: a gentle smile that says he might offer me a treat from his outstretched hand at any moment. I want to crumble that smile between my fingers.

"We need a plan." He walks away from me, down the long street. I get the sense he wants me to follow. No, not wants—expects.

I look instead to the dirt lot where Armina is doing . . . who knows? The Huntsmen have churned into a flurry of activity, but it's too far away to discern any meaning. Though I interpret the lack of screaming as a good sign.

"Canto." Renn turns around, still wearing that frustrating smile, though it's grown tattered at the edges. "We're moving."

When my feet remain planted on the cracked concrete, Renn returns to my side. He shoves his hands into his pockets, shoulders squared—the almost-guilty body language of a Huntsman about to do something he doesn't want to be caught doing.

"We can't afford to stand around," he says. "This area stinks of magic, and while Pierce has a full platoon distracted by the truck, I doubt he enlisted every Huntsman in the city for this task."

I'm not short, but Renn's taller, and I hate having to crane my neck to look into his face. "I'm not taking orders from you."

He looks tired. A bone-deep exhaustion that has nothing to do with when he last slept. I've never known a Huntsman to be tired. "Now is not the time to argue."

"This isn't a 'now' thing," I say. "It's a forever thing. Either you agree to follow *my* lead"—his face scrunches—"or we'll take a moment to discuss our next steps."

"We don't have a moment—"

"We'll make one." A truck engine roars to life in the dirt lot. "Although I suppose we should get off the road."

He throws up his hands and stalks away again. "What did you think I was doing?"

I jog to catch up, annoyed that I have to adjust my pace to fit his long strides. He ducks into a side street, and I hurry after him. "How did you escape the truck, anyway?" I ask. "I suppose you must have really pissed off the other Huntsmen if you want to help me, so what? Did they unchain you and give you a head start? We both know Huntsmen love a chase—"

He rounds on me. My palm finds the wall beside me in case he changes his mind about this tentative partnership and I need an enchantment. My other hand grips the mageblade I don't know how to use.

"Valaina let me go," he says.

My fingernails scrape the brick. "Let you . . ."

"Yeah." He leans against the wall beside me, head tilted down to watch my reaction. "She works for the Huntsmaster. Or she used to—said she killed that Averard guy, and afterward, Pierce reneged on some promise he made to her."

No. That can't be right. I sink down the wall to sit on the ground.

Renn looms above me and crosses his feet at the ankles. "Something you want to share?" he asks.

"Why would Valaina . . . Averard *raised* them."

"I gathered that."

"No, you don't get it. They were a family. Especially for Armina. I mean, you've seen that coat she wears."

"That was his? Makes sense; it's three times too big—"

"You've seen the blood on it."

Renn falls silent.

I try to concentrate on the places where my body hurts—all the little cuts from the exploding sidewalk, my bruised throat from Renn's arm, the throb in my blood from today's enchanting. Scrutinizing my physical aches means I don't have to linger on the more abstract ones. On the sheer volume of the betrayal Renn just unveiled.

"I guess the Huntsmen took something from Armina, too," Renn says. He sounds almost melancholy—a funny emotion for a Huntsman to have about a little thing like betrayal.

"Like you care," I spit.

"Even Huntsmen can care when bad things happen to good people, and she seems like a good person. The kind of person whose first instinct is to help, even before they understand the situation. More than I could ever say for myself." He shrugs. "Sure, she was a weird case. Thought she was a mage at first with how much magic she gave off, but I guess it was a byproduct of living in the truck all her life."

I raise an eyebrow. "You thought she was a mage?"

"You didn't think so? Magic rolls off her very similar to how it does off the mages I've met. Like it's part of her. In her blood."

I press my forehead against my knees with an incredulous laugh. Huntsmen must perceive magic differently from mages. For me, magic is an energy that needs to be explored. I'd have to touch an enchanted object and pick apart the threads of its enchantment to fully understand it. On sight, one enchanted object wouldn't appear different from another, so surrounded by artifacts and wearing a coat with a magic lining, Armina wouldn't have stood out to me.

Maybe for Huntsmen, magic is more tangible—visible, or even scent-based, judging by what Renn said earlier about the area stinking of magic.

There's only one thing about Armina that would have set her apart from other normal people.

"She's enchanted," I say.

I hear a sharp shift of movement and lift my head, only to see Renn crouch beside me. His eyes widen, and I sense he wants to do something—maybe grab and shake me. His hands twitch at his sides, but at his sides they remain. "She's *enchanted*? To do what?"

It's secretly gratifying to see the horror painted on his face, though I hate how similar our reactions to finding out this information were. "She doesn't know."

"Shit. Canto, we—"

"Stop." I stab my nails into my elbows and ignore the incredulous glare he sends my way. "I don't like it either, but we'll figure out what to do about it after she's safe." I meet his eyes. "Her rescue is one of my conditions for cooperating."

Renn shakes his head. "Fine. Maybe it'll even be great to have an unknown weapon on our side. She could be a good distraction."

"She's one of the people we're *saving*."

"That doesn't mean she can't make herself useful."

I hate Huntsmen.

"So," he says, "can I make suggestions for what we do next, or is that against your rules?"

I hate this Huntsman in particular.

"I know what we need to do next. We need to get into Perishing."

"You've skipped a few steps. Such as getting *to* Perishing."

"We take a car."

"Have you got one of those hiding somewhere? Surely, you can't fit it up your—"

"All we need to do is find one," I snap. "I can enchant it to get us anywhere; we won't even have to drive."

"Enchanting a car is going to draw the Huntsmen's notice faster. I don't know what fresh magic feels like to *you*, but I can detect an enchantment on that scale from several blocks away. Setting that aside, I don't know the patrol routes in the city. Say we managed to enchant a car; that does nothing if we're caught trying to leave. You stick out like, well, like a mage."

"If we can't take a car, then what? We walk?"

"It's almost a day by vehicle, and the road is mountainous. The parts that aren't mountain are desert. We can't walk."

"Then what do you suggest we do?"

He smirks. "I thought you'd never ask."

Heat creeps up my neck when I realize I've been tricked into handing him the reins. I want to punch him, drive my fist into that handsome face until it's all blood and missing teeth.

"Armina mentioned she was taking you to a contact of hers. Some safe place for mages," he continues. "We should go there. If this contact is the kind of person who can smuggle mages out of the city, they may have a means of moving us out of it, too."

"No."

The response falls from my mouth before I even have a chance to think about what he's suggesting. The very idea of taking this man to Georgian, to *Kateryna* . . . Kateryna has probably never seen a Huntsman at a distance closer than a quarter mile, and while Georgian might give Renn a challenge in terms of strength, even she wouldn't last long against a Huntsman.

I can't defile their safehouse like that.

"No?" Renn asks, like I've said something unreasonable. "Do you have a better idea?"

"We . . . we could leave the city on foot. If we're careful, I'm sure we could avoid any Huntsmen patrols. Maybe we'll run into another vehicle on the road that can give us a ride."

"*Hitchhike*? Canto, you're a *mage*."

"I'm aware. If we make it to a rest stop outside the city, we—"

"We won't make it that far. I don't know about you, but if I don't address some of these injuries soon, they're likely to get infected. I don't think my festering corpse will be much help getting you into Perishing."

Blood mats his tattered shirt, and the cuts I dragged through his skin have ragged, raw edges. They're glossy wet under the glow of distant streetlights. He isn't actively bleeding anymore, but I don't know anything about first aid other than "put pressure on the wound and pray it stops bleeding before you have to ask the Huntsmen for help".

If life were fair, if it were easy, I could just enchant his wounds closed. But that's impossible. Magic can do a lot of things; healing isn't one of them. Fixing an injury with magic isn't as simple as enchanting the wound closed—one would need to enchant the person's entire body. There's no guarantee a mage could keep their focus long enough to heal without poisoning the injury with some other intent. The patient they were trying to save would become a victim, just like Armina. Even in a matter of life and death, no mage I know would try.

He'd be useless to me dead—absolutely *useless*. He's right that I can't walk to Perishing, that I can't enchant a vehicle without the risk of being caught. But worse, he holds all the knowledge I need in that stupid blond head of his. Without him, I'll never safely breach Perishing's walls. I'll never find my mother or Armina.

I swallow the nagging doubt inside myself that this is a terrible plan because Renn has a point. Georgian and Kateryna could get us out of Crotalus. They could tend to Renn's injuries. And, selfishly, they might be able to soothe the growing buzz in my brain, the panic that comes from having no plan, that comes from allying myself to the one thing I hate most of all. Georgian is steady, and Kateryna is well-meaning, and I miss my mother.

I stand and brush sand off my thighs. There's no time to flounder with my decisions. I have to make even the bad ones with confidence.

"Fine," I say, "I'll take you to them."

Renn pushes off the ground as well, with a smug, triumphant expression.

"But first . . ." I point at the remains of his shirt. "Give that to me."

He doesn't move, and that smug expression becomes confused as his fingertips brush his chest.

"I'll take you to Armina's contact," I continue, "but I have to mitigate the potential damage as much as possible. You're going blindfolded."

A muscle twitches in his jaw.

I hold out my hand, and I'm pleased when it doesn't tremble.

I think he's going to argue or insist on a different plan, but after a moment, he undoes the few intact buttons left on his shirt. Then he shrugs it off and tosses the bloody fabric into my outstretched hand.

He stands there in his tattered undershirt and crosses his arms over his chest, shifting from foot to foot. I wonder if he's cold or just uncomfortable.

The fabric smells like sweat and blood and dirt as I wrap it around my fingers. Magic and my own blood sink into the material as I begin my enchantment.

Renn mentioned that Huntsmen can sense fresh magic from far away. I wonder what this enchantment must feel like to him, standing so close. I don't look up to gauge his reaction until the material turns fully black, a night sky against my palms.

"Come here," I say, finally meeting his gaze.

That muscle in his jaw twitches again. "Let me do it."

"No. I made the fabric opaque, but I still need to be sure your eyes are fully covered. This may be the kind of partnership that requires trust, but sorry, we aren't there yet. So come. Here."

He stands still, blinking down at me in the alley's half-light, and for a moment, I think he's going to turn around and walk away. That maybe he should, because this is a stupid idea, a doomed partnership between two people who will never, ever trust one another.

Then he lowers his body toward me in a half bow.

His shoulders tense when I loop the fabric over his eyes. Every nerve in my body is on fire. A Huntsman bowing to a mage. A Huntsman letting himself be fettered. Either he is the world's greatest fool or he wants something more than most Huntsmen want power. I understand how strong a motivator revenge can be.

I adjust the blindfold over his eyes, my fingers lingering a second too long as I revel in this impossible feeling of control. "How's that?"

"Awful." He straightens. "How am I supposed to navigate like this? I doubt you're going to lead me by the hand."

"Can't you follow my magic?"

"With a fresh enchantment on my face?" He waves a hand over the blindfold. "Not likely."

"Then listen to my footsteps. I'll let you know if you're about to run into something." I take a few steps forward, then pause. "Maybe."

The walk back to Georgian's home feels longer this time. Renn keeps muttering low curses whenever he scrapes against a wall, which he does more often than I expect. Not that Huntsmen are supernaturally gifted at avoiding obstacles, but certainly, his other senses should make up for the loss of one. That's what drinking all that blood is for.

We eventually fall out into Georgian's neighborhood, where the radio still plays an energetic beat and the red lights gleam from nearly every window. There are more people on the street now, and one or two women in tight dresses point at us and titter behind their hands. I ignore it until some couple pinned against the side of a building moans very loudly and Renn pulls up short.

"Where the fuck are you taking me?" he asks.

"We're almost there."

I shove his arm in encouragement, and he continues tentatively forward until we reach the wooden steps of Georgian's porch. Renn slams the toe of his boot against the bottommost step and flinches.

"Stairs," I say.

He grits his teeth. "You have no idea how hard this is." He reaches out his foot until it bumps the step. He climbs up one.

"Please." I scale to the top. "Do you honestly think the Huntsmen at my Community never played with us like this?"

He pauses his ascent of the second step, although his face is still turned toward the ground as if he can see his feet. "What do you mean?"

"Little games. Poke and prod and stab until one of us snaps. Feel justified in the subsequent bloodletting. Consider yourself lucky. Parading around blindfolded sounds almost fun."

His mouth curves into a sharp frown as he attempts the third step. "They're not supposed to do that."

"I guess no one ever told them not to."

He reaches the fourth step, and his face is on level with mine. "I would never allow that." I abhor the honesty in his voice. "But I'm not the Huntsmen who hurt you."

"It doesn't matter." I move out of his way. "You weren't born a Huntsman, Renn. You chose to be one. And so you're complicit."

He says nothing, but he doesn't continue climbing either. Instead, he stays where he is, staring straight forward as if he can still see my face. His shoulders move with his breathing, but I watch the tendons in his wrists tighten as he clenches his hands.

When he does move forward again, his steps are even more uncertain.

At the apex of the porch, we face the door together. Renn picks at the skin on his fingers and asks in a weary voice, "Where are we?"

"On a porch," I say. "In front of a door."

Standing under the light, with the *tink* of tiny bugs smacking into the bulb, I feel like I'm being interrogated. I've brought a monster to Georgian's home; I'm causing an upheaval in their careful lives. It's worse than selfish, but I don't know what else to do. There are only so many people I trust, and they keep getting taken away from me.

My eyes glue to the wall's peeling paint when Renn reaches out and taps his fist on the wooden door.

"What are you doing?" I demand.

"Knocking." He reaches out to do it again. "Why, did I miss?"

I grab his fist and press it back to his chest. "You can't just—"

The door creaks open, and Kateryna peeks out. In the hour or so since I saw her last, she's pulled her blonde hair into a puffy ponytail and changed into pajamas. "Canto! We weren't expecting you back. Come—"

Her eyes fall on the blindfolded Huntsman beside me. She slams the door shut, and I hear her footsteps retreat down the hallway.

"I take it your friend wasn't happy to see me?" Renn asks.

I don't have a response for that. All my energy is focused on the cold dread settling into my chest.

A moment later, the door swings open again, this time with force. Georgian blocks the entrance, wearing a scowl I didn't even think her face capable of forming. She grabs the neck of my shirt, hauls me into the house, and closes the door.

"How dare you"—she backs me up against the wall, and her finger pokes into my collar—"bring *that* to my home?"

A swell of discomfort rises in my chest at her proximity. I clutch my hands together by my throat and try to make myself small. For the Huntsmen in my Community, anger is a game they play. But I don't know how to handle anger I agree with and understand.

"I'm sorry," I say. "I'm really, really sorry. I need your help."

"And why should I help you? You just endangered my *family*."

"I can hear you, you know," comes Renn's muffled voice through the door. "I promise I mean no harm, so may I come inside? It's cold out here and, uh, I can't see. And I would really like to clean some of these wounds." He pauses, then adds a hopeful, "I'll keep the blindfold on?"

The ire seeps out of Georgian like steam from a kettle. She releases me, and it's all I can do not to collapse onto the floor. "Why did you bring him here?"

"The Huntsmen took Armina and the *Blackblood*," I say. Georgian sucks in a sharp breath and leans against the wall. "I don't know what happened between the Order and this Huntsman, but he wants some sort of revenge against them. He told me he'd help save Armina. And my mother."

"And you bought that?"

I fidget my hands together. "I think the information he's given me so far is accurate, so I've chosen to use him for now."

Georgian frowns down at me. "You've chosen to use him. Now you're choosing to use me."

The accusation stings worse than my shoulders after she slammed them into the wall. It stings because it's true, even if I didn't think about it that way until now.

"I don't want . . . I never wanted to upset your life. I promise, he's been blindfolded all the way up to your door. There's no way he could retrace his steps."

"A blindfold . . . Do you really think that's good enough?" Georgian's eyes meet mine, and I'm rooted to the floor as if the dirty wooden boards have been enchanted to swallow me. "I know you don't get it, kid. Just like Kateryna doesn't know what it's like to live in a Community, you don't know what it's like to live outside one. But Kateryna understands what a Huntsman at your door means. I thought you would, too."

I bow my head before her fury, my excuses and justifications all dried up. I've always been ready to kill Huntsmen to save my mother, always been ready to die myself. Somewhere along the line, I forgot that the world is bigger than my Community, and that not every person has the same values and justices that I do. Armina, Georgian and Kateryna, even Renn: I had no right to drag them into my fight. But I did. I *did*.

Georgian heaves a sigh and nudges me out of the way. "Stop wallowing and live with your decisions. We'll figure something out for now, but if anything happens to my wife, I'm holding you responsible."

She throws the door open and inspects Renn as he stands at attention with his arms plastered to his sides.

"Get in," she barks.

He gives a bowing tilt of his head and steps over the threshold before Georgian closes the door.

She stomps past us, down to the patch of light at the end of the hallway. I nudge Renn in the spine, and he stumbles forward. The overhead lights flicker. Something about the dim pall they cast feeds my growing shame.

Everything in Georgian's workshop is the same as it was an hour before, save that Georgian put her tools away and cleaned the detritus from her workspace. Kateryna is tucked into a corner. She has one arm wrapped around her stomach, and the other holds a nail gun. When Renn enters, she makes a small noise at the back of her throat and trains the makeshift weapon between his eyes.

Georgian turns toward her. "It's all right, Kateryna. Why don't you get some water and bandages for the kid? If he dies on our property, we'll be worse off."

Kateryna clutches her nail gun to her chest and backs slowly out of the room.

Georgian fixes us with a stern look that Renn can't see but that I drown beneath. She folds her hands on the tabletop. "What, exactly, is your plan?"

I open my mouth to speak, but Renn steps forward. He smacks his knee into one of the storage crates by the door. "W- we need transportation out of the city," he says as he rubs his leg.

Georgian settles deeper into her seat. "You think I can give you that?"

"Armina said you move mages."

"She did?"

Renn frowns. "Not exactly. But it was obvious."

"Why's that?"

"She was talking to her crewmate, said she would be visiting a contact. Then she said that she would return without the m— Canto, provided that she was assured of their safety. Harboring a mage is dangerous, something I doubt the average Crotalus citizen would be equipped to do on such short notice. So either you're some naive do-gooder—in which case I doubt Armina would feel comfortable leaving Canto with you—or you're well-established with moving mages and evading the Huntsmen." He stands up straighter. "Seemed a safe bet."

Georgian rubs a hand across her mouth, glaring at the pair of us. "You're not a normal Huntsman. Too clever."

Renn's jaw tightens, and his shoulders tense. "I just like to pay attention."

Kateryna returns holding a pitcher of water, a small stack of towels, and a white box. She drops the items on the desk, then stands behind Georgian. She lifts the nail gun again, and this time, her hands don't tremble.

Georgian tilts her head toward the stack of objects and meets my eye. "Well? Take them. He's your Huntsman."

I place my palm on Renn's back and direct him toward the bench where Armina and I sat earlier tonight. When his knees bump it, he throws out his hands and pats downward until he locates the surface, then carefully sits. I approach the desk— keeping my eyes trained on my feet—retrieve the stack of goods, and return to Renn.

I direct his hands to the pitcher and towels, and blessedly, he picks them up. He peels off his undershirt and begins cleaning himself.

I tear my eyes from the sight of bloody water and torn skin and open the box. Picking through its contents, I withdraw the needle. It's curved and sharp, and I'm not sure whether I want to stab him with it or myself.

"I'm really all right," Renn whispers as he sets aside a bloodied rag and picks up a new one. "The longest wounds need four or five stitches at most. Keeping them clean is the more important part."

I don't like him trying to be nice. I wonder instead if driving the needle into his skin would ease some of the tension in the room.

"Just take the blindfold off," Georgian says. "It's pointless now."

He pauses in cleaning the wounds on his leg, then reaches up and lifts the blindfold from his face. He rubs the back of his hand across his forehead and passes me the blackened fabric. I twist it in my grip as he gives Kateryna and Georgian a look over. The pair study him back, and Kateryna levels the nail gun at his forehead once more.

"She's an excellent shot," Georgian says.

"I can tell." Renn grabs the suture kit and picks through the threads.

I distract myself by watching the movement of his hands as he threads his needle and locks it into the clamp. He picks up the forceps and draws back the wound before puncturing one side. He pulls the thread through, then gives a low, rumbling laugh. "You like this sort of stuff?"

With a jolt, I realize I've bent so far forward to watch that I'm practically in his way.

I clear my throat and sit back, face burning. "I've never seen anyone get stitches before. Seeing it isn't the same as reading about it in books."

"You don't have to be embarrassed." He snips and ties the thread.

"I'm not."

He moves up the wound to make the next stitch. It's high on his chest, toward his collar, and the drag of my enchanted claws down his skin springs to mind. His arms strain at the awkward angle, and with an annoyed grunt, he lowers the tools into his lap. "Guess that one will have to do without." His black-eyed gaze turns toward me. "Unless you'd like some first-hand experience."

"Excuse me?"

He holds out the needle and forceps. "I'm saying I could use a little help."

I stare at the tools. "And I'd say you'd be an idiot for trusting me to do so."

"You can't possibly make it worse."

He gestures the forceps at me again, and I no longer have the words to protest.

My hands don't shake as I take the tools from him, as I nudge the skin of his wound aside with the forceps and puncture the needle point through his flesh. I'm much slower than he was, but he sits still as I carefully tug the needle through. The memory of the barracks all those weeks ago springs into my mind, only now I'm stitching things together instead of slitting them apart.

Puncture. Tug. Knot. His pulse thumps, rhythmic and unconcerned, beneath where my fingers stabilize against his chest. He's fearless. He doesn't even blot out my magic.

I hate his calm.

My stitches don't look as nice as his, but I hardly care. I'm furious at him. I'm furious at myself. These wounds will scar, and there's a vindictive pleasure in knowing that no matter what happens, he will never forget what I did to him.

"Good job," he says when I finish tying my last knot.

"I don't need your praise."

"No one *needs* praise. But it's kind of nice, isn't it?"

He washes the sealed injuries once more before covering them with gauze and tape from the suture kit. He stands and twists his torso, then addresses Georgian. "You ladies wouldn't happen to have a change of clothes I could borrow?"

Georgian shakes her head. "I should let you walk around like that." Then she pushes out of her chair. "But I'm not that petty. I'll see what I can find."

She leaves the room, but not before giving Renn a very stern and pointed look.

Renn collapses back onto the bench. He prods one of his bandages, then rinses his hands in the pitcher's now-pink water.

"Huntsman."

Kateryna's arms haven't wavered. She stands with the desk between us, and her blue eyes narrow to nothing. "Why are you doing this?"

Renn picks up one of the clean towels to dry his hands. "You're skilled at hiding from the Huntsmen. That's what Canto and I need: a way out of this city without getting caught. A way into Perishing."

Kateryna's mouth curves into a deeper frown. "You're not going to hurt Canto, are you?"

No, no, no. Don't care about me.

Renn folds his hands between his knees and finally looks up at Kateryna. Their eyes meet, and she doesn't flinch. "I'm not going to hurt Canto."

When Georgian returns, she crosses to the bench and drops a stack of clothes beside Renn. "Should fit well enough that you won't look like you've clawed your way out of a shallow grave."

Renn stands and pulls off his ripped pants. I turn toward Georgian and Kateryna, shielding my face with my hand. I don't need to see that. It was weird enough with Armina.

Kateryna speaks again, her voice flat. "The Huntsman says they need a way into Perishing."

Georgian pinches the bridge of her nose. "Canto, I think what you're doing is damn foolish." She lowers her hand and fixes me with her most serious glare. "But you coming here hasn't given me much choice but to participate in that foolishness, regardless of whether or not I trust your new friend."

I shake my head. "I swear, he's not—"

She holds up her hand to silence me. "I'm gonna choose to trust *you*. I'll get you out of this city, but what you do after that is your business. If you ever make it back to Crotalus, Kat and I won't be here to greet you. And if you manage to find us again, I hope you won't be expecting any more favors."

Georgian's response is cold, but it's more than I deserve. I've never had freedom, and while some part of me resented Kateryna before, I hope I haven't doomed her to a future where she loses it.

"Come with me." Georgian jerks her head toward the doorway. Renn and I follow into the dingy hallway lined with its stained wallpaper and flickering lights. At the end of the hall is a steep set of concrete steps that end in one final door. Georgian holds it open while we enter.

I think it's a garage. It's a good deal tidier than the workshop, although there are neatly stacked toolboxes lining some of the walls. There are a few bulky objects covered in gray tarps, one of which I'm certain is a car.

Georgian leads us over to a smaller tarp-covered object. "You'll leave tonight in about an hour—that's when the Huntsmen have a shift change, so they won't be as vigilant. Move fast; don't do anything stupid to attract attention. I'll mark up a map with the safest routes to follow—follow *only* those routes. Don't stop to speak to anyone. Don't stop to bicker."

She grasps the tarp and removes it, revealing a flash of black metal. At first, I think it's enchanted, but then I see it's only been coated in years of grime and rust. Still, its two wheels appear in excellent condition, as does the black leather of its seat.

Georgian pats the handlebars of the motorcycle. "You get on this, and you ride. And you don't look back until Crotalus City has disappeared behind you."

19

ARMINA

Pierce drives through the night.

He stops around hour six to refuel. As we pull up to the pump, my heart leaps, thinking I've finally found my chance to escape, but he doesn't even leave the truck. Instead, I watch through my side mirror as one of the other Huntsman vehicles pulls up alongside us and refuels for him. Pierce's eyes never leave my face, even as I glare out the window and try to pretend he doesn't exist.

When we return to the road, Pierce's attention continues to alternate between his driving and where I'm sat scrunched against the door, still debating whether or not I want to throw myself out of it.

It'd be pointless: I'd either get banged up or dead. If I get hurt, Pierce'll stop the truck and put me back in the cab, and I'll be worse off than when I started. If I die, then I won't be of use to anyone anymore.

"You're quiet," Pierce says around the eight-hour mark of our ride. The Onyx Mountains started looming ahead hours ago, but now we're well within their slope.

"So are you," I mutter.

We take the rocky road slow as it twists upward.

"I'm out of practice." He turns the wheel too sharply around a bend, and the truck protests beneath us. I grit my teeth but don't say anything, preferring to stare into the darkness. Patchy grass pushes through the black dirt at the side of the road. "The other Huntsmen don't make great conversational partners."

I snort, and my breath fogs the glass. "Guess you made a bad career choice then."

He doesn't have an answer for that more than a humorless chuckle. His fingers drum the steering wheel in a familiar rhythm Averard used a thousand times, right before he jumped into some story or another. It sets my teeth on edge, but after a moment, I realize for the first time that I don't understand how Pierce is driving the truck.

Oh, it's not difficult to start a semi and get it moving—not more difficult than a regular car, at any rate. But if you're not prepared for the weight or the differences in visibility, then you're basically driving a diesel-powered death machine. Pierce navigates the rocky landscape with ease, going far too fast around the type of turns even I'd use caution with. Maybe he's driven a truck for the Huntsmen before.

But as his fingers drum that pattern, my stomach starts to sink.

Then we round another bend in the road, and Perishing drifts into view.

If it weren't for the truck's flashing headlights, I probably wouldn't have been able to distinguish the building from the darkness. Cliffs rise on either side of it like the walls of a cradle, and the building's four spires puncture the sky with black stone darker than the nighttime surrounding it. As we draw closer, my eyes separate a black wall surrounding it from the green-gray forest shadows, and I notice that one of the cliffs and the adjacent spire is partially destroyed, bits of both scattered along the slope of the mountain.

The road inclines, and the wheels creak beneath us, and I push myself deeper into my seat, as if gaining a few inches of distance will make it so we never reach our destination. But that wall draws closer and closer, and the wheels keep turning, and eventually, I make out a massive gate in the black stone wall and two Huntsmen sentries at either side of it, standing at rapt attention.

Pierce leans out the broken driver's window as we approach and slows the truck to a crawl. The moment the sentries recognize Pierce, they freeze like rabbits spotting a coyote. One pulls a radio off his vest and speaks into it, and the iron gate creaks upward with the distant rattle of chains.

Pierce nods to his men and drives through. The truck trundles across a small courtyard until Pierce pulls it alongside a broad outbuilding. He straightens the wheel and cuts the engine, then turns to study my face. His mouth screws into a half smile. "Welcome back."

I scoot against the door and grope for the handle. We're not moving anymore, so maybe if I run fast enough, I could hide in the shadows, wait for an opportunity to escape.

"I don't know what you're talking about," I hiss, squeezing up on the handle as quietly as I can. "I've never been here before."

Pierce's smile cracks into a grin, and a warm laugh falls from his throat. It makes every hair on my arms stand on end. "I guess you wouldn't remember. And if Averard never told you, well . . ." He shrugs and leans back in his chair, stares out the windshield. "It can't be helped."

In the bleak darkness, this far away from the city, there are a million stars. The Viper's bright tail reflects in Pierce's eyes.

"How do you know Averard?" I whisper.

He shakes his head and throws the door open. "We'll discuss this in my office. And I wouldn't recommend trying to flee." He turns toward me again, and all humor in his face has died, replaced by an ugly, twisted, inhuman snarl. "Do you know how many Huntsmen I have here? If I told a single one about your enchantment, do you know how thrilled they'd be to slay you like the mistake you are?"

"How did you know about—"

But he slides out of the cab and slams the door in my face.

I'm crumbling. Pierce just snapped apart the thousand threads that comprise the tapestry of my life, snapped them like they were meaningless. But they're my fabric, my skin, my comfortable coat and the rumble of my truck. Who am I if I've been to Perishing before? Who am I if Pierce knew Averard?

I thought Averard's death meant the end of his story. His was always a mythos that only ever existed in unconnected pieces, in fables about stars whispered on long drives through the desert. He's gone, so he'll never be complete. His story'll never be able to end.

But if Pierce knew him, maybe he could fill in those missing paragraphs. Knot those threads he already cut.

I hop out of the truck.

The lot we sit in's busier than a wasp hive. Headlights bob as trucks drive around the complex or toward the gate. Huntsmen shout orders to one another; street lamps flicker and hum. The spired building still seems so far in the distance, and between us and it is another looming wall, though this one's made of normal gray stone and not magicked black. I swear, in this courtyard alone, you could fit half of Wallton.

I round the back of the *Blackblood's* trailer, and there Pierce waits, hands in his pockets and a half dozen Huntsmen standing at attention around him. None of them touch me or even approach, but their hollow, black eyes land on me as one.

Pierce jerks his head and starts toward the gray stone wall, and the Huntsmen follow on either side. They catch me in their flow as they pass, and I find myself at the center of their pack like the weakest sheep in the flock.

Pierce lifts an arm in greeting to the guards at the gate, who stiffly step aside and allow us through. The unerring movement of the group of Huntsmen ushers me inside. Their bodies jostle me, and I draw Averard's coat tighter. I've been scared since the moment they caught me, but it was the kind of terror that could be brushed aside while I figured myself out. There was room to make plans. Space to flee.

I take my first steps into the onyx city of Perishing, and I know all those chances are gone.

I always thought people were exaggerating when they called it a city. Headquarters sounded too militant, I guessed, or too small. I imagined a single huge structure, like a massive library or a town hall, maybe with a few smaller buildings outside. When I saw the distant spires, I thought it might be some kind of fortress, like one of those castles I've heard about across the ocean that rich folk used to live in.

This is like we've entered some kind of nightmare version of Crotalus.

We're on a long street that stretches forward at least a mile and ends in the fortress itself. Every step we take closer makes the building seem higher, bigger than what should be possible. The main street branches off in a webbed network of side roads, each lined with run-down houses. The gray wall we came through is the only thing here not made of pitch-black material.

The city is absolutely silent.

I feel like I'm part of some dark parade, interrupting the death-like peace of the city to put on our own macabre show. Our boots echo on the cracked pavement, and there are no trees to intercept the wind as it howls through the empty alleys between houses. Dim streetlamps illuminate the path forward, but none of the buildings cast light at all.

As we pass a house at the edge of the street, our marching bodies reflect in its window. Between a spidery crack that runs through the glass and the dilapidated wooden sill, I spot a little face pressed against the pane. Their black veins stand out even in all this gloom.

One of the Huntsmen in the pack spots the child and veers off as we pass.

I curl my fingers into Averard's coat and squeeze my eyes shut. Nothing breaks the world's eternal silence.

We reach the spired building, and nothing feels real anymore. It's taller than the Tidal Wall and somehow a deeper black. It looks like you could fall right through if you accidentally touched it—fall into the void and float endlessly in the nothing.

No Huntsmen guard the doors, so one of the pack rushes forward to hold them open. Pierce waits for me to step through, then follows at my heels.

Inside are more black walls, this time with black tile floors instead of asphalt. The air smells stale and smoky. Unlike outside, there's noise everywhere—the resounding drumbeat of footsteps, gruff chatter, and shouting and laughing and screaming. A PA system from somewhere overhead intones a schedule of tomorrow's blood draws and exsanguinations. I glance around at the Huntsmen, but none of them even blink at the casual announcement of deaths and suffering. They continue to follow past closed doors and cracked marble pillars.

When Pierce raises a hand, they watch him like dogs.

"Your presence is no longer required," he says.

The Huntsmen break formation, and the hall rings with their retreating footsteps.

I try to memorize the path Pierce leads me down, but it's long and winding. We climb a staircase, then go down a hall, then through a room that's big enough to house banquets but currently houses dusty office furniture. Through a dozen more winding halls, then Pierce finally directs me through a large wooden door.

It must be Pierce's office. I'm basing that mostly on the fact that there's a desk with a chair behind it. Otherwise, it doesn't look like any office I've ever seen. Bank tellers always have stacks of paperwork and family photographs, and Georgian has her tools and her wires. The only thing Pierce has other than his desk and his chair is a ratty old map on one wall, pinned there like an afterthought.

He gestures for me to sit in his chair. When I instead lean awkwardly beside the corner of the desk, he sighs and closes the door. He rests his back against it.

"First of all," I begin, "how'd you know about my enchantment?"

His mouth twitches into a smile again. "Oh, Armina. We *could* start with that," he says. "Or we could start with how to get rid of it."

"Don't say my name like you know me."

"But I do know you. Do you think I regularly give a damn about magical experiments like yourself if there's nothing in it for me?" My face burns, and he tilts his head, still unerringly watching. "I simply thought you might want to get the more time-sensitive matters out of the way."

"It isn't like it's going to explode."

"You know that for sure?"

I wish he had the enchantment attached to *his* body, so we could see how much he enjoyed it when I gloated over his pain.

"Fine. How do we get rid of it?"

He hums pleasantly and walks forward. He stops before me and reaches down to grasp my calf and jerk it upward. I scrabble to keep purchase on the desk and kick at him with my free foot, but he bats it away as he rolls up my pant leg.

"Granted, it's little more than a theory at this point, but it's a strong one—one I've spent the last decade working on. It's a simple matter, really: we need to override your enchantment with a new one." His fingers on my leg pause when they encounter metal, and his eyes narrow. "Veins and Vipers, Averard," he whispers. "What have you done?"

I wrench my leg away from him and leap off the desk. "You want to enchant me *again*? Isn't once bad enough?"

Pierce shakes his head like he's clearing cobwebs. "Yes. Replace the first enchantment with a second, less volatile one. It doesn't need to be particularly complex, just strong enough to compel the original magic to lie dormant forever. An enchantment *on* the enchantment if you will. It requires a powerful mage to do the spellwork, but I've had one such mage brought to Perishing just for this purpose."

"How do you figure that would even work?" I ask, edging along the wall. There aren't even any damned windows in this place; the only way out is through the door behind Pierce. "Seems a bit of a logical leap to assume one enchantment will heal the other. I'm not interested in being a test subject."

Pierce laughs, a deep, warm rumble, like I've said something funny on purpose. "A test subject, yes, which comes with its own dangers, but you wouldn't remotely be my first. Do you think I have zero connections outside the Huntsmen? No free mages to manipulate into working for me? There are very few depths people won't stoop to protect their loved ones, Armina, and a mage on the outside would commit all manner of magical sins to make sure their family on the inside stays as . . . whole as possible."

He crosses his arms over his chest, and a sneer rises to his face. "Your friend Valaina—our little Huntswoman hopeful. I believe she encountered a few of my mages herself. She was the perfect test subject: young, no family to miss her, blood untouched by magic. We could have learned so much from her if Averard hadn't intervened." Pierce's words come out in a hiss. "They gave her to him. Rest assured, I made sure those mages remember what happens when they disobey orders."

The words are like a slap, or the stroke of a knife. I imagine the welts on Valaina's arms, those promises of magical enchantment. All along, all her suffering . . . it was Pierce.

"Of course, once Averard found out about the experiments, he knew it was me. He spent the next decade hunting down my mages across the Federation and putting them into hiding, convincing them not to aid me further. I believe he found the last of them this year. A waste of his time, considering now I have you."

"But we don't smuggle mages," I say blankly, trying to latch on to the pieces of my life as they shatter apart around me.

"Maybe the *Blackblood* doesn't," Pierce sneers, "but Averard was always bigger than his truck."

The enchantment in my leg sends an unbidden spark of pain through my hip. I grasp my thigh as the anger and confusion of it all bites through me. "And what would you know?" I snarl. "How do you know Averard, anyway?"

Pierce's black eyes spark like flint in the dull overhead light. His amusement takes on a cruel bent, a sardonic twist of his mouth. "Oh, did your precious captain like to keep secrets? Prefer to pretend he was always the holy man, protector of mages and sinners alike?" Pierce sits on the desk right where I did a moment before, arms crossed and glowering. "Let me shatter that illusion. Averard and I were friends. In fact, we became Huntsmen at the very same time."

20

ARMINA

Pierce's words make no sense. My lungs burn like I've hit the last mile on a race I didn't know I was running. For the first time since he abducted me from Crotalus, the wounds on my face pulse with pain.

"He's not a Huntsman." A shiver runs up my arms like it's cold in here, even though my blood's boiling beneath the surface. "He had blue eyes."

"The eyes wear off after a while. A year or two at most and he'd have been back to boring normal. He left the Order, oh, almost twenty years ago." Pierce gestures once more toward his chair. "Sit. It's a long story, even if you aren't tired."

I honestly don't have a clear enough head to refuse him. I cross the room and collapse into the chair.

Pierce twists around to stare at me. "Averard left because he couldn't handle the pressure," he says. "Or the expectations the Huntsmaster put on him."

"The Huntsmaster before you?"

He nods. "A man named Richard Mason. Fond of Averard's cleverness and constantly trying to pick his brain for ideas and knowledge. Ideas for what a real Huntsman Order could look like—a thing which did not exist before him."

My fingernails stab into the already-scored leather arms of his office chair. "The Huntsmen have been around for centuries."

"The Huntsmen have." Pierce stands and paces toward the map on the wall with his arms folded behind his back. "But the Order? With its rules and regulations, its Communities and outposts? That was Richard Mason's child."

Pierce spreads his hand out on the map. He's got Perishing framed between his thumb and forefinger. "Before Mason, those of us who called ourselves Huntsmen were little more than peacekeepers. Nomads who went town to town to settle disputes between mages and regular people. We didn't drink as much blood in those days, just enough to overpower if necessary—not much different than carrying a revolver."

Pierce shrugs. "Don't know how long Mason took planning, but within a few years, he'd amassed enough loyalty to start his takeover. When it became clear that the old ways were dying out and that we were either with him or against him, Averard and I joined up. After that, it was endless years of combing the desert and herding the mages we once worked with into the Communities where their powers were Mason's to exploit." Pierce scowls. "Not that he ever did."

I clutch Averard's coat closer. For the first time, it feels less like the comfort of a hug, and too hot. Itchy. "That's impossible. No one . . . no one talks about a time *before* the Order."

"Oh, I'm sure they do, in whispered, huddled secret. But history is decided by those who live to write it, and Mason made sure his narrative was the ones fed to the youth. I'm surprised Averard never mentioned the truth to you. Maybe he wanted to protect you from it. Or maybe he wanted to protect himself."

Narratives I thought I knew about my world stutter and clash. The war against Tempestor wasn't waged by a centuries-old peacekeeping organization, but a fledgling company. Most of the mages in the Communities weren't born there at all.

"How did Mason manage to round up all the mages in a couple years?" I ask. "Didn't anyone resist?"

"Oh, there was plenty of resistance, but Mason was a professional at propaganda and manipulation. It is surprisingly easy to spread fear, and once that fear takes root, it's difficult to dig up again. Now those that remember don't talk about it, and those who were too young don't know." He tilts his head toward me. "Just like you."

"Why are you telling me this?"

Pierce shoves away from the wall and walks toward me. "Because you wanted to know about Averard. And I want you to know that as perfect as he may have tried to appear, he was nothing more than another sinner desperately trying to escape the things he'd done."

I shake my head. I don't want to believe him. I *don't*, but . . .

"He left," I insist—a last straw to grasp onto. "If he really was a Huntsman, you said he left decades ago."

"He did, but it wasn't to spite the Huntsmen." His lips curl into a snarl that makes his face appear leonine and predatory. "He left to spite me." He gestures to my leg with a sharp point, and a phantom pain triggers across my missing muscles. "He left, and he took you."

The world buzzes in and out of focus—or maybe that's the sound of the overhead lights. Nothing feels tangible anymore, not even the seat beneath me or the surrounding walls. The conversation I had with Georgian comes back to me in painful bursts. When Averard escaped Perishing, when he smuggled all those mages out . . .

Did he also smuggle me?

Pierce paces, and it doesn't occur to me to interrupt him. I watch, numb and confused, as he tugs at the high collar of his dress shirt.

"There was a skirmish," he says. "A rebel mage leader known as the Wanderer and her cohort came to take Perishing. Killed a lot of good men and women and almost broke through our defenses, but we pushed them back. Captured a whole slew of her forces, including her top lieutenant. The Wanderer attempted to flee through the woods, but Mason set his best men on her tail: Averard and me."

Pierce's footsteps abruptly stop, and he turns his face toward the light. "We caught up to her, but wouldn't you know? Our enemy had a great secret. She'd led us right to her camp, where a few of her followers stood watch over the group's supplies—and the group's children."

Dread trickles through me as the pain in my leg ignites further.

Pierce's black eyes burn. "Have you ever encountered a brown bear and her cubs? One could not have fought more fiercely than the Wanderer in that moment. Averard felled the other mages one by one, but I took her on directly. She could stop bullets with a wave of her palm, and my blade bounced off her skin. When her hands wrapped around my throat, I found myself unable to bind her magic even as it bit into me, even as it spiraled through my blood."

He reaches up again and tugs down his collar, and for the first time, I see the expanse of his throat. Black as a void, as if part of his neck were missing and replaced by midnight.

"Averard managed to wrestle her off me as backup arrived. The Wanderer, realizing she was cornered, grabbed one of the babies from the group and tried to shield it from us. When we finally managed to pull her away, the baby's leg had turned as black as my neck."

My hands wander to my own leg, and I meet Pierce's eyes. Understanding passes between the two of us, alongside a swell of sudden horror. "Was she—"

"Your mother," Pierce hisses. "And, facing capture, she decided to make you into a weapon." He approaches the desk again, looks down at me with complete coldness. "But little did she know you were more a parting gift for me. You didn't inherit her magic, but her blood is in you—and better yet, her enchantment. With you to experiment on, I could find a solution. Something to pull her vile magic out without risking myself in the process. But Averard, ever the bleeding heart, didn't like that, and so he stole you from me. You, the Wanderer's lieutenant, and a few of the other resistance mages." Pierce's mouth splits into a nasty grin. "Eventually, we got the rest of *them* back."

I don't know what to feel. I'd never given much thought to who my parents were because I had Averard, and he was enough. I don't remember my mother, or this lieutenant, or any other group of mages. I only remember the thrum of the *Blackblood* and the soothing sound of Averard's stories.

"I wanted Averard tracked down," Pierce continues. "I wanted you *back*. But Mason, the idiot, loved Averard and wouldn't authorize the hunt, and I couldn't risk telling anyone about my enchantment. It lay dormant, waiting, every day gripping me tighter and tighter until sometimes, I couldn't breathe. I conscripted the free mages to help me seek a cure, but we always came back to that same best solution: you." His eyes trail to my leg once more. "I see that Averard mutilated you in his quest to destroy your enchantment. But that was never going to work."

"Mutilated . . ." I glance down at my leg and run my fingers over where metal meets skin. My prosthesis. Georgian meeting Averard not long after he escaped Perishing.

Pierce stops before me and puts a hand on my shoulder. It takes all my force of will not to kick him.

"We can work together on this, Armina. I'll destroy that enchantment for you, give you what Averard never could. We'll both be free."

Averard wanted to save me, but he couldn't. He tried to save those mages, but they were all taken back in the end. I feel like I'm still missing pieces of him, and I'm somehow more unsatisfied than I was before.

I can't possibly work with Pierce. Not after what he did to Valaina and every single mage inside the Communities and out. Still . . .

A cure for the enchantment, for the terror that's been lurking beneath my skin all my life—could that be worth aligning myself with this monster? It wouldn't have to be forever, of course, just until I'm fixed. Like Pierce said, I didn't inherit my mother's magic. Her world of freedom fighting and enchanting babies isn't mine. I fix my leg, I go home to the *Blackblood*, and I pretend none of it ever happened.

"I'll think about it." I haven't slept in almost two days, and I won't be of any use if my brain's too scrambled to function. "I want this thing off my leg, especially if it means you'll leave me alone afterward." I glare into his eyes. "If you'll leave the *Blackblood* alone."

He snorts and leans back, finally releasing me. "The *Blackblood's* all you kids think about, isn't it? Don't worry, I get it. It was my home once, too." Pierce's smile becomes kind and gentle, like a doting father gazing upon his precious child. "You can take the *Blackblood* and go on to live whatever life you dream of, no Huntsmen at your heels and free of the fear and burden of enchantment. And I . . ."

He crosses the room to look at the map again, and while I can't see his face anymore, he gives off the impression of a god surveying his creation. "I'll do all the things Mason was too cowardly to try."

He lifts a hand and caresses the line of the continent's eastern shore. His thumb follows the inky black curve of the Tidal Wall. "He was so shortsighted, never thinking beyond the Federation. Communities and blood drinking are all well and good for sentimental men who lie to themselves, but why have all this power at our fingertips if we do so little to exploit it?"

Something in the warmth of his voice makes my stomach churn, and I swallow hard and grip the desk to avoid dry heaving. I think of Canto huddled by the *Blackblood's* wheel, trembling and angry and terrified; of bloodstains on the sands outside the Tidal Wall. I think of my own mother, desperate enough to enchant me rather than hand me over to them.

"My vision is clear," Pierce continues. "Having the Federation under our thumb is only the beginning of what we could accomplish. What if we fed more blood to our ranks? What if we harnessed our mages' powers, forced them to fight alongside us on pain of death? An army of the caliber I could create wouldn't be stopped by a wall. Tempestor will fall beneath the number of bodies I can throw at them."

The image of a landscape of bodies flashes through my mind. Canto's dead face sticks out from where it's crushed beneath a tangle of limbs. Pierce stands on top of the ruined Tidal Wall, coated in black blood except for the whites of his gleaming eyes. An army of Huntsmen cheering before him, and at his back lie more bodies, a country of them.

And where am I in all of it?

Hiding in my truck with my leg repaired, pretending at normal.

Pierce steps back and nods toward the door. "I have several things to set up for the enchantment, but as a show of good faith, I'll send someone up to tend your injuries. In the meantime, don't think of running. There will be a guard stationed at the door."

Then he leaves, leaves me to the silence of the room and the screaming of my thoughts.

21

RENN

Canto hasn't spoken since we left Crotalus City.

The whipping wind and roaring engine are the only sounds keeping me company. Canto's arms are stiff around my waist, and their forehead presses between my shoulder blades. Whenever we stop to refuel, Canto stares out over the dunes, as if they can't bear to remember I exist.

I've been driving hours longer than I should, but even though the glare from the headlight makes my head ache, even though my eyes burn from trying to keep them open against the sand, we can't stop now. The rocky silhouette of the mountains looms above us. I can almost see the metal spires of home.

The road bumps beneath our tires, and Canto's grip tightens. Distantly, I hear them say their first words in hours, but their voice is so soft I can't make it out over the engine as I grip the clutch and shift into a higher gear. I twist the throttle, and Canto makes a distinct noise of displeasure as our speed increases.

"What?" I keep my eyes on the road. We're still miles out from the building itself, but Huntsman patrols aren't uncommon at the mountain's base. I don't know who Pierce has doing the duty roster in my absence—if he even has anyone doing the duty roster—so we'll have to proceed assuming the worst. The bike makes too much noise; we'll drive as near to Perishing as possible before we ditch it.

Canto leans closer, and I grip the bike harder with my knees so we don't overbalance and careen off the road.

"I said," they hiss in my ear, "maybe we should stop."

The smell of magic makes it difficult to concentrate, as does the sensation of their heart beating where their chest presses against my spine. I squeeze the clutch, shift us slowly back to neutral, and pull to a stop.

We're resting in the shadow of the Onyx Mountains, in a valley of blackened boulders. The motorcycle rumbles beneath me, and Canto falls silent again as their arms slip from my sides. The places on my body they're no longer covering grow cold.

Canto's palms press against the back of their seat for balance as they stare toward the mountain's peak. "You must be tired," they say. "It has to have been over a day since you last slept and several days since you've slept comfortably. And no, that's not altruism—if you drive us off a cliff, I'll die too."

"Sooner we get there, sooner we rescue your mom and Armina." Sooner we get to Pierce.

Canto reaches around me. Before I can blink the exhaustion out of my brain, they've turned off the ignition and stolen the key.

"You're of dubious use to me at your full wits." They shove the key into their coat pocket. "We're about to infiltrate the most dangerous Community in the Federation. If you think we're doing that without a fight, then you're not as smart as you've made yourself out to be. I can't do this on my own; I need you at your brutish best."

I lean forward and rest my head against the handlebars. The truth is, even if I get a full night's sleep—doubtful at this point—I'm not sure how much help I'll be in a fight. A Huntsman's power and skill are directly tied to when they've last consumed mage blood. The longer it's been, the more human their strength. It would take years for that strength to wear off entirely, but only a few days for its potency to dull.

It's been weeks for me. The others drink every day.

What good is a Huntsman without the blood? I can't even make the drive to Perishing in one shot without exhaustion creeping in.

Canto's magic burns behind me like a beacon in the dark.

I slam down the kickstand and push myself off the motorcycle. Canto gasps and clutches the seat as if they're about to fall into the abyss without my weight keeping them balanced. It's hard not to smile as they slide forward, placing their feet firmly on the ground as if it's about to slip away from them.

"Need a hand?" I ask.

They find their footing and shoot me a nasty glare before rising on their tiptoes and swinging their leg wider than necessary to clear the seat. They move like a wet cat that doesn't want any of its fur displaced, and when I let out a tired bark of laughter, they round on me. Unfortunately, their gold eyes, their sneer, and the way they've squared their shoulders don't eliminate the cat impression, so I can't quite stop the laughter.

"You're right," I say once I compose myself. "Perishing is an hour or so by vehicle. Several hours on foot. We'll need the break." I grab the handlebars of the motorcycle and begin to wheel it off the road.

"Here?" Canto follows after me with that stubborn, dignified walk.

"You see an inn?" I lean the bike in the shade of one of the blackened boulders. "Don't be picky."

Canto laughs. I've heard them laugh before, but that was a dry, sarcastic sound. This almost sounds genuine. "Sorry, did you think my objection had something to do with the decor?

The lack of plumbing? The ambiance? Huntsman, I grew up in a Community. My house was a single room with a bed and a toilet in it. I relish the opportunity to camp—more legroom in the wilds."

There is no winning with Canto Keer. I'm not sure why I even tried. "Then what's the objection?"

They approach the shadow of the boulder I've stopped beneath and press their palm to its surface. They look past me, further into the valley where the rocky domes of the other boulders grow like the spines of some great beast. "There's a lot of magic here. Screaming."

"Sounds more like a buzzing to me." I gesture for Canto to follow me deeper into the valley. "The nice thing about it is that none of the Huntsmen will track you in here."

"Why? Does it hurt?" Their footing isn't as steady on the slope, and they've thrown out their arms to maintain their balance.

"No. It feels more like a head cold." I wince as we pass a particularly large slab of rock. "The newer an enchantment, the worse that feeling gets. Like the blindfold you put on me. Think of it like wet paint—the fresher the coat, the worse it smells. After a while, that smell fades, and after a longer while, it may disappear entirely."

Canto frowns at the surrounding shadows. "This doesn't feel like new magic."

"New in the grand scheme of things. Been around as long as I can remember, but probably not much longer. This kind of reek isn't pleasant, but it's tolerable. It's definitely not somewhere I'd want to go if I didn't have a reason, though. You'll be able to sleep."

"I'm not worried about *my* sleep. I was never going to be much help against the Huntsmen."

"What makes you say that?" I spot an empty stretch of dirt in the middle of a few jagged rocks that almost look like they could be walls. They're not made of that same black as the rest of the stone, and stepping between them brings a wave of relief. "You almost entombed me beneath Crotalus City, the very last place I'd want to be laid to rest."

"That's because you let me."

I take a seat on the ground. "I hardly let you."

"You think the Huntsmen in Perishing are going to hesitate to take my magic, let alone offer to return it?" They lower themself across from me and huddle into their coat. "I am many things—aggressive and reckless chief among my less savory qualities—but I am not foolish enough to think I can defend myself unarmed."

I lean back in the dirt and pillow my arms beneath my head. The stars have returned since we left Crotalus City. I only recognize two constellations on sight—the Crooked Viper and the Magistrate's Branches. I seek them out now, follow the familiarity of their patterns. I'm not much of a navigator or a dreamer, but it's nice to have something to cling to in the dark.

"I gave you my mageblade," I say.

"A weapon I don't know how to use."

"You put the sharp parts in the person you're trying to kill. Want a quick lesson?"

They draw the blade and grip it clumsily in one hand. "You're offering to let me stab you?"

I sigh and roll to a seated position. "You're holding it wrong. It's a longsword—two hands on the grip."

They follow my command, their fists making contact on the black leather.

"A little further apart. Now, let me see you swing."

"You'll mock me."

"I'd never. It isn't as if I'm the best swordsman in the world."

Canto stands and adjusts their footing. Their stance is . . . almost right. A close enough approximation. It could be that they've read about sword fighting in books. Or maybe they're copying a stance they've seen the Huntsmen take. I try not to dwell on that possibility as they start swinging.

It's immediately clear that they've never held a sword before, but they move with such ferocity that I can't help but pity whoever will stand in their way.

"Who's the best swordsman?" they ask.

"Hmm?" I tear my eyes away from where they overextend their swing and almost topple themself to the ground.

"You denigrated yourself with such confidence, which means you must know who the best swordsman is."

I motion for them to stop, and they do so by dropping the blade, chucking their woolen coat across the clearing, and collapsing to the ground. Their panting has a soft, pathetic wheeze to it.

"I only know the best swordsman in Perishing," I say.

Canto tilts their head toward me. They're close enough I could reach out and touch them.

"Iva Iverson, the Huntsmaster's second in command. You'd think she was born with a blade in her grip."

Canto rolls onto their back. They hold their hand in the air above them, long fingers splitting the sky. "I want to be like her."

"No, you don't. She's a terrible person."

"I don't care. I want to be powerful and ruthless and strong. I want to drive that sword through the hearts of every person even tangentially connected to the ones who hurt me."

"I understand—"

"You think so?" They roll to their feet and grab the sword. Their thin chest still heaves, and their arms shake as they lift the blade off the ground. They cross the space I hadn't dared to and stand above me, press the tip of the sword against my throat.

I should feel afraid. I should.

"I can teach you to understand, if you like. Maybe, if I cut you in enough places, I can make you feel a fraction of the terror I've known." They lean harder on the blade, and my breath catches. "A . . . a fraction of the terror we made Kateryna feel."

They pull the sword away and slam the tip into the dirt. "Every day, since the time I could speak, I woke up wondering if that was the day they'd kill me. Or if it was the day they'd kill my mother, or our neighbors. If it was the day they'd separate us. I'd wonder how much pain I'd be put through, or if I'd just have to live in fear of it until I woke up the next morning to start over again."

They crouch down to my level and lean on the sword for support. "Everything about the Order is designed to cause pain. To revel in it. These blades, for example." They run their fingers down the sword's edge, and my breath catches, suddenly terrified they'll cut themself. "These aren't weapons. These are *lives*. Each and every one a mage the Order slaughtered for some made-up crime. When you wield it in pursuit of your *justice*, all you're doing is proving that this was never about such lofty ideals as safety and prosperity. We are *objects* to you, Huntsman. Do you really wonder why I want to kill?"

Their eyes are brilliant gold in the low light from the stars. They're looking at me, unblinking, unflinching, even as they shake.

All the world weighs heavy on Canto's weary shoulders.

"No, I don't wonder," I say. "It makes perfect sense to me."

The anger, the barbs, the fear—they all make sense. I can't even look at the mageblade now where it stands stalwart and silent between us. I never gave it much thought, always just considered it *mine*. My weapon. My symbol of allegiance. The blood it's composed of and the person it came from never crossed my mind.

And now? With Canto's words and their face broken by the impossibly heavy weight? Now I will be haunted by it.

When did I stop thinking of mages as people? When did I start thinking about blood as part of a daily routine and not something the Huntsmen had to harvest? I could pretend that my father hid the truth from me beneath stories of honor and duty, but the reality is that I hid that truth from myself.

I don't work with mages. I don't go to exsanguinations. I don't have time for any of that; I'm too busy with my paperwork.

"The sword," I say, trying to impress upon Canto, or maybe upon myself, that the world has shifted. "It's yours now. When all this is over, you can do as you please with it. A burial, perhaps."

They glare at me out of narrowed eyes. "And you'll be there. To apologize."

I nod. "I'll be there."

Canto sits down and folds their elbows against their knees. Their frown is still deeply etched on their face, but their shoulders relax. They watch me, half their face obscured from view by the black blade.

"What's waiting for you in Perishing?" they ask.

"What do you mean?"

"You agreed to help me, and I needed help badly enough that I didn't question it much at the time. But I'm questioning it now. You said the Order took something from you. What was it?"

My muscles tense, stitches pulling painfully as I momentarily forget how to breathe. "The Huntsmaster had my father murdered."

The words hurt to say out loud.

Canto sits up straight, like a child getting read a bedtime story. "Was he a mage?"

"No. He was . . ."

I hesitate. Canto's eyes gleam, like I'm about to deliver an interesting tidbit of information they can tuck away for later. I know that look because I wore it a thousand times before I realized people don't like it when you let them know you're using them.

I also hesitate because this truce I've formed with Canto stands on a very unstable foundation, one that's been tested more than once tonight. Knowing I'm the previous Huntsmaster's son might send the whole thing crumbling down.

"He was a Huntsman," I say. "Disobeyed orders, and Pierce had him exsanguinated."

Canto sucks in a breath. "I'm surprised you're still alive."

"Well . . ." I lie down because I can't bear looking into their face any longer. "I don't think Pierce intended me to be."

Canto crawls back across the dirt and grabs their coat, then pulls it over their body and flops down. They reach into their pocket like they're digging for something, but their hands come out empty. "What do you think Pierce *does* intend?" They tilt their fingers this way and that as if fiddling with something.

"I'm not sure. Iverson implied they were hunting down the *Blackblood.*"

"Maybe he wanted something on it."

"I suppose, but what could—"

I'm taken back to Pierce's office what feels like a lifetime ago. *Arrest the captain. Bring her here.* No mention of the truck; no mention of its contents at all. In a normal smuggling circumstance, we'd take in the entire haul of artifacts, organize and catalog them. But the only thing Pierce specified was Armina. Alive.

"He was after Armina," I say.

"What would he possibly want with a nineteen-year-old artifact smuggler?"

I turn toward the mountain, my eyes following its distant trail up and up to where Perishing lies nestled. "I only know he wanted her alive." I scowl at the peaks where they interrupt the stars. "If Pierce hadn't commanded it, it would have been far easier for me to kill–"

The words die in my throat. The potent stink of rust sullies the air, followed by the head-splitting sensation of magic. Canto glares at the sky, squeezing their hand open and closed. Blood trickles down their wrist.

"Canto." My fingers dig trenches into the dirt.

They turn their head to look at me. "What?"

Drinking blood isn't a compulsion: it won't kill me or drive me crazy if I don't. It's a temptation. The temptation of enough strength to get my revenge and help Canto get theirs. And it's lying on the ground six feet away.

"You're bleeding." I plunge my fingers deeper into the earth.

Canto stares down at their hands. Then they scramble away and put an extra dozen feet between us. Their back is against one of the stone walls, and their eyes keep flicking between me and the mageblade they've left impaled in the dirt by my side.

"Stay over there." Their voice has lost its commanding tone and risen an octave as they press closer to the stone. "Stay over there." It sounds almost pleading this time.

"I'm not going to hurt you." I disengage my fingers from the dirt and tug the blade out of the ground. I slide it toward them so it stops a few feet from their knees. "This isn't the first time you've bled around me, and it wasn't an issue then, right? Have I not followed all your rules so far? You have my mageblade. I haven't touched you."

"You have."

"*You've* touched *me*. I did your whole blindfold thing; I let you give me stitches; I listened when you said we needed to stop driving." My voice drops, and now I'm the one who sounds like he's pleading. "I know you don't trust me, but I'm not going to jeopardize our goal."

Canto slowly unfolds. They reach out and grab the mageblade, pull it toward themself. "You haven't had any blood in days."

"Weeks, actually." I run a hand through my hair and try to steady my breathing. "I'm not really the type who expects to go on big, cross-country adventures on a whim, so I may not have stuck to the strictest schedule."

"What happens to a Huntsman who doesn't drink blood?"

Their eyes pin me down, and they have the perfect grip on the mageblade. If they came at me now, they could probably cleave me in two. Maybe I'd let them.

"They stop being a Huntsman. Eventually."

"So, you're not a Huntsman anymore?"

There's some kind of wonderment in their voice, something that I hate to crack apart.

"I still am. Takes more than a few weeks to get it out of your system. I still have all the skills a regular Huntsman does, just not as fresh. Not as strong."

Their grip on the mageblade loosens. "A weak Huntsman and a mage try to infiltrate Perishing. Sounds like the start of a joke."

"I grew up in Perishing; I know more of its secrets than anyone. You and I are going to do this." I juggle what I'm about to say next, then blurt it out all at once. "If you let me have some of your blood, I can be back to fighting strength. If that's a worry."

I wish I hadn't said it. I even falter at the end, trail off into oblivion as Canto's blood *drip, drips* into the dirt and their grip on the mageblade tightens again.

"No," they say.

"Right. I didn't think so, but I figured it wouldn't hurt to ask. Cover all our options up front so we're not arguing about what's best or what could have been later." I'm speaking so fast even my own brain can't keep up with my prattle, and my face may well catch fire. "It'll be all right; I'm bigger than most of the other Huntsmen, so maybe that will even up the—"

"It's okay?" Canto asks. All my words die in my throat at the look on their face: a mix of that previous wonderment and confusion. "'No' is okay?"

The cold night air fills my lungs, and suddenly, everything hurts. "Of course it's okay."

Canto studies me a minute before falling back in the dirt and curling around their coat. "Good. Because if it wasn't, this would be the end of our partnership." They roll onto their side, turning their back to me. "Get some sleep, Huntsman. We need to retain at least a portion of your usefulness."

I lay down as well, watch the staggering rise and fall of their shoulders against a backdrop of boulders and mountains. The metallic tang of their blood still rests heavy in the air.

"Canto." The word spills from my mouth as my thoughts try to catch up.

Their shoulders seize, but then they turn toward me.

"How did you cut your hand, anyway?" I ask.

They hold out their open palm. "Old habits."

Their skin appears bloodstained but empty. "I don't understand."

They lift their hand to the meager starlight, fingers pinched as if they have something trapped between them. "It was my mother's. And her grandfather's, and presumably his grandparents'." They frown and clutch their invisible object tighter. "Sometimes I take it out and hold it. It feels like a connection. A tip-of-the-tongue memory of something I've lost."

"I can't see it."

They scowl at their hand, then their expression breaks, and they let out another one of those genuine laughs. "Of course. I enchanted it to be undetectable by Huntsmen so they couldn't take it from me. I didn't realize that would manifest as it becoming *invisible*." Their grin is wild, and their teeth look sharp. "Magic is *wonderful*."

Magic is terrifying.

"Do you always bleed when you hold it?"

Their laughter dies, and they pull their hand back to their chest. They're quiet a long moment before they say, "Recently."

"Have you given any thought to the possibility that it might be taking blood on purpose?"

They don't respond.

I rise as dawn breaks, casting our valley in shades of brown and gray. There's a fine mist everywhere, and I swipe dew off my shirt as I stand. Canto still huddles beneath their coat, presumably sleeping, so I decide to do a swift walk around the perimeter of our camp to stretch the soreness out of my bones.

The air hums with magic, making my nose run. I imagine that, in another decade or two, this area will lose the sting of new magic and creep into the territory of old magic.

Old magic doesn't cause sinus pressure and headaches. But old magic is clever. Old magic bends its creator's rules, and sometimes, it can warp them until the enchantment is no longer recognizable for what it was intended to be. That's one of the reasons Huntsmen exist—to destroy old, broken enchantments before they become more than the average person can handle.

I glance back at Canto's still-dreaming form, at the blood drying between their clenched fingers.

Then I return my attention to the mountain, where Perishing's black spires absorb the morning sun.

22
CANTO

I have decided that I don't like walking.

Trees and outcroppings of black rock surround us, and we pick our way through brush and roots and a carpet of pine needles. Renn refused to follow the clear dirt road, which I suppose was sensible of him, but I'm covered in enough scrapes and bruises that I'll be sore for the next eternity. I may have left my leg muscles behind miles ago, and now I'm walking on the skeletal remains.

Renn, however, seems fine to go forever on five hours of sleep and the bag of dried meat he stole during one of yesterday's pit stops. It tasted like ashes, but Renn shared it with me, which was enough of a shock that I didn't complain.

Huntsmen don't share. They don't teach you how to hold swords. They don't offer to carry you when they notice you're tired, and they certainly don't ask permission before they take your blood. I don't know what Renn is, but he doesn't behave like a Huntsman.

"When all this is done," Renn says, doubling back when he realizes he's gotten too far ahead of me again, "I'm going to teach you how to walk properly."

"I know how to walk." I stumble over yet another fallen branch. "Pardon if I'm unused to a half-dozen hours combing rough terrain—we didn't have hiking trails in my Community."

"You're almost done." He somehow manages to sound both encouraging and deeply condescending.

Perishing peeks above the tree line like a shadow. Too solid to be a shadow, though. Too impossibly dark. Its spires pierce the clouds in a way that's uncomfortable to look at for too long, as if parts of the sky have been scrubbed away to reveal the emptiness beneath. I've been staring at my feet instead, afraid to see it and remember that it's real.

Renn stops short, and I walk into his back. He holds out an arm to corral me behind him, then crouches to the ground. I follow suit, welcoming the blissful relief from the burn in my calves.

"We clear these last few trees and we'll be at the east side of the exterior wall." Renn's voice is low, and his eyes haven't left Perishing. "This wall has two entrances: one in the south—which is considered the main gate—and one in the east, which we'll use."

"What makes the east gate special?"

"Well, first, since it isn't the main gate, there's no foot traffic, no supply delivery, no Huntsman patrol. Second, it's isolated. There's a guard on it, but most Huntsmen *hate* eastern door duty—it's dead boring. You're by yourself for hours with nothing to do but stare at the trees." Renn smirks. "I used to schedule Huntsmen who pissed me off to work it for weeks at a time."

I pick up one of the pine needles from the ground and shred it apart. "What's the plan?"

"You're going to stay out of sight, and I'm going to talk to the guard." Renn stands again, and after a moment, I do as well. "If Pierce hasn't denounced me to the entirety of Perishing yet, I can convince whoever's up there that I'm taking the shift."

"That isn't going to work."

"You underestimate how much people loathe this rotation. And if it doesn't work, all that means is I need to take down one Huntsman. This is our safest option."

"Are you sure you can fight them?"

"Have a little faith. I may not be at peak strength, but drinking mage blood doesn't replace skill."

He trudges up the hill, and I scramble to keep a few feet behind him. Wherever his confidence comes from, I wish I could borrow some. As the trees thin and the black walls continue to reveal themselves, I suppress a shudder.

We're not even inside yet, and I can already tell that Perishing is haunted.

"Stay here." Renn gestures toward an enormous oak, the trunk more than thick enough to hide my frame. "Don't come out for anything, okay? If something goes wrong, head back down the mountain."

If something goes wrong. Maybe he isn't so confident.

I reach out and prod his arm with my fingertip. "Nothing is going to go wrong."

His lips twitch, and his eyes gleam, and I wish they were a color I didn't fear. "I'll be back soon."

He disappears around the side of the tree, and I slide to its base, hugging my knees. I still have the mageblade clutched in my grip, but it feels less like I'm armed with it and more like I'm burdened. The long walk has left a quiver in my limbs and an ache in my feet. Worse, we've finally arrived at our objective, and I'm too afraid to look it in the eye.

We're about to enter Perishing. We're about to either find my mother and Armina or die. I'm voluntarily going into the most dangerous building in the world, and the only person at my side is a Huntsman who doesn't act in any of the ways I expect. I'm out of my element. Perhaps I never had an element to begin with and I've always been drifting.

Every inch of the world seems designed to cage me. If something goes wrong in Perishing, they'll put me back in my box unless I fight and fight and make myself so sharp that they have no choice but to kill me. I cannot be caught again. I refuse to bleed anymore because someone else demands it.

Something scrapes through the wet earth in the direction of Perishing, followed by a *thud*. A *thump*. A *crash*. I squeeze my eyes shut. Renn said not to come out for anything. He said to stay hidden.

But he's taking too long, and I never agreed to follow his orders anyway. I peek around my tree.

Renn is on the ground. There's another man on top of him—equal his size—with his thick arm pressed against Renn's throat. Renn grabs the man's head, but the man keeps his eyes and nose out of Renn's reach while applying more pressure. They're both covered in dirt and smeared in red blood.

That Huntsman doesn't know I'm here, but the moment he's done with Renn, he'll find me. I could get far enough away in the several minutes it will take Renn to die that I might be safe. I'll return to the valley of boulders, figure out the motorcycle—the key still rests heavy in my pocket. One lone mage on the road might not attract much attention. I've burned my bridges with Georgian, but there must be something, someone, that can help me. I'll find another way to rescue my mother and Armina. A safer way.

All I have to do is let Renn die.

The magic bursts from me before I even think to channel it properly. My fingernails dig into the oak tree's bark, and the enchantment spirals outward and down, down, down into the dirt. The Huntsman pauses his assault, his shoulders and head lifting while he keeps Renn pinned. His eyes land on me.

The ground explodes in a shower of dirt and water and worms as the oak's roots unanchor themselves. They knot together in a mass of wood and tendrils, blackened with magic, and surge forward. They strike the Huntsman atop Renn, driving through his torso and lifting him into the air before slamming him against Perishing's stone wall. Blood streams from his mouth in tiny rivers. I think he's still alive. He won't be for very long.

Renn chokes for breath as he stares at the roots impaling the Huntsman to the wall.

"The human body is very resilient," I say as I approach. "One would think that should have killed him instantly. Alas, fate is cruel."

"*You're* cruel," Renn wheezes, but it sounds almost affectionate.

"Such a charming way to say thank you."

Renn staggers to his feet, massaging his throat. "Thank you. I mean it. Unfortunately, this reeks of magic, and it's going to have half the Huntsmen in the Community wandering out here soon enough. We need to get inside."

I turn toward the door. It's a heavy-looking thing, black iron, fit neatly into the wall's stone archway. I grab the ring handle and tug.

It doesn't budge.

"I, uh . . . I think he had the key," Renn says.

We both glance toward the man, only to find that he has finally died, his body slumped against the wood. The roots I summoned tangle around him like a cage: some push through his chest, while others wrap around his legs and torso, crushing him to the wall. Blood and meat splat to the ground in slow, steady drips.

Any keys he may have had in his pockets are now either destroyed or unreachably trapped beneath the knotted roots.

I return my attention to Renn. "Can you break the door down?"

Renn taps his knuckles against the iron door. "I appreciate your faith in me, but kicking down a metal door *might* test the limits of even my bountiful strength." He bends and peers into the keyhole. "I could pick it, but I've never done that before. Can you enchant it open or something?"

I approach the door. "A black like that means it's already enchanted. I might be able to do it, but I'd need time, and maybe even blood. And since you get mopey when I cut myself . . ."

"I do *not* get—"

I rest my hand against the cold metal and try to feel my way through the ancient enchantment. The moment I do, however, I hear a *click*, and the iron vibrates beneath my palm. I grasp the ring again and pull. The door flows soundlessly open.

"What did you do?" Renn inspects the hinges, then my hands, like he expects to see them dripping blood.

"Nothing." My palm tingles but remains otherwise unchanged. "Maybe it was just stuck?"

"Stuck," Renn mutters with a frown. He slides his hands along the doorframe, but eventually, he does step through and into the darkness beyond. I follow, stretching my palm as the sensation lingers.

The wall is thicker than I imagined, and there's a little alcove behind the iron door where we stand in shadow.

"This is as far as most outsiders get." Renn speaks so softly that I have to lean closer to hear him. "There's a second, interior wall, but it only has one gate. We'll need to do something slightly more dangerous to get past."

"More dangerous than putting a hole through a Huntsman?"

"Much. I'm going to need you to put a hole through the wall."

"But you said the enchantment I did reeked. Won't enchanting a new hole make things worse?"

Renn grimaces. His feet shuffle. "Yes, but it'll take the Huntsmen longer to notice. The interior wall leads directly into the Community. The magic from all the mages on the other side will cover your enchantment to an extent."

All the mages on the other side. Several thousand people suffering as I have—so close and I can't save them. Renn is asking me to *use* them.

Again.

"Renn," I hiss.

He tilts his ear closer to listen.

"Those aren't distractions on the other side of that wall. They're *people*. They're people like *me*."

His eyebrows knit, and his eyes drift from my face to the mageblade at my side.

"What happens to them after we rescue who we've come to rescue and kill who we've come to kill?"

"I don't know." Darkness cloaks his expression but not the twinge of guilt in his voice. "We'll figure something out."

"Something" can have so many meanings. From a Huntsman, "something" sounds like a return to status quo. To the normalcy of the Order and Communities and bloodletting rooms. And I can't have that. I *can't*. If I'm going to keep using people to get what I want, there has to be something in it for them, too. Life has to get better.

"I'm adding a new stipulation to this partnership," I say. "We're saving my mother and Armina. We're killing Pierce. Then afterward, when the dust settles, we're tearing Perishing down. The Huntsmen legacy crumbles *today*."

Renn's breath hitches like I've slapped him again. His delayed response comes out strained. "I . . . we'll try."

"We'll *do*."

He steps around me, and even the shadows of his face are no longer visible. His voice, however, floats back toward me, empty in tone.

"Okay," he says, then pokes his head through the opening in the wall.

I don't have time to hash out his response, as he glances both ways before waving me forward.

We exit into the sunshine together, and I finally see the full scope of Perishing's welcome. We stand between the interior and exterior walls, and in the distance, trucks rumble and people shout. Huntsmen move and march in the same rambling pattern as flies, skirting through the courtyard on whatever daily task they've been assigned. Renn and I run away from them along the alley between the walls. Renn keeps us going further and further back, so when we finally stop, my legs are screaming again.

"Here's good," Renn says. "There should be a building right on the other side that will keep us blocked from view."

Magic comes naturally to me, and even though this context terrifies and worries me, I find comfort in the gentle tug on my blood as I press both palms flat against the wall. The new stone, gray and rough beneath my skin, is perfect for enchantment. I imagine the layers of it peeling apart, and the rock beneath my hands blackens and flakes away, curling in on itself in wide strips. I make a hole big enough for myself to walk through comfortably and for Renn to squeeze through if he really puts in the effort.

"Go," Renn urges, and I duck across the threshold.

On the other side, I blink sun out of my eyes and come face to face with a mage.

He's about my height, with a shock of white-blond hair and blue eyes. We're standing in a dirt yard, and there's a house behind him, all blackened brick and roof tiles. He has a tub of water and scrub board and appears to be doing his laundry, although his hands have paused mid-task, water soaking through the linen of his rolled-up sleeves. He's my mother's age, perhaps a little younger. His veins stand out against his skin, and he has an angry black bruise at the crook of his arm.

He looks at the hole, and I see the question forming on the tip of his tongue: what kind of mage breaks *into* Perishing?

Renn comes through a moment later, and the mage gasps and fumbles his washing. The whole tub spills to the ground and puddles on the black earth.

"You couldn't have made it a little bigger?" Renn grouses as he extracts his shoulder from the wall. "Some of us have—" He stops when he sees the mage's horrified face.

I'm feeling some of that horror myself—the warm, sticky dread that comes from being surrounded on all sides. The forty-foot walls tower above us, and the rows upon rows of little houses bring to mind the house I left so far behind.

The mage's head bows the moment he sees Renn, and his hands clasp together. My own palms meet, some unconscious part of me ready to join the display. It's safer to appease the Huntsmen. Sometimes they'll decide they can't be bothered to punish you.

"At ease," Renn says, which only makes the mage cringe more.

My hands clasp together harder until my fingers sting. It's Renn; it's Renn. He promised not to hurt me.

The mage shoots a quick glance in my direction before fixing his gaze somewhere around Renn's collar. "I apologize for breaking lockdown, Huntsman. My . . . my son got sick in the night; I needed to clean the bed linens; I thought it would only be a minute; I—"

"You're forgiven," Renn says. "Keep this hole in the wall our secret and we won't have any further issues."

I know these lines. I don't like this Renn.

The mage gives a halting nod and retreats into his home.

The snap of his door breaks something inside me, and I tear my hands apart and round on Renn. My fingertip meets his chest, and I prod him hard until his back presses against the stone wall.

"You told me there was a building on the other side," I snarl. "You didn't tell me it was someone's *house*."

"I can't see how it matters—"

"It matters because if the Huntsmen find this hole before we take the Huntsmaster out, they'll think the mages who live here did it. The Huntsmen will *kill this man's entire family*."

Renn's face turns crimson. "Could we close the hole?"

I draw my fingers back to my chest and step away from him. For the second time in as many days, I am complicit in ruining someone's life. "You've seen magic. You *know* magic. What good is closing up the hole when there will still be a big, black, *magic* stain? Is your head empty, Renn? Do you not think?"

"I didn't think," Renn admits. "I'm not . . . I don't come out here much. It's rare I even interact with a mage in my day-to-day life; I don't know what—"

"You should know. All Communities are like this. There are thousands of mages and one very enchantable wall. What do you think keeps us inside?"

Renn pauses, his eyes glued to the back of the mage's house. "I'm sorry."

It's a very heavy sort of sorry.

I grunt in acknowledgement. "We needed to move fast before. Now that we've put these people in direct danger, we need to move that much faster. What's next?"

Renn steps past me, but his walk is stiff, as if he's forgotten how to use his arms. "The initial plan was to go through the front door."

"Just like that?"

"Yeah. No guards stationed directly at the entrance; the rotation takes them through the Community, so if we time it right, there won't be anyone to see us enter." He presses his knuckles to his lips. "But the plan also included getting the keys from the east gate's guard. Now we don't have those, so we'll need to find a guard and somehow trick them into splitting off from the others, which won't be easy if the Community really is on lockdown as the mage said. I don't think I have the strength to take out an entire—"

"*Renn*." I grasp his shoulder, and his mouth snaps shut. "Let's try the front door first before we panic. Maybe one of them left it unlocked."

"That would be a huge oversight and breach of—"

I stalk off alone across the mage's meager lawn. To Renn's credit, he hurries after me.

This Community is big. Easily ten times the size of my own. The sea of black buildings stretches on and on, the streets neat and orderly but also empty. At capacity, this could house a hundred thousand residents. Maybe more.

I keep my eyes on the mage houses as long as I am able, but all too soon, Perishing itself draws my gaze. Even with my head tilted all the way back, at its base, I cannot see the top. The structure is a strange mix of metal and stone and glass, and as Renn promised, the double doors are unguarded.

Renn reaches the door first and grasps the handle. He tugs, but it remains firmly closed. "Thought so. All right, new plan. Pierce took his best soldiers with him to Crotalus City, so it's possible those on duty now are—"

I step up and touch the blackened wood, and I hear that same resounding *click* as before. My palm buzzes again, and my head spins with a lightheaded dizziness so reminiscent of having my blood drawn that I need to lean against the door for a moment to regain my balance.

"How are you *doing* that?" Renn presses his own hand against the door. "It doesn't feel like an enchantment."

I glance down at my fingertips. "I have no idea." I shake my head and clench my hand into a fist. "We can worry about my new lockpicking skills later. What's the plan?"

Renn runs his hand up the ancient metal. "I really don't like this."

"You don't have to. *What is the plan?*"

He grasps the door handle once more, but he's still scowling. "Once we're inside, we need to get to the library. That's where the archive is; I'll double check the file on your mother and make sure I haven't missed anything. There's also a chance someone has dumped something about Armina into the intake bin."

"What if there are Huntsmen in the library?"

"To be honest, I don't think half of them know the library even exists. People usually just put things in the intake slot and are done with it. We should be okay." Renn ushers me into the entrance hall, his chest inches from my back. "We should be okay," he repeats.

At first, the emptiness of the building surprises me. Not that I expected grand tapestries or gilt vases, but not a single object decorates the cavernous hall. Not even a rug. Instead, the walls and floors and ceilings are empty; the only things interrupting the sameness are the occasional marble columns stretching into the darkness above.

All that empty makes the hall echo. The smattering tap of our footsteps mixes with those of patrolling Huntsmen, but Renn still needs to stop and pull me aside several times throughout our journey, pressing me deep into the shadows of columns and stairways as someone stalks past.

Eventually, Renn draws me from careful walking to almost sprinting, his hand wrapped around mine. My shins burn as he drags me down a side corridor and toward a set of black wood doors. He throws them open, and we rush inside before Renn closes them quietly behind us once more.

Renn leans against the door, one arm wrapped across his chest, the other pressing his hand to his forehead. He's breathing through his teeth, and I rest my shoulders beside his.

The room smells of books and paper and dust. Dozens of shelves holding thousands upon thousands of volumes both ring the perimeter and stand in neat rows throughout. There is a small step down into a section of tables—only one of which has a lamp perched on its surface—and a wall of filing cabinets.

"Welcome to my office." Renn pushes away from the door and hops down the step, crossing to the table and switching on the lamp. "Maybe there's something in the bin about Pierce's agenda." He heads over to a wide metal box beneath a slot in the wall.

While he fishes through it, I take a moment to wander the shelves.

I thought my Community's library was the biggest in the world until I saw all the crates in Armina's truck. Then I thought certainly, *certainly* there couldn't be more.

The contents of both those libraries wouldn't fill a single shelf in this one.

I run my fingers along the spines, bursting clouds of dust into the air. Some of them are so ancient that the titles are no longer legible. There are paperbacks and hardbacks, books bound with leather and with cloth. Books that have lost their covers entirely and now sit with their glue and binding exposed to the world. Most are ordinary. Some are black with magic.

"All right," Renn calls, shocking me from my reverie. "I double checked your mother's file, and it's as I remembered.

Nothing in the bin about Armina, though. Not even basic intake forms."

"What about for Valaina?"

I hear more shuffling, then a grunt of surprise. "There's one here, but she's—"

His voice cuts off as the door swings open so hard that it bounces against the wall. My pulse rings in my ears as I duck down and creep forward. I keep a shelf between me and the door and peer through the books.

Two people enter the library. The first is a young man, broad, his hair somewhere between ginger and colorless. He glances around—not as if he's looking for something, but as if he's expecting something.

The second one I know.

Unkempt beard and broken leg; the Huntsman who dragged me from my Community limps into the room.

Renn grows very still where he'd been sifting through papers on the table. "Baker," he says.

"Mason," Baker replies. "Good to see you up and about and arresting yourself." He steps into the archive and snatches a stack of papers off Renn's desk, thumbs through them.

The other Huntsman takes a step toward the stacks. I move in tandem with him, edging myself deeper and deeper into the shadow of the shelves.

"I came back because I've done nothing wrong," Renn says. I no longer see his face, but I hear the way his voice falls flat.

"We'll see about that, won't we? In the meantime . . ."

The other Huntsman reaches the first shelf and places his palm on it. I realize what he's about to do a moment before he does it, and I scramble out of the way, behind another shelf, as that one crashes down. The thunder of falling books and tearing paper rends the air, as well as an explosion of centuries of dust.

Baker laughs. "Carrie is going to keep pushing down shelves until we find your little snack."

23

ARMINA

True to his word, Pierce doesn't leave me alone for long. No one comes into the room, but I hear boots shuffle on the other side of the door and that same door creak like someone's leaned on it. With only a desk and a chair and an ancient map to keep me company, I've no choice but to play the waiting game. To dig through my own scrambled thoughts for a way out of this incredible mess.

I fold my arms on the desk and bury my face between them. I'm not about to help Pierce or let him take any of my blood, even if it means living with this enchantment until it kills me. I don't remember anything about my mother, but if she thought it necessary, shit . . . maybe it is.

Would Averard have ever told me the truth? Sat me down and said, *By the way, I stole you from my ex-best friend, who may come back for you someday, upending everything you care about?*

Maybe I wasn't a daughter to Averard, instead just another piece in his collection of enchanted trinkets gathering dust in the back of the truck. I'm gonna be left with that big, gaping unknown for the rest of my life, another wound I can't hold closed long enough to heal.

I guess I doze off at some point because meaningless nightmares chase through my head: Desert scenes dyed black with blood and smoke. Broken legs and broken promises and broken families and a thousand other things Averard left shattered in his wake. A skeletal horse and a woman astride it, black blood dripping from her empty eyes and mouth.

I jolt awake with a gasp. The yellow overhead light buzzes and flicks, and through the shadows, I realize there's someone else in the room.

Valaina sits in a chair opposite me, her legs propped on the desk. She stares at the ceiling with her arms crossed. Her dark curls stick out every which way, and she has bags under her brown eyes, as if maybe it's been a minute since she's slept too.

"Morning," she says.

"I don't want to see you."

Her eyes fall from the ceiling, and her legs slip off the desk. "You sure? I brought gifts." She reaches down and picks a first aid kit up off the floor. "Need to get that lip cleaned and stitched. You're already looking at a scar."

"I can do it myself." I hold my hand out for the kit.

"You fucking can't." Valaina sits on the desk and slides across toward me.

I push away in my chair, but she slams her foot down on one arm of it. "Come on, Mina. How many times have I stitched you up?"

"Dunno." I try to stand, but she drops her other foot on the chair's other arm, caging me in. "How many of those times have been directly after I found out you betrayed me?"

Valaina rolls her eyes and opens the kit. "Don't be dramatic."

"You sold us out." I shove the chair from under the soles of her boots and step back. "I heard you. You have some kind of deal with Pierce—"

"You brought a mage onto my truck, so as far as betrayals go, let's call ourselves even." Valaina starts pulling things from the kit—cloth and a glass bottle of alcohol and a needle. "Now, are you gonna let me clean you up, or are you gonna let your mouth rot off?"

"I think I'll take the latter option."

She uncaps the bottle of alcohol and pours some on the cloth. "I'll tell you what you want to know"—her voice takes on a singsong note—"if you let me fix you."

"Valaina, even when I loved you, I didn't trust you. What makes you think I'll start now?"

"Because I've got all sorts of secrets." She rests her elbows on her knees and smirks at me. "And I'm tired of keeping them from you."

I hesitate, but the truth is, I miss Valaina. I miss what she represents—a member of my little pirate crew, someone I spent half my life caring about. *Family*. The word flits across my mind, and I try to stuff it down again. But it doesn't work. Valaina's home in the same way the *Blackblood* is, and I crave that familiarity in this awful place.

"Fine." I lean against the edge of the desk because I'm afraid she'll trap me again if I sit in the chair. "Get talking."

She hums and tilts my face with her fingertips. She presses the cloth to my lip; I'd been able to ignore the injury over the last couple hours, but I'm instantly reminded as the acidic sting runs through half my face and the sharp smell makes my eyes tear.

"Been thinking about joining the Huntsmen for a while," she says. The thin metal of the forceps touches my mouth. "Not because I care much for their mission, but because I thought they could offer the *Blackblood* something. Protection, even if it was from themselves. Averard never wanted to work with them. I thought he was wrong."

The needle pierces my upper lip. I breathe through my nose and drum my fingers on the desk as Valaina tugs the needle through the other side.

"Pierce offered me a position if I proved myself," she says. "So I did. Worked real hard doing whatever menial tasks I could without drawing Averard's attention. But then Pierce wanted me to do a harder job, and for that, I demanded something more than a place in the Huntsmen." She ties off the stitch and puts the materials back into the box. "I did what he asked, and then he reneged on his end. Not much more to it than that."

"What was the job?"

I reach up to touch my mouth, but she smacks my hand away. "Doesn't matter. Now stop picking at it! You'll ruin my hard work."

I clamp my hands at my sides, but I want to rip the stitches out, just to show her she doesn't get a say in what I do anymore. My lip's fixed, I'm rested, and I'm ready to go.

"There a guard at the door?" I ask.

Her eyebrows raise. "Nah. Told him he could take a break, and he seemed keen to do anything but door duty."

"Perfect. Let's go." I push away from the desk and head toward the door. Dunno what I'm gonna do about Valaina yet, but that all can wait. We'll grab the truck and get out of here. Actually cross the Y'ashtrian border this time. Lay low forever if need be, or until Pierce's enchantment swallows him whole. If there's still a way for me to stitch the ripped-up shreds of my life back together, I'll take it, betrayal or no.

Val doesn't move to follow. "Aw, but Mina, you haven't finished hearing me out. Isn't that what you wanted?"

"You can tell me the rest once we're on the road. Forget this Huntsman shit; let's get out of here."

She whistles low. "Damn, you think it's gonna be that easy, huh?"

"It's not gonna be anything if we don't try."

"You really do sound like Averard."

I flinch and cross the room faster. I have to get out; the air in here stinks of alcohol and bad memories. "If you stay here, I'll assume you don't want to be part of my crew anymore."

"Everything I do is for this crew." Valaina's voice is all sorts of quiet, like a poised viper. I hear a loud *thunk* on the desk behind me. "Maybe I'm more like Averard than you'll ever be."

I whip around because I'm tired, I'm so damn *tired*, of people using him like a weapon against me. Before I lash out, however, I see what made the sound against the desk.

There's a black-bladed knife sunk into the wood.

"I think people forget a lot of times that he was my father figure too." Valaina collapses into Pierce's chair and prods at the handle of the knife with the toe of her boot. "I mean, he's the only parent I remember having. But you? You're the only one who was his daughter. You were Armina and Averard: artifact traders and desert explorers. I was just Valaina: a scared little girl who was nothing without the *Blackblood*."

My eyes roam down the edge of the blade. "Where did you get that?"

"Where do you think?"

I've stopped breathing; my heart has stopped beating; my skin is burning right off my bones. A knife through my own throat would be less agonizing.

Valaina's always known how to hurt me best.

"Why did . . ." I trail off, unable to find the words in the seething tangled mess of my brain. Instead, the question comes out like a scream. "*Why?*"

Every muscle in my body shakes as Valaina tugs the knife from the wood. She spins the tip on the desk, and the black metal whirls. "Pierce told me if I killed Averard, I could have anything I wanted."

"What could you possibly have wanted that bad?" I grip my lapels and tighten Averard's coat around my chest. The leather smells like diesel and the desert, but even that comfort isn't grounding enough. "What'd be worth this?"

The knife stops spinning. "I wanted to make sure nothing threatened our home again. That you'd be safe." She glares at me. "I wanted the people who hurt me to suffer."

In the stretching silence, in the wake of the world crumbling apart, it occurs to me that I've spent a decade pretending Valaina doesn't feel pain. I know the scars carved into her skin, obvious and irrefutable, but Valaina . . .

She hid it so well.

She smiles when she doesn't mean it. She laughs when she's angry. She'll tell you all the pretty things you want to hear so that you never, never focus on what's decomposing beneath her skin. We don't talk about Huntsmen; we skirt around our scars. But pain festers. It rots. If we ignore it too long, it shapes itself up in all kinds of ugly ways.

I try to keep my response calm, reasonable, even as my own rot threatens to breach my surface.

"Averard rescued you," I say. "He kept you safe from the people who made you suffer."

"He let them *go*." Valaina's grip on the knife tightens, and the tip gouges deep into the table's wood. "He let those mages go free and then kept *me* in a cage."

"You weren't kept," I insist. "You were free to—"

"Free to *what*, Armina? Free to leave the *Blackblood*, get a job, live in the Federation like any of its lazy, cowering citizens? I was twelve. I wasn't free to do anything. And by the time I grew up, I didn't know how to do anything but travel alongside someone else's dream."

My fingers curl in the hems of my sleeves. "I didn't . . . you never—"

"I didn't want to upset you." She glances away, picking up the knife and finally storing it in her pocket. The memory of it remains like the imprint of the sun after glancing at the sky a second too long. "You're the only thing that's ever made my life good. Being with you is like a blanket put over a fire just before it burns everything down." Her eyes meet mine, and her teeth set. "I loved you; I love you; I always will."

She's told me she loves me before, but it's always been in prettier places: camped out on a dune overlooking the mountains; on the roof of a little settlement tavern, high above the sounds of music and laughter; alone in the truck, surrounded by magic, giggling as she pressed her lips to mine. An empty Huntsman office after telling me she murdered my father is not a pretty place, and it isn't worthy of us, either.

I love Valaina too. Despite all the things she's done, despite all the things she wants to do, you never really stop loving someone once you properly start. I want her to be happy, and I want her hurts to go away.

But I don't ever want to see her again.

"Let Pierce help you," she says, so gentle it doesn't even sound like her. "Let him fix your leg; then we can run away. To Y'ashtria, as far away from mages as possible. Or across the sea. If spending your life with me sounds unappealing, then think about yourself. You do this, and you'll never have to worry about your leg again. You'll never have to worry about being powerless. You can kill all your little problems." She hesitates, then places a hand over her heart and smiles. "You can kill me."

I shake my head and back away from her, wringing my fingers together. My gut feels so empty, like I've lost Averard all over again—except worse somehow, because when Valaina leaves, it really will just be me, the *Blackblood*, and the road. And I realize now that isn't a family at all.

My fingers grasp the doorknob behind me, and I wonder when she'll drop her act. When she'll lunge across the desk toward me with her knife or with Averard's pistol. But she stays put, and I'm thankful for it.

"I'm sorry, Val," I say, and the words stick in my throat. "But I don't . . . I don't think this is good for either of us anymore. Pierce doesn't care about me or you or anyone other than himself. I'll keep my enchantment if it means leaving one more weakness in his armor to exploit. I'm not about to let a bunch of innocent people die just to make my life more comfortable."

I glance up at her one last time and take a deep breath. "Those mages who hurt you? Pierce was threatening them. I'm not saying what they did was excusable, but he would've killed them and their families if they hadn't obeyed." I pull the door open, and a waft of cool air sweeps into the room. "Pierce doesn't care a single bit about protecting anyone from magic."

I duck out the door before she can respond, before she can reel me back like I may secretly want her to. Instead, I rush away, letting Perishing's dark halls swallow me like a predator's monstrous maw.

24

ARMINA

Perishing's ceilings vault overhead. As someone who's used to spending her days in the close quarters of a truck's cab, I may as well be lost in an abyss. It doesn't help that my thoughts're still scrambled, but I try to put what happened with Valaina aside. Distracted worrying won't help me escape, not with Huntsmen milling around the place like fleas on a mangy stray.

The first time I spot the looming shadows of Huntsmen, I head in the opposite direction and around a corner as swiftly as possible. I doubt I could retrace my steps from Pierce's office if I tried, so instead, I seek out a different route, changing direction any time I hear the slightest noise. I walk down a long hall lined on either side by empty rooms, then through another, identical hall, except these rooms are fully furnished. The furniture's coated in dust and grime, molding apart as if no one's so much as breathed on it in years and years.

I climb down a staircase and tuck into a corridor, keeping to the walls and shadows. Pierce and I only climbed one set of stairs, so I must be on the first floor again. If I somehow find the entrance, I'll sneak out and collect the truck, hotwire it if necessary to get out of here. I can drive that truck better than any Huntsman in any vehicle. I'll outrun them, report back to Georgian and Canto. We'll figure something out together.

A crash reverberates through the hall, making a set of wooden doors on my left jolt. My shoulders hunch, and I instinctively freeze. Echoes of the crash recede, replaced by voices in heated conversation.

"I came alone," says a muffled, irritated, *familiar* voice.

Renn? How did—

"You can't honestly believe I'm working with mages and smug—"

Another loud crash.

"Can you please stop destroying my library?" Renn snarls.

"*Your* library?" says another familiar voice. I picture yellow teeth bared in a nasty sneer. Baker. "Last I checked, you don't own Perishing. Not even your father did, regardless of what he may have thought."

"Don't talk about my father again unless you want me to break your other leg."

"So touchy. Most Huntsmen worth anything would've denounced a parent like him, but I can see that you're keen to follow in his footsteps. Partnering up with a mage to kill a sentry and breaking into Perishing . . . I'll ask again: where is your mage?"

There's a different sort of crash then, smaller, and curiosity gets the best of me enough that I push the door open and peek into the room.

It may've been a library at one point, but books and papers are scattered everywhere like a dust storm blew through. A young Huntsman peers around the shelves he must've knocked over, his hands already finding purchase on the next. The opposite side of the room's blocked from my view by the door, but I hear bumping and scratching and snarling.

This's none of my business, Huntsmen bickering. Better for me if the three of them kill one another. But as I go to close the door, I hear a cry of alarm.

The young Huntsman drags Canto out of the shadow of the next shelf. Canto's covered in dust and scratches, black blood oozing from a slice in their forehead. They have a thick book clutched to their chest and a mageblade in their opposite hand.

"Let them go," Renn snarls out of sight, followed by more scuffling.

The young Huntsman ignores him and hauls Canto off the ground.

I shove the door the rest of the way open and jump into the room. My hand shoots for my revolver, but too late, I remember it was stolen back at the lot in Crotalus City.

Ah, shit.

"The captain," comes Baker's snide voice. He struggles with Renn in an alcove surrounded by overturned furniture, a toppled desk the only thing standing between them. They're both sporting bloody noses and wild eyes. "I owe you a broken leg."

I throw up my hands and back away—toward Canto. "Trust me, you don't. The Huntsman you're fighting already got that particular revenge, but my legs heal quicker than most."

Baker wipes the blood on his face in a great red smear. "Let's do something more permanent, then." He lunges toward me.

To my great surprise, Renn launches forward and tackles him to the ground.

A howl of pain erupts behind me, and I whip around to see Canto trying to stab their captor with the mageblade. The angle's awkward 'cause of how they're being held, but they get a few good slices in before the Huntsman throws them across the room. They slam into one of the shelves, and books rain down.

The Huntsman checks the shallow cuts on his arms, then advances toward Canto again.

With several hurried strides, I leap onto the Huntsman's back. He reaches to rip me off but only gets a handful of Averard's coat. I tighten my arms around his throat and try to force him away from where Canto is struggling to their feet. When the Huntsman fails to throw me, he draws his own mageblade, but his angle's worse than Canto's was. The blade batters uselessly against my metal leg.

Something whizzes past my head, and I smell burning leather as it singes Averard's coat. A second bolt strikes the Huntsman on the side of his face, and his flesh sears and crisps as he screams.

"Armina." Canto's voice is deadly calm. "Let go of him and back off."

Canto stands among the rubble of books, the tome they were clutching to their chest now open in their hands. Their long fingers splay across the page, and as they start reading, another bolt of white light streaks from the vaulted ceiling and hits the Huntsman square in the chest. He stumbles, and I leap away before his falling body crushes me. He strikes the ground as his clothing singes and pops with embers.

"What're you doing?" I shout at Canto as I scramble toward their spot by the shelf.

"Perishing's library is proving more interesting than I could have anticipated," Canto says. They flip to the next page, revealing a diagram of the sky, constellations carefully labeled in smooth white ink over a field of black. Their fingers follow the trailing lines of the Crooked Viper, trickster god and magic thief.

Great, undulating coils slither and plop from the pages of Canto's book.

It's not nearly as big as it appears in the sky, but as the constellation unravels onto the tile, the Huntsman stops patting his singed chest and starts to back away. The Viper's body glitters with stardust, and its muscles bunch as it slides across the floor toward the Huntsman. He strikes down at it with his blade, but the Viper's skin breaks in a burst of light, spewing a jet of white flame that spreads up the mageblade and makes the Huntsman drop it with a horrified shout. Then the snake turns on him.

I don't want to watch, but it's hard to look away from someone both burning and being devoured at the same time.

When the Huntsman has been reduced to ashes, the Viper curls in on itself and sinks into the ground, leaving behind a coiled burn somehow even darker than the tile itself.

The library falls awful silent in the wake.

Renn, who'd been shoving Baker against one of the filing cabinets, lets his arms fall slack. His eyes move from the burn on the ground to Canto, who leans against the shelves and flicks through the pages of the book. Baker pushes past Renn, but Renn seems too stunned to stop him.

"What've you done?" Baker limps up the step to the library at large.

"I borrowed a book from the Huntsmen's library." Canto's eyes snap up. "Would you like to hear another story?"

Baker's hands clench and unclench at his sides as he watches Canto out of watery eyes.

My own eyes return to the coiled burn, where I watched a man go up in smoke and starlight. It'd been nearly soundless other than the screaming. I can't imagine the kind of pain that—

Something cold touches my neck.

"Since someone stole my mageblade, I'm reduced to this." The edge of the Huntsman's knife presses closer to my throat.

Renn comes to life again. He jumps up the step toward us, but Baker pulls me tighter against his chest.

"Take another step," Baker snarls, "and the blade'll bite. As for you, mage"—Canto's hands curl into the leather cover of the constellation book—"if you even try to summon something, she'll be dead before you read the first words."

It's a weird feeling, knowing I have to trust Canto's patience and Renn's discretion. Canto's eyes narrow. Renn's breathing grows heavier. I've got about half a minute before one of them breaks and my blood's on the floor.

"That's it." Baker's knife burns, it's so cold. "I think we've all played enough games for a lifetime. Mason, you and I are going to escort your mage down to the bloodletting room. It's where they were headed anyway before they escaped." His grin widens against my cheek. "And when that's done, I'm sure Pierce'll want a word with both you and the little captain."

What would Averard do? Maybe he'd talk Baker down in the hopes of reaching some kind of compromise. He'd spin a yarn, make a friend. Baker would be charmed, let us leave whole and healthy. Everyone would go home smiling.

But Brother's Blood, I'm tired of trying to reason with people. I'm sick of compromise. I'd rather die now than spend my life waiting for something to happen or relying on the charity of people who don't have any to give and who don't deserve my own.

I slam my head back into Baker's skull at the same time I stomp on his foot, catching his broken leg with my heel. The knife jerks away from my throat, but as I duck, the blade plunges down again and slices across part of my face and upper arm.

Hot, wet blood pours down my cheek. But a worse pain shoots up my hip like lightning, spiraling along my veins and chest toward my heart. My pulse pounds in my leg like a phantom limb, and my vision whites out. I hear a thud from somewhere far away as I clutch my thigh and fall to the tile.

My vision returns in patches of light as the pain subsides. Someone's hand presses against my arm, and they grip harder when a whine of agony curls from my throat. After a few moments, Canto's face swims into view.

"Are you okay?" Their eyes flick to something behind me before returning to my face. They run a hand over the cut on my cheek, and I wince to see red blood stain their fingertips.

"I dunno." Something about the pain is hysterical, and I start giggling. "Are *you*?"

Canto scoffs and helps me sit up.

I inspect my injuries with exhausted hands—for the most part, they're shallow; neither my cheek nor my arm'll require stitching, although Averard's coat might. As the last of my blurred vision sharpens again, I see Renn crouched over Baker, who's splayed across the ground.

"How'd you subdue him?" I ask. I roll to my knees, and another sharp pain lances through my leg.

Renn turns away from Baker. His eyes're wide, and he looks afraid.

Canto draws me closer against their chest, and I don't protest. If they weren't holding me upright, I'd probably collapse again anyway.

"What are you thinking, Renn?" Canto asks. "Something stupid."

Renn sighs and stands, and the frightened expression dissipates. "Don't answer your own questions."

"It was an easy enough answer."

"I was thinking," Renn continues, "that now we know what her enchantment does."

A wave of dizziness rolls over me, and my fingers dig into Canto's coat. "Why do you know about my enchantment?"

"Canto told me. Explains why I thought you were a mage." He frowns, crosses his arms. "The enchantment's powerful, and it's in your blood."

"And you think you know what it does?"

Renn gestures to Baker. "Take a look."

I push out of Canto's arms to my feet, wobbling as I limp across to Baker. Renn steps away when I approach and joins Canto on the floor. I'd spend a second wondering why Canto's letting him get so close, but something about Baker holds my attention.

Or, rather, something about Baker's corpse. Because he's dead—that much is certain. When I stoop to investigate, I find he's not just dead, but stiff and cold, as if he's been gone for days. It's like every little bit of life's been vacuumed out of him at once, only there's no sign of injury. His eyeballs bulge, and his blue veins stand out stark on his forehead.

"The enchantment did this?" My hands fall to his chest. It's like touching stone.

"I can't think of any other explanation," Renn says. "You pushed him away, and he swung at you, and the next thing I know, you're both on the ground."

My mind returns to the dirt lot, to the Huntsman who punched me, to the Huntswoman's startled face as she inspected the body.

"I don't understand." I rejoin Canto and Renn, but Renn shies away like I'm venomous. "If the enchantment kills Huntsmen, why aren't you dead? Or Pierce?"

"Maybe they have to attack you," Renn suggests.

"You *did* attack me." The events of the last few minutes settle into the pit of my stomach. I'm glad Baker's dead, but what I'm not so happy about is that I didn't have a choice. What if the trigger's something impossible to control, or—

"They have to make you bleed." Canto's voice rings across my panicked thoughts. They gaze at Baker's body, absentmindedly thumbing the cut on their forehead.

"How do you figure that?" I ask.

Canto shrugs, but their expression's gone hard. "The instant his knife cut you, he fell. Whoever cast the enchantment must have had an incredible sense of humor, let alone an insane magical prowess. A Huntsman dying the moment they draw blood? It's a mage's dream."

My hands fidget in my lap. "I know who cast it now, but . . ." I glance at Renn. "Why're the pair of you together?"

"We were looking for you," Renn says. "Although it seems you've rescued yourself. Helpful, to be honest."

"*You* were looking for me?"

"Partially. You, Canto's mother, and Pierce."

I rub my upper thigh, trying to massage out the pins and needles. "That doesn't explain why you're here *together*. I'm guessing there's no love lost for the Huntsmen we just killed, but last time we spoke, you seemed plenty pleased with the Order itself. And the pair of you were trading barbs and punches on the *Blackblood*. Now you're . . ."

I trail off because I'm not sure how to describe them. They sit side by side, not quite touching but close enough they could. Canto looks agitated, I guess, but from the way they're glaring at Baker's corpse, I don't think it has anything to do with Renn.

"Renn and I have an agreement," Canto says.

"And whatever my feelings for the Order used to be," Renn continues, "I don't much care for Pierce. He killed my father."

"Ah," I say. "I guess we have that in common."

It's uncomfortable to lay out the truth, to explain all the weird things that've happened over the last two days. I tell Canto and Renn about Pierce, about Averard's theft, about Valaina. I explain about my unknown mother, about the enchantment she placed on me and on Pierce, about how Pierce wants to experiment on me to destroy it.

"I dunno why my mom did it." I tap on my leg. "But I guess that's why I'm in this mess. Why we all are."

"She was protecting you," Canto says.

"Was she?" Renn asks. "Or was she making herself a weapon?"

Canto falls silent, but their mouth twitches like they have something they want to say and can't bring themself to say it.

Another twinge of pain from my leg shoots across my skin, and I get the most awful feeling that the enchantment's crawled further up. I rise and am surprised when both Canto and Renn reach out to steady me. I hold up a hand to stop them. My knee quakes, but I don't topple over.

"So, what now?" I ask.

"We still need to collect Canto's mother," Renn says. "It's important we get her to safety before Pierce decides to grab her."

Canto gazes up at Renn with wide, horrified eyes. "Why would he do that?"

"Armina mentioned Pierce brought a powerful mage to Perishing in the hopes of dissecting her enchantment. If he was going to abuse his power to move mages around, he'd try to keep the paper trail as small as possible." Renn taps Canto on the shoulder and gestures toward the filing cabinets. "Which leads us to your mother's devastatingly sparse file."

"You think he brought my mother here to enchant Armina?"

"I'd say it's the only possible explanation. So, we need to get to her before Pierce does. If she's moved from isolation, he could take her anywhere in Perishing, and Perishing's too big to explore on no information."

"Then let's go." Canto hefts their tome on constellations back against their chest and retrieves the mageblade. They hold it out to Renn.

He looks down at the sword. "But I thought—"

"Look, we both know it's near useless to me. If you're really serious about rescuing my mother, then you should wield it. One last time."

Renn takes the grip in his hand. He gazes down at it reverently. "One last time."

Canto nods and moves toward the door. "Now, lead the way, Huntsman."

Renn smiles as if he's been called a pet name instead of his title and trails after Canto.

The pain must still be getting to me—it's the only explanation for the upside-down world I've stumbled into.

But there's something familiar about their bickering and banter. Something warm. It makes me miss Valaina that much more, and Averard, and the life we used to have. I want that camaraderie back. Watching Canto and Renn, I can almost picture the *Blackblood* with a crew of three again.

Makes me think that maybe getting my old life back isn't so outside the realm of possibility.

25

ARMINA

Renn pushes the library door open, and the three of us lean out to inspect the empty halls. Huntsmen footsteps echo, but they sound distant enough that Renn beckons us out of the room with a grim, determined expression. We creep down the hall in a pack so tight we're almost tripping over one another, but as claustrophobic as it may seem, I can't deny it's a comfort to have allies so close.

"The fastest way to the isolation chamber where Canto's mother is being kept is past the entrance and down one of the side stairs by the courtyard," Renn whispers. Our eyes watch for roaming Huntsmen, but we encounter none as we pass the grand staircase near the entrance. My footsteps sound far too loud on the tile floor: each step I take echoes like a gunshot. "From there it's only a short walk, but while there aren't guards on the room itself, there are undoubtedly Huntsmen we'll need to avoid if we don't want another fight."

A shout comes through the entrance's double doors right as we pass them, then another. Renn throws out an arm to stop Canto and me. We listen as the shouts grow louder, more surprised, and then—

Crash. The splintering of wood and stone shrieks from behind the closed doors, followed by the *pop* of gunfire. Then, like the voice of an old friend, I hear the sound of an engine growling. Brakes squeal, and wheels thump to a rhythm I know as well as my own breathing.

Before I can stop myself, before Renn can stop me, I throw myself toward those double doors.

My shoulder hits the heavy wood, and the doors spring open, revealing watery afternoon sunlight. The Community looks less grim today than it did the night before, but only enough that its buildings seem like actual houses rather than graves. At the closest homes, several mages open their doors to peer out. They make confused eye contact with neighbors before turning their attention to the cause of the commotion.

There, twenty feet away from Perishing's entrance, sits the *Blackblood*. Its engine rumbles and coughs. The ground behind and around its beautiful trailer is littered with a half-dozen Huntsmen corpses. Some have been dragged beneath its wheels, looking closer to paint smears than people, and the few who escaped that particular fate have the round burn of a bullet hole through their heads.

Val's always been a better shot than me. That's why she kept Averard's pistol.

The driver's side door opens with its familiar *creak* as Valaina kicks it with her boot. She jumps down into the dirt and strides around the side of the truck. The hatch gives a thunderous rattle as she throws it open and climbs through, disappearing inside the trailer.

"What is she doing?" Canto hisses, pushing their way past Renn to stand beside me in the sunlight.

Renn's hands fall on our shoulders and tug us gently but firmly backward. "It doesn't matter. We don't have time to play around here; whatever she's doing won't go unnoticed by the Huntsmen for long, and if we want any hope of rescuing Canto's mother and killing Pierce, we need to get going."

It feels like my boots are stuck to the ground. Did Valaina change her mind, then, about becoming a Huntsman? Maybe we could . . .

No. We can't. Not after everything.

Valaina hops down from the truck a moment later, her boots splashing in what's left of a Huntsman sticking out from under the back wheel. In her arms she cradles blackened books and knitting needles, chefs' knives and gardening tools. She takes a few steps away from the *Blackblood* and dumps the artifacts into a pile at her feet. The surrounding mages' eyes follow the objects, then look up to Valaina in clear disbelief.

Valaina tosses her hair, the wind picking up her curls. She tucks one hand against the pistol at her hip. A smirk rises onto her face, her eyebrows furrowed and eyes narrowed, but I see through the confidence. She's never been surrounded by this many mages. If her pride would let her get away with trembling, she would.

"I'm only gonna say this once, and that'll be all I owe any of you." Her voice echoes in the silent yard, louder than the *Blackblood's* engine and equally as powerful. Like the sting of a slap, her gaze strikes me for a split second before turning away. "I don't like mages. Despite what someone might say, you've got the power to hurt whoever and however all up inside you. It's not like a gun that can be disarmed, and no number of excuses will change my mind." She scowls and taps one of the gardening tools with her boot. "But I guess if I've gotta be fair, there're worse monsters out there."

She glances up again, eyes steely. "What are you all waiting for? You've got five minutes before I drive this truck out of here forever. I have artifacts for sale, and I'm willing to give 'em out on loan."

The yard remains silent for a long moment, during which Renn glances over his shoulder and tries again to pull us back into the building. My feet're rooted to Perishing's front step, and I'm not sure a sandstorm could move me at this point. The *Blackblood* sits there, grumbling worse than Valaina. My truck.

My home. I've gotta get in there and fight Val before she takes this one last thing from me. Drive away to where it'll be safe.

Seeing her standing there dredges up a memory of the first night Val came to us. She was twelve and covered in scars and bruises, and I was ten and infatuated with her. I'd never met another kid my age, at least not long enough to form any sort of meaningful connection, and I thought she was the most beautiful person in the world. She hadn't spoken yet, just clutched the blanket Averard had given her and stared at the artifacts surrounding us with fear and discomfort. Between us sat a bowl of candied fruit which she couldn't even look at. I tried to coax her name out, but between shivers and scowls, the only words she managed were—

"Where are we?"

It was enough of a victory to make me smile like I'd won a thousand games of cards against Averard. "We're home. This is your new home."

Our truck. Our home.

A mage steps out of the crowd. Her vibrant red hair rests in a single braid down her back. She approaches Valaina with a blank face and even gait, reaches into the pile of artifacts at her feet, and withdraws a pair of knitting needles. She turns toward the steadily growing group and gestures at a pair of identical twin mages: two tall, burly men with dark skin and hazel eyes.

"Start the signal," she says in a voice rusty with disuse.

The twins show no signs of acknowledgement other than turning and disappearing between the shadows of the buildings. At this command, however, the other gathered mages descend upon the *Blackblood*, whispering to one another as they sort through the artifacts of a long-dead business.

Over the din, Valaina's eyes meet mine. She doesn't speak, but I hear her. I always do. Her expression says she's given me everything she will to make things right. Everything owed an ex-lover and an ex-friend. And for that sacrifice, she'll take the *Blackblood*. She'll take home.

"Let's go," I say, grabbing onto Renn and Canto. Valaina turns and pulls herself back into the driver's seat. The mages haul armful after armful of artifacts out of the trailer.

"Are you okay?" Canto asks as we return to the relative silence of Perishing. Through the now-closed doors, I hear nothing of the amassing mage army outside. If I didn't already know about the impending mutiny, I'd assume things were like they always were and always would be.

But things are changing around here. Around everywhere.

"I'm fine," I insist. "Now, let's get to your mom before the chaos starts."

26

CANTO

We don't get a dozen steps down the hall before the PA system above us screeches to life. We tuck ourselves into a corner shadow to listen to the crackly announcement.

"Attention," says an irritated male voice. "All available Huntsmen to the Community. I repeat: all available Huntsmen to the Community. A volatile pro-mage group has broken into Perishing for unknown ends. Consider these insurgents armed and dangerous and kill any who interfere with attempts to reinstate control, our subjects included should they resist." His voice crackles out.

Before the announcement, we'd heard shuffling Huntsmen and the occasional low tone of voices. The moment the announcement ends, the sound of dozens of bodies running through the empty halls reaches us. They whoop and cheer as if they're about to attend a party or a game, not as if they're about to do battle with the very people they've kept prisoner for so long.

It makes the magic in my blood sing. I want to see all those smiling Huntsmen faces before I rip them apart. Behind us, the mages Valaina armed respond with howls of their own, full of fury and determination. The joy of vengeance prickles up my spine, and there's nothing I'd love more than to join them, to help them spill all the blood they're owed. My limbs quake with it; my fingers clench around my book, and my free hand finds my mother's pendant in my pocket and squeezes.

Renn tugs me in the opposite direction of the entrance as the first Huntsmen round the far corner, mageblades and pistols wrapped in their hands. Renn backs down the still-empty hall, his own mageblade out. He's right to be terrified. Consequences have finally come to Perishing.

A scream erupts from the doorway as the Huntsmen reach it. The door bursts off its hinges, flying across the foyer and slamming so hard into the grand staircase that the wood embeds itself in the stone. The Huntsmen at the front of the group, shocked by the ferocity of the explosion, fall in a wave of blood and tile shrapnel as the floor beneath them explodes. A pack of mages leaps inside, dust settling around their shoulders as they face the Huntsmen who weren't obliterated by the initial blast.

I teeter on the edge of joining the massacre, ready to drag the Huntsmen down. I take a step toward the mayhem. Another.

"Canto," Renn says.

That one word slots into my senses, and the whole thing falls apart.

The three of us turn and flee. One day, I may come to regret it, but today, Armina, Renn, and my mother need me more.

We move quickly, not quite sprinting but fast enough that my already sore legs burn anew. Every time we reach an intersection in the corridor, Renn tucks himself against the wall and looks both ways before allowing us to continue.

"What's the plan?" Armina asks, peering around a corner before we sprint away at high speeds.

"Well," Renn says, "there are ten thousand mages in the Community and about four hundred Huntsmen. Even if we're generous and assume fewer than half the mages are capable of fighting, the Huntsmen here can only contain them so quickly, if at all. There's going to be a lot of death, and we can't afford to get caught up in it."

"Then let's take advantage of it," Armina says as Renn makes a sharp left and leads us down a side hall. "If the Huntsmen're distracted at the front, we'll find Canto's mother and get out."

We pull to a stop at the end of a hall as a trio of Huntsmen round the opposite corner. We sink into the shadows, but their focus is clearly on reaching the Community as swiftly as possible. When they pass, Renn speaks, his voice barely above a whisper. "No. If we want to give the mages a chance to take Perishing, we need to kill Pierce. If they can hold back the Huntsmen long enough for us to track him down, taking him out will destabilize the other Huntsmen, make them scatter. With the fortress under siege, he wouldn't have more than a rudimentary guard on him, so this will be our best bet."

His words burn in my mind, and my steps falter. "You want to help them?" I ask. "The mages?"

Renn frowns, his concentration less on my question than on the path ahead. "I told you we would, didn't I? Now, let's focus on your mother first."

He had said *okay*, but I didn't think . . . I couldn't imagine . . . I . . .

A Huntsman who keeps his word isn't a Huntsman at all; I'm certain of it. As the screaming and the fighting and the pulse of magic from behind us grows stronger, I can't help the smile that drifts onto my face.

We start down a new corridor, Renn's head swiveling even as he continues to speak. "If Pierce hasn't moved her, then Canto's mother will be at the lowest level." We jog toward a dark stairwell that leads downward. "Since the riot's at the entrance, all Huntsmen that would normally be—"

The door at the bottom of the stairs bursts open. A pair of Huntsmen charge upward, taking the steps two at a time. Renn pushes Armina and me against the far wall as the Huntsmen crest the top of the stairs. They barrel past us at first, but then the woman in the pair grabs her companion's elbow and yanks him to a halt. His eyes, which were trained on the end of the hall, fall on us.

His lips curl.

"Mason." He unsheathes his sword. "Are you the one behind this? Like father, like son."

"I had nothing to do with this." Renn raises his sword, still blocking Armina and me with his body. "But you know what? I'm starting to wish I had."

The Huntsman lunges, and his blade clashes against Renn's. Renn pushes him away, leaving Armina and me with the Huntswoman. She glances between us and must decide I'm the bigger threat. She stalks toward me, and I fumble with my constellation book as I back away.

She speaks, so softly that I barely hear her over the swordfight and the distant thunder of battle. "I don't know what will happen to Perishing now," she whispers, "but at least I'll get to kill one of you."

Before I can move, her sword arcs down and slices clean through the left cover of my book.

It also slices through the tips of two of my fingers.

I bite back the pain as blood splatters down my boots and across the remaining pages. My vision blurs, but I try to focus beyond my own body and into the present, where the Huntswoman grins. She lifts the blade parallel to her lips. She licks my blood off it.

Then she eats a mouthful of sword as Armina kicks her legs out.

The Huntswoman falls, spitting blood. Her blade clatters to the floor, and Armina punts it away. It spins in a circle like the arrow on a compass until it embeds itself harmlessly in the wall.

When the Huntswoman staggers upright, a thrill runs through me. Her jaw hangs open, unable to close properly after the sword sliced her mouth at the corners, and her taunts have died, considering she's lost a good chunk of her tongue. She pounces for Armina and pins her against the wall with an arm pressed to her throat. Armina's fingers latch onto the woman's injured mouth, and together they struggle, trying to cause one another as much pain as possible.

Renn, meanwhile, has hit a stalemate with his Huntsman. Their blades lock them in place, muscles straining. I flick through my book—leaving blood on the ancient pages—and run my hand across the magic. The pulse of it burns my injuries, but I ignore that as I concentrate on summoning a new constellation.

The beast's head and hooves and trunk explode from the page in a graceful arc. It lands silently, tossing its exposed skull as it rears onto its hind legs. The stars that comprise the cosmos of its body gleam and flash as it lowers its head and charges.

Its skull connects with the torso of the Huntsman Renn is fighting, and it throws him into the air. White flame licks up the man's skin, but the crack of his neck as he hits the tile floor is what ultimately kills him. His body smolders where it lies.

The Huntswoman stares at the scene, mouth agape for reasons other than her injuries. Renn wipes his chin on the back of his hand before sauntering over, ripping the woman off Armina, and driving his sword through her chest.

The constellation canters back toward me. Its magic isn't fully spent, but I can't have it following us like a beacon.

I point it toward the curve of the hall. "Go help someone else. One of the mages."

It tosses its gleaming mane and then gallops away, around the corner and out of sight.

Renn stares after its comet tail. "That's the, uh . . . the Wanderer, right?" he asks.

"The Wanderer's horse," Armina says. "She's the goddess of death."

"Makes sense." Renn shifts his sword. It drips blood onto the floor, and I wonder how many mageblades have drunk that much red blood.

The door at the base of the steps erupts open again, spilling forward another handful of Huntsmen. I grip my book and flip through the pages. I can't summon the horse back while it's still running around somewhere. Should I call the snake again?

I'm about to run my fingers along the trail of a constellation shaped like a bull when footsteps sound behind us.

"More over here!" calls a woman's voice. Down the hallway, the Skeletal Mare bursts back into sight, leading a whole contingent of mages. At the front sprints the redheaded woman with her knitting needles. The moment she's upon us, she stabs them toward Renn's head. He yelps and ducks, and the Skeletal Mare bursts past him down the stairwell, through the pack of Huntsmen. When it crashes into the door at the base, it explodes into starlight.

One or two Huntsmen escape the molten flame, but when they crest the stairs, the mages launch their attack.

The redheaded woman glances up at me as she drives her needles through a Huntsman's eyes. "Well? Are you going to help, or are you going to stand there and gawk?"

"Canto!" Armina shouts. She and Renn have maneuvered their way down the stairs behind me. They're pressed against the walls to avoid the still-smoldering Huntsmen.

I toss the woman an apologetic grimace, then leap down the stairs to follow. We rush through the door and into another hallway.

The redheaded woman doesn't call after me, but I have to wonder what she's thinking. I ran off with a Huntsman, left her and her group to clean up the mess. Am I a coward in her eyes? A traitor? After everything that's happened, maybe I deserve both those titles.

"You okay?" Armina picks up my hand and examines the wounds. The top joint on my left ring finger is gone. Part of the pinky, too.

"I've been better." The pain is distant, floating somewhere in the depths of my mind rather than on the surface. I wish once more I could enchant the wounds closed, but my thoughts are so scattered that I'd undoubtedly do more harm than good. As we run, I rip out some of my book's paper and enchant it to be sturdier, then wrap it around my bleeding fingers as a makeshift bandage.

Renn is on even higher alert now as we pass through the underground. He's quick to pull Armina and me out of the way whenever Huntsmen run past. More than once, we encounter mages and Huntsmen tearing into one another, puddles of black and red blood mingling and slick on the tile. They pay us no mind, too engulfed in their war with one another to notice us fleeing in the opposite direction.

"How did they get down here before us?" Armina asks as we skirt around another skirmish.

"Perishing is . . . weird," Renn replies. "There are numerous entrances to the subterranean levels. Probably more of them than even I know about."

Eventually, he tugs us down a final set of stairs. We crowd together in the dark, claustrophobic stairwell. I feel their hearts beating, erratic rhythms not quite in time with my own.

"She'll be in here," Renn whispers. A bead of sweat rolls down his chin, and while his hand rests on the doorknob, his eyes stay pinned to the top of the stairwell. "Stay alert, all right? There shouldn't be a guard in here, but with all the chaos happening above, anything's possible."

"I've been meaning to ask," I say. "Why aren't there any guards?"

"You'll see." Renn twists the doorknob and pushes it open. We all stumble apart into the new space.

It's like stepping into the mouth of one of my constellations—scalding, screaming starlight. A blinding pain strikes my eyes, and I try to squint through the tears streaming down my face to make out our surroundings.

Every other room I've seen in Perishing so far—every floor, every wall, every ceiling, every fixture—has been the tarnished black of magic. This room is a blazing, painful white. From inch to scorching, identical inch, it's difficult to make out where the floor ends and the walls begin.

But sitting at its center is a cube.

It's taller than Renn and a matte black so deep that it looks like someone cut a hole in the stark-white walls. It does not move or make any noise.

It fills me with dread.

"It'll be locked." Renn strides toward the box. He settles his hand on one of its sides, and somehow, it doesn't absorb him like I feel it should. "Canto, think your magic lockpick skills could help us here?"

Bile burns up my throat, and I take a step toward the salvation of the door we came through. This object, this *abomination* . . . it's the same kind of pure magic as a mageblade, but entirely more precious. Entirely more cruel. It makes sense as a prison: the amount of blood a mage would require to enchant it open would exceed that contained in a single body.

Exceed it by *gallons*.

"Your mother is in there." Renn's hand drops, and he returns to my side. "We're so close. You just need to open the door."

Open the door. Mother is drowning in corpses, and I just need to open the door.

Armina's hand falls on my back. "I dunno what that thing is, but I'm not gonna let it hurt you, okay?"

Renn grasps my shoulder. "We're both right here. You're going to be fine."

I swallow the fear and approach the box. Distantly, I feel their hands still on me. Guidance. Support. Something I didn't think I would ever have again after the Huntsmen ripped my mother from me.

Then the cube looms above, and my vision fills with void.

I lift a quaking, bleeding hand and press it against the wall. When the pad of my palm touches the impossible surface, there comes a gentle *click*. Renn leans over me and pushes it open. Light floods into the dense darkness.

My mother sits at its center, scribbling in a notebook with an open flame in her opposite hand. She's smaller than I remember, her hair shorter. She squints up at us, shielding her brown eyes from the painful whiteness of the room.

"Canto?" Her voice is choppy and strained. Her gaze slides over Renn and lands on Armina. "Averard?"

Then she shakes her head and goes back to scribbling on her notepad. "Too small."

"Mother." I step toward the cube, fear of it forgotten. My mother is alive. Heart still beating, still able to speak, not tortured to endless oblivion. How could anything be frightening when we're together?

She holds up the hand with the pen in it. "One moment, sweetness. Mother had an idea."

I crouch to watch the swiftness of her cramped writing, the way ink stains her fingers and sinks into all the lines and crevices, spreading like water. "What sort of idea?"

"A fantastic one. As unpleasant as this whole business has been, the solitude has brought its own sort of productivity. Why, I've come up with a dozen new ideas, and it's only been a few days."

I wrap my arms around my legs, tilt my head against my knees. It's as if my magic has been blocked all this time, and now the warmth of it has finally returned to my limbs. "It's been several weeks."

"Has it? My, time does fly." She dots the end of her sentence with a particularly hard flourish.

She looks so normal. She's acting so normal, just like she would at home at the end of a long day. We'd sit together inside our house's dim twilight, and she'd instruct me on the principles of magic for hours. Now, as she tucks her pen and a strand of hair behind her ear, I notice her fingers trembling.

The anger scorches through my chest again.

Renn clears his throat. "Ma'am, why don't you step outside? I can't imagine you're comfortable in there."

A hesitant frown creeps onto my mother's face. Her hands twitch where they've come to settle in her lap, palms clenched together. "Sorry, Huntsman, but I've grown tired of following orders."

"It wasn't an order, Mother," I say. "He was just making a suggestion."

"Oh. Well, yes, I think I'd rather prefer to be out of here." She stands and crosses the threshold of the box, steps into the room. She's only an inch shorter than me, but she's become bitterly thin since I last saw her. She used to be plump and soft, a comfort to hug, but now her cheeks are sharp, and her clothes hang around her middle. She takes a few steps into the room and folds herself back onto the floor. "I must admit, that box was dreadful. But I suppose that's by design."

She flips through a few pages in her notepad and holds it up. She's drawn the box with ruler-perfect precision, complete blackness captured as photographically as her pen could reproduce. "I dabbled in pure magic in my youth, but this is on an entirely different scale. Do you know how much blood they would have needed to make that room? If we assume that each wall is seven inches thick by eight feet long by eight feet tall times six walls, we get a total volume of 387,072 cubic inches. That's approximately 6,343 liters, or 1,268 bodies."

I slide to the ground to sit beside her, and she taps me on the knee with her book. "Thank you for coming to fetch me; I . . ." Her jaw tightens, and her eyes flick to the box once more. "I don't think I could have endured it much longer. Pierce had some wild scheme he wanted me to take part in, and when I refused, he put me in there. A few more days and I might have acquiesced."

"I'm . . . I'm so sorry," Armina says. She lowers herself to the ground beside us. "Pierce brought you here to experiment on me. My leg—"

Mother sits up on her knees and reaches out to Armina. She claps her hands on either side of Armina's jaw and draws her startled face closer. She hums as she inspects Armina's face in the same way she used to inspect mine every morning before I left the house. "You're Armina, aren't you? Kestrel's daughter?"

"I . . . who?"

Mother releases Armina's face. "Couldn't be anyone else's daughter; you look too much alike. Let me see your leg."

Armina rolls up her pant leg with stiff fingers. Mother taps her nail against the metal. "Oh, this is nice work. I have a few ideas for improvements, if you'd like. Strengthening the material, making it lighter. Or!" She flips to a new page in her notebook and tears the pen from behind her ear, starts scribbling. "Would you like it to shoot bullets?"

A strange noise winds out of Armina's throat, and she places a hand on my mother's knee. "The prosthesis isn't the issue, ma'am; it's—"

"Calliope, if you please. You too, Huntsman, since my baby seems fond of you."

"*Mother*," I snap, but Renn guffaws and takes a seat beside us.

"What? I've been alone long enough, and I'm glad to meet your friends. I only wish it were under better circumstances." She eyes Renn up. "You're the old Huntsmaster's son. What was his name . . . Mason? Reginald Mason?"

Renn's laughter dies. He pins his eyes to the floor, even as I stare at him. "Richard."

"Right, right. You look just like him, minus the beard. I do not recommend the beard."

"Your father was the previous Huntsmaster? *That's* who you want to avenge?" I demand, and Renn winces and leans further away from me. My hands tighten into fists. I could strangle him. "You didn't think that was pertinent information?"

"Leave him be, Canto," my mother says. "It's very easy to overlook one's own parent's sins. It's difficult to stop loving people who are good to you just because they've hurt someone else."

"Calliope," Armina interrupts, "why did you . . . how did you know my mother?"

Mother waves a dismissive hand, her pen drawing a curve through the air. "I used to be part of her group before we were captured trying to retake Perishing." She smiles, and her eyes flick to the ceiling in reminiscence. "The Wanderer's right-hand woman, whether she liked it or not. She wasn't very good with numbers, you see, and I am very good with numbers. Every resistance group needs a numbers person."

Before I can question Mother on why she never told me she was part of some wild rebellion, Armina says, "You said Averard's name earlier." She grips her ratty coat closer. "Did you know him, too?"

My mother blinks, as if Armina has swerved the conversation off a cliff. Her eyes wander down the length of Armina's coat, and she nods knowingly. "Sorry if that caused any confusion. You're wearing the coat I bought him, and with all the commotion and the blinding lights, I'm afraid I thought he came to rescue me."

"The coat *you* bought him?" Armina asks.

Mother closes her eyes. "Oh, yes. I bought the fabric off a Y'ashtrian merchant and used some saved-up coin to get it tailored for him. It was a Rabbit's Day present in exchange for him giving me a place to stay." She laughs and plucks at the ends of the worn leather. "He was so fond of it. Never took it off; said it felt like a hug from me. When Canto was born, he even used it as their bed for a time, as we didn't have a crib on the truck." She turns to Armina and smiles. "You were already old enough for a proper mattress by then, though."

Armina goes quiet. Her fingers curl against her knees.

"Is . . . is Averard my father?" I ask.

My mother taps her pen on her notepad. "Oh, no, no, no. Not at all. I was already pregnant by the time he rescued us and Armina from Perishing. Your father died in our failed rebellion." She frowns at me, her head tilted. "I'm certain I told you he was dead."

She did tell me that, but that man always seemed such a distant thought to her that I imagined him as someone she cared about only in memory, in a dim and fleeting smile of something long gone. But Averard . . . listening to her talk now about Armina's smuggler father, she looks young again. Beaming and laughing.

Mother closes her notebook and slides it inside the front pocket of her dress. She folds her hands on her lap, rearranging her laced fingers over and over. "I suppose Averard must be dead too, if you have the coat and he isn't here with you. I had hoped we'd meet again someday."

I take her hands between mine.

She blinks down at my touch. "Oh, *oh*, Canto, you're hurt; I—"

"It's okay."

It isn't. The pain is fine, but nothing else makes sense. My mother loved him. She loved this man, and he lived an entire life letting her do so behind a wall.

"I can't believe you knew me," Armina says. "Averard never mentioned . . . I don't remember you at *all*."

"Well, you wouldn't," Mother says. "Canto wasn't even a year old yet when the Huntsmen recaptured us, and you were barely two."

"How did they . . ."

"With great difficulty." Mother bares her teeth in her most wicked smile, the one that looks like she could tear a person apart with them. "They questioned me about Averard's whereabouts, but when I gave them nothing, Huntsmaster Mason had us stuffed into a Community as far away from Perishing as possible. I never learned what happened to Kestrel. I wish I could tell you; she'd love to see how you grew up."

"You're not upset?" Armina asks. "That he never came looking for you?"

Mother's smile doesn't dim, but its quality does change, taking on something wistful and sighing and distant. "Averard is not someone you love without understanding how he operates. He told me once that he would do whatever he needed to do to protect you from Pierce. That he would sacrifice everything. I understood what that meant, and I hold no grudges."

I can't take it anymore. The sunshine smile on my mother's face, the way her shoulders relax—it hurts to see her so ready to brush away the happiness that could have been *hers*.

"He didn't sacrifice anything," I snap. "He decided *we* would sacrifice everything instead. When he left us to the Huntsmen, that man stole our chance at freedom."

My mother's face falls as I continue. "If he loved you, why did he leave you? Why did he let us get taken in the first place? He was there when I was born, gave me that precious fucking coat to sleep on, but we weren't good enough to look for? Everything that's happened, every indignity and injustice we've endured, he could have stopped. We suffer because he decided one life saved was enough for him."

Renn slides his fingers across the tile floor, and one of his knuckles taps against my knee.

I glare at him. "What? Is he somehow your father, too?"

Renn's face turns pink. "No, I . . . uh . . . that was my very bad attempt at comforting you, I guess."

I don't need his comfort. Not now, not when everything is needles and teeth directly through my armor. I haven't got the time to appreciate pity, not when I am so full of fire.

"Oh, Canto." My mother reaches out and touches a knuckle on my knee, right beside Renn's. "I promise, no one is trying to steal your suffering away from you."

I don't have an answer to that, but all the blood rushes to my face. The world is hot, explosive, and I cannot look at my mother or else I might scream. I turn to Armina instead, not sure if I want to lash out at her or cry, but I find her watching me with wide eyes, her fingers picking at the hem of her blood-flecked coat. Her shoulders tremble. The fire burning through my chest sputters and dies.

"If it helps," Mother says, leaning away. Renn's fingers remain pressed against my knee. "Averard and I *did* talk. We had contingency plan after contingency plan, and I told him in no uncertain terms that if it were impossible to rescue us without endangering himself or Armina, he wasn't to attempt it. She was enchanted, defenseless. If the Huntsmen found her, they would have killed her, and I couldn't let that happen to Kestrel's little one."

A moment later, the serious expression flits away from my mother's face, and she rubs her hands together. "Speaking of, let me see the enchantment."

"Here?" Armina's voice is faint, and her gaze flicks to Renn.

"We haven't the time to go anywhere else, have we?"

Renn catches Armina's eye. He grimaces but gives her a nod and spins to face the far wall.

Armina removes her pants and leg. My mother picks up the prosthesis right away, examining it from every angle, flexing the joints, and making calculations in the air with her finger. Armina sits on the tile as if all her will has drained out of her body. She stares at her amputation.

The skin is tarnished from scar to hip. Tendrils of the enchantment have started to edge beneath the hem of her shirt.

"Hmm." My mother sets the prosthesis aside. "This does look quite a bit nastier than it did when I saw it last. Averard hypothesized that cutting away the enchanted tissue might alleviate the problem, but I should have known better than to let him go through with it. Kestrel was too clever to be stymied by something so simple. Do you know what it does?"

"Knocks a Huntsman dead," Armina says, "if they make me bleed."

"Well, that's fun."

I interrupt. "What will happen if it keeps spreading?"

Mother tilts her head this way and that like a little bird. "I'm not sure. It depends on how the enchantment was woven, what kind of thoughts went into it. Knowing her baby was unlikely to survive an encounter with the Huntsmen, Kestrel must have wanted to do the maximum amount of damage. Only, since Armina wasn't expected to survive, Kestrel probably didn't prepare for what could happen if the enchantment was given time to grow. If the spell consumes her body, Armina's sole focus will be carrying out the conditions of the enchantment. So, if the parameters state that any Huntsman who damages her body will die, she might be compelled to *find* Huntsmen to kill, at the expense of all else—eating, sleeping, living."

"So, my mom *was* trying to create a weapon." Armina places her head in her hands, rubbing her eyes with the heels of her palms. "Why would she do something like this? Didn't she love me?"

Mother's eyebrows furrow. "Of course she loved you. She loved you so much she wanted to exact revenge on anyone who would dare hurt you."

The enchantment on Armina's skin is so powerful that it's making the air around it blur like a mirage. Heat seeps from it. "Can you enchant over it?" I ask.

"Maybe." Mother places a hand on Armina's leg but withdraws it quickly, shaking her fingers and wincing. "I knew Kestrel's magic better than anyone, and it's possible she left room for me to exploit. But we'd need a lot of blood."

"Is that really the only way?" Armina grabs her prosthesis and reattaches it, turning the socket until it clicks into place.

"Hmmm." Mother pats her hands on her thighs. "You could ask Kestrel. She knows how the enchantment works and would certainly have an easier time weaving over it than I would. She may not need any blood at all, or at least considerably less."

"We don't know where she is, or if she's even alive." Armina stands and pulls on her pants. "I wouldn't know where to start looking."

I turn to Renn, who's remained conspicuously silent throughout this exchange. "Your favorite pastime is to drone on and on about your paperwork," I say. "Do you know where the Wanderer was held?"

Renn's shoulders flinch when I address him. "Sort of," he says. "She was held in the Prickweed Pine Community to the north. But that Community is . . . well, it's been destroyed. Allegedly by my father, though I have my doubts. She'd been held there for almost twenty years with no behavioral problems, so hers wasn't a file I dwelled on long." He pauses, his nose scrunched in thought. "But if we catch Pierce, I'm certain he'll have more information for us."

"That's an excellent idea." Mother rolls to her feet. "What are we waiting for?"

"But we don't know where he is," Armina says. She keeps patting her thigh.

"I have a few ideas for where to start," Renn says, "although most of them are difficult to get to. Guards—if there are any still manning their stations—locked doors . . . though those don't seem much of a problem for Canto."

Mother smiles at me. "So, you still have my grandfather's pendant?"

My hand falls to my coat pocket, and I withdraw the hunk of metal. It's as much a void in my palm as the cube is in the room. A tiny bead of blood wells up where one of its spindles pricks my finger. "The pendant is unlocking the doors? How is that possible?"

"Because Perishing is *ours*." She smiles and grabs my hand. "I've told you about it a thousand times. My childhood home. A city built for mages."

"*What?*" Renn and I say at the same time.

I meet his horrified confusion and say, "But . . . but mages have been captive for *centuries*."

"Don't be silly. Of course we haven't."

I glance at Renn, who looks a little ill, and Armina, who frowns. "Wait," I ask. "Did you know?"

"Pierce told me," Armina mutters. "I didn't know whether to believe him."

My cheeks warm. "The Huntsmen in the Community said mages had been living under their rule for hundreds of years."

"The Huntsmen told you all sorts of things, sweetness," Mother says. "You certainly never believed *me* when I tried to tell you otherwise. Seeing Perishing now, do you really think the Huntsmen capable of building such a city? Towers of shining black absorbing the setting sun. It used to be a bastion, a beacon. Thirty-two years ago, the Huntsmen, united under Huntsmaster Mason, attacked us. My grandfather, Perishing's last magistrate, died defending it. Collapsed half the cliff face along with himself, hoping to bury the invaders."

"And the pendant?" I ask.

"It's the key. The key to the whole city. Not a door here it can't unlock, not even ones the Huntsmen installed after their takeover. The magic resonates, see?" Mother reaches out and curls my fingers closed around it. "Blood on blood on blood. It belongs to you."

"Belongs to me." I feel an unpleasant wetness on my palm.

Mother pulls me close. As she does, the hand holding the pendant presses against my chest, over my heart.

"I'm so glad you kept it safe," she whispers. "It'll unlock more than doors for us, after all."

"We should start moving." Renn looks perturbed, his eyes glued to the black stain growing over the red wool of my coat. "The longer we wait, the more time the Huntsmen have to regroup and strategize."

"Yes, of course." Mother loops her arm through mine and smiles. "Lead the way."

As we exit the room, a confusion of feelings mixes inside me: relief at my mother being with me again, curiosity at what mage society once was only a generation ago, and a sickening dread that the other pleasant emotions can't squash.

Perishing is ours. But some part of me worries that it's been too badly tainted over the years by all the bloodshed.

I take a moment to shove the pendant into my boot. I'm getting tired of cutting myself open every time I stick my hand into my pocket.

We climb the narrow staircase, and Renn turns his head to whisper. "Most likely, Pierce will be observing the proceedings from somewhere he can issue direct orders and where his marshals can rapidly deliver him news." We crest the top of the stairs, and Renn leads us down a hall on the left. "If I had to venture a guess, I'd say he's probably—"

An arm slides around my stomach and lifts me into the air, preventing me from hearing the end of his sentence. My constellation book tumbles from my grasp and slides toward the wall. A hand claps over my mouth, but I sink my teeth into flesh until I taste blood. The person jerks their hand away, and I scream, "Renn!"

But Renn is preoccupied. Five Huntsmen stand in the hall. One holds me. One tussles with my mother, who has stabbed her pen into his side. Two more have Armina crowded against a wall.

The final Huntswoman stands before Renn, sword clutched in her freckled hand. Her short, dark hair curls around her ears, and she has a smear of black blood running down the corner of her mouth.

"Mason," she purrs, licking her lip clean. "I'm going to make you bleed."

27
RENN

I guess I thought we won.

Not that I imagined the rest would be easy, but things looked like they were heading in our favor. The Huntsmen are distracted. I know the lay of our territory within Perishing, regardless of whether or not it's always been *ours*. Canto's book is a weapon more dangerous than any I've seen, and Armina can kill with a drop of her own blood. We've rescued Calliope. We know Pierce is cornered and distracted somewhere in the building. The hardest part is supposed to be over.

But if I look away from Iverson's face, she'll kill me.

Behind me, Canto swears and scuffles with the Huntsman holding them.

Iverson rolls her eyes. "It's one mage, Garrick. They're scrawnier than you by half. And you," she snaps at the Huntsman wrangling Calliope. "Just pick her up."

The Huntsman does as he's told, although Calliope makes him work for it. Her fingernails dig into flesh, and she kicks, punches, bites. She's muttering something about arteries and pressure points as she drives her pen deeper into his side. Eventually, the Huntsman fists his hand into her short hair and hits her so hard I feel my own teeth rattle. Her nose erupts in a fountain of black blood.

Is this what the Huntsmen are? Is this what we've always been?

Canto screams, and the fighting behind me grows louder. Armina tries to duck between the arms of her captors, but they sweep her legs out, and she crashes to the ground.

"Careful with that one," Iverson says. "Not sure how, but I saw her kill a man without a word."

The Huntsman finally subdues Calliope with her arms gripped tight behind her back. He wipes her blood off his face with his free hand and licks it, then marches her behind me.

I hear Canto, but I can't turn around to look at them. I can't reassure them. For all my collected knowledge, for all my carefully crafted confidence and nonchalance, I am utterly unprepared for the wrench in my gut when they scream my name for help.

"Pierce is in the observatory," Iverson snaps. "Take them there and wait. I'll be right along—I'm more than a match for Mason." She catches my eye again and smiles. "Pierce sent us to collect the captain and the prisoner. Thank you for gathering them for us. It leaves me free to kill you."

The hall grows silent as Calliope and Canto are dragged away. The remaining Huntsmen—Barrowe and Hayes, two of Iverson's favorites—have Armina pinned against the ground. They're not exactly gentle with her, but they aren't using enough force to cause any damage. If they just made her bleed a bit—

Iverson swings her sword at me, and I barely move in time as it whistles through the air.

"You're awful quiet, Mason. That isn't very fun. Would you like to hear how much your father bitched when we took *him* in? Maybe that'll rile you up." She thrusts her sword. I dodge, and the blade strikes the marble wall and skitters off. "Kicked up a fuss when he realized there was no coming back from the coup. Sure, he killed a whole lot of us before we took him down. But we did take him down."

"My father"—I pull my sword from my belt before her blade can bite my hand—"never destroyed the Prickweed Pine Community. That charge was entirely fabricated. Either that, or it was perpetrated by Pierce. You're loyal to the wrong man."

"Whyever would you think I'm loyal to Pierce?" Iverson asks. "Because I helped him stage his coup? Please, Mason. I, like all Huntsmen, am loyal to *power*."

I block one of her strikes, but the force behind it is enough to send me stumbling back. I spot Armina struggling against the boot pressing her to the floor and note the wild gleam in her eyes. Whatever she has planned, I hope she gets to it soon.

"Then why betray my father? He had plenty of power—"

"*Magic* is power, kid." Iverson laughs and hops away from me as I slash at her. "The people who control it control the world. Your father knew that. I know that. Pierce knows it better than anyone. I suspect deep down, past your stuffy optimism and your file folders, you know it too. If I could carve out a little of that for myself—control the man who controls the power—why wouldn't I take the opportunity?"

I feel the pain before I register it happening. The edge of her blade catches my side, embedding itself in the flesh in a stripe of agony. Then she rips it out, and the pain flares tenfold, along with an intense heat and the wetness of blood.

"Where shall I cut you next?" she asks.

I deflect her blow, but barely. Whenever I so much as twitch my torso, the pain blazes anew. I go on the offensive, trying to keep my strikes powerful and controlled, and she parries and blocks with a casual looseness to her limbs. Like we're training together. Or playing a game.

"You'd make a better Huntsmaster than Pierce, I won't deny that," she says. "You're adorably committed to the fiction your father sold the general populace." She slides to a stop, lowers her sword. "We could work together if you want. Stop the pathetic tantrum taking place in the Community and arrest Pierce for letting it happen. You could be Huntsmaster. Follow in your father's footsteps."

"I'm not—"

"You are," she hisses. "You very, very much are. We both know you'd do anything to go back to the way things were. Anything for a bit more power. Anything for *control*."

She isn't wrong.

I want to go back to a year ago: Perishing's familiar halls, my quiet library, my father's office full of life and color. I would give anything to talk to him again, to hear the truth from his mouth. The Huntsmen are not supposed to be this way— violent, murderous, cruel. We're supposed to be a force for peace. We're supposed to protect.

My paperwork this past year has been the same as always. Mages come and go through Perishing. They join the Community. They face trial. There are executions and births and intakes and deaths, all outlined in black ink on white paper, and it never, ever changes.

I think of the crumbled boulders at the base of the mountain, the destroyed side of Perishing that we've tried unsuccessfully to patch over the years. The labyrinthine halls full of empty, moldering rooms. The mageblade in my hand. The pristine whiteness of the isolation chamber and the black cube inside. One thousand two hundred and sixty-eight bodies.

This is not a problem that started with Pierce.

Iverson swings at me again, and I bring my blade up too slow. As her sword scrapes across my arm, my vision blurs in and out of focus.

What do I want? Not this. Not *knowing*. I used to think I knew everything, but now I sorely wish I didn't. I want to return to the comfortable lies my father sold me. To my own sense of superiority. I wish I'd never gone after Armina. I wish I'd never met Canto.

But I did, and I have, and now there's no comfort left.

"Come on, Mason." Iverson twists her hand and slams the pommel of her blade into my upper arm, snapping me awake. "I'm offering you the chance of a lifetime: revenge, and the opportunity to step right back into the role your father planned for you. You can doll Perishing up however you want, make it all pretty and harmonious or whatever sad sap shit you pine over."

It's probably all I'm good for: following orders.

She grins as she lowers her sword once more. "You can repair his legacy. Make him proud."

He would have loved to see me as Huntsmaster. He would have loved for me to pick up the mantle. I think of us sitting together on the parapet, legs swinging over the void.

It's yours, he said. *All of it*.

But that was a dream.

There's a shout behind us. Armina has managed to wiggle her arms out of her loose coat sleeves and slip her hands under her enough to shove the Huntsmen away. She pushes off the ground, and Hayes lunges for her, but he slips on her discarded coat and falls to one knee. Armina throws herself toward Hayes's sword, but as her palm touches the blade, Barrowe aims a kick at her stomach that launches her away. Then Barrowe crumples.

Armina wails in pain as she crashes to the tile. She clutches her leg, panting, but a moment later looks at me with a savage grin. She holds up one shaking hand, which has a thin slice clean across the palm, a perforated cut with the barest hint of red.

"I'm not my father," Armina says as she struggles to her feet. "And you aren't yours."

"What are you *doing*?" Iverson snaps at Hayes. She turns back to me, teeth bared. "Change of plans." She drives her sword toward my chest.

I'm not my father. It's like a moment ago, I was being crushed beneath the mountain, and I suddenly remembered how to dig myself free. My father's legacy, his mistakes, his crimes and cruelties—they aren't mine. I'm not beholden to them, and I never was.

There's still time for me to make a different choice.

I bat away Iverson's sword and follow through with my own strike. Armina scrabbles out of Hayes's reach as he gropes toward her. She snatches her coat off the ground.

"You're . . . a fucking . . . waste." Iverson catches my blade with her own and leans into the strike. "You had all that power force-fed to you, and still you weep and wallow and hide yourself away so you don't have to see the truth. You pretend it's nobility, but in reality, it's *cowardice*."

"You're right." I jump back from her blade, and in that moment, Armina lunges. She loops her coat around Iverson's throat and yanks her backward. Iverson chokes and drops her sword to claw at the offending fabric. I take the opportunity to thrust my own sword through her chest.

Armina leaps out of the way at the last moment, pulling her coat with her. I shove Iverson until, with a final burst of effort, my sword punctures her back and cracks the marble wall behind her.

She hangs there a moment. Her eyes fall on the blade sticking through her ribcage, then a bubble of blood bursts from her mouth and dribbles down her chin. She slumps against the wall and slides to the ground.

Hayes—who seems to have regained his wits—freezes, his mouth agape at the sight of Iverson's body. I scoop up Iverson's discarded sword and take a step toward him, but he turns tail and flees.

Armina puts on her coat. She steps over to Barrowe's body, then unsheathes his sword and shoves it into her belt. It's hard not to stare at her as she crouches and rifles through his clothes. My heart leaps and screams, and the adrenaline might pound my head apart, but she pulls out coins and lint from Barrowe's pockets with the same focus as someone digging up rocks to skip across a lake. Every time her weight shifts to her false leg, she winces, and when she stands and looks down the hall, she rubs a stiff hand over her hip.

"Iverson said they're in an observatory? You can lead us there, right?"

"Of course I can. I'm glad she confirmed it, but the observatory's one of the first places I would have checked anyway. It has an overview of the entire—" I pause. Actions now. No more hiding. "Let's go."

I retrieve my sword from Iverson's body before leading Armina deeper into the building. My fingers find and probe the wound on my torso. While it's painful and bleeding more than I'd like, it's also fairly shallow. Something to worry about later, after all this is done.

Our footsteps echo in the empty halls of Perishing's underworld, the rest of its inhabitants and assailants far off above us. The echo is the same as always, just as Perishing is the same—incomprehensible, strange, empty, familiar.

I cannot be the Huntsmaster here; I cannot stitch together the mess my father left behind. But Perishing is still my home. No one knows its secrets quite like I do.

At least, none of the Huntsmen.

28

CANTO

Maybe I *will* die in a Community.

The Huntsmen drag my mother and me through Perishing's endless halls. I see fighting in my peripheral vision as we pass, hear screaming and shouting, but I am doing my own screaming and shouting and do not have time to register someone else's pain. The Huntsman carrying me has me thrown over his shoulder. The one tugging my mother along has her forearm in an iron grip. Blood patters the ground where it drips from her nose.

They carry us up several flights of stone steps before finally arriving at a plain wooden door. My Huntsman throws it open and yanks us into the room.

It's circular, perhaps one of the city's spires. The black walls are crumbling in places, and the ceiling opens to the dusky sky. Ivy and moss crawl down the stone walls alongside mold and the remnants of bird nests. Rotting books carpet the ground, and what might have once been a rug but is now so threadbare and weatherworn that it more resembles dirt. There are a few chairs in one corner, but otherwise, no furniture.

A rickety set of stairs curls along the inside wall, beneath which sits a single wooden door that must open onto the rampart. The stairs end in a platform, and on that platform sits an enormous, blackened telescope. It points not at the heavens, but at the ground far below.

Pierce pulls his eye away from it when we enter.

With a loud thump, he hops down from his perch and strides toward us. I struggle and push against my Huntsman's grip, but he laughs and shifts me higher onto his shoulder.

"Let us go," I spit at Pierce as he crosses to stand in front of my mother's face. "Haven't you done—"

"Enough," Pierce says. "No more fighting, no more arguing, no more nitpicking and babbling. You have no rights and no power, and you are going to do as I say."

Mother laughs. "You have nothing left to bargain with. You have taken my freedom, my magic, and my city. You've taken my best friend and killed my love. You even tried to take my notebook—and I'll point out you weren't very successful—"

"You fail to understand," Pierce hisses, "that there is no rock bottom. There are always greater depths to which you can sink." He gestures to my Huntsman.

The Huntsman crosses the room and throws me into a chair, then kneels on my thighs to keep me seated as he tugs open the buttons on my red-wool coat. He pulls it off and tosses it aside, then lifts the straps connected to the armrests and cuffs me to them.

A bloodletting chair. My stomach lurches. I try to pull away, but he buckles me tight. He stoops to cuff my legs, and before I can kick his face, he grabs my ankle and forces it against the chair leg. When my feet are properly strapped, he stands, resting his hand on my shoulder to keep my magic at bay.

No, no, no, no. This can't be happening. They can't take this from me again. I've fought too hard.

My mother wails and lashes out at the Huntsman holding her, but both of our magic is blocked, and there's little we can do against this unstoppable force. I see the calculations racing through her mind as if they're projected on a screen before me. A dozen threads she's following, each one ending in failure.

"This isn't a hostage situation," she says, shoving against the Huntsman's arms. Through the streaked blood, her lips quiver. "You're going to do as you please to us, and no level of obedience will change your mind. You will not get your enchantment from me, Huntsmaster."

Pierce stares at her, and then his mouth curls into something so much crueler than a smile. He crosses the room and reaches behind my chair, bracing himself on my arm as if trying to break it. The Huntsman holding me bows slightly and retreats toward his fellow, grabbing my mother's other arm and helping hold her upright.

Pierce retrieves a wooden box and takes a seat on a folding chair directly beside my own. "You're good with numbers, Keer." My mother and I watch his hands as he removes the coiled tube, the needle, all while keeping his arm pressed against my own. "Tell me: how much blood do the Huntsmen typically draw from the Community mages?"

My mother's fingers curl against the Huntsman's sleeve. "A pint every month."

He nods along to her voice as he removes a plastic bag from the container. It's several times the size of the average blood bag, and I yank against my restraints as he calmly unfolds it and connects it to one of the coiled tubes. He hangs it on a hook at the side of the chair. "And how long would you say that process takes?"

Her lips barely move as he connects the needle to the other end of the tubing. "Fifteen minutes."

"Right. That's a good estimate." Pierce takes a strap out of the box and ties it to my upper arm. He knots it tight enough that my pulse pounds in my elbow. "How many pints of blood does a person have in their body?"

"It depends on several factors. I can't—"

"An average will do."

She swallows. "Ten."

He pats the crux of my arm, feeling for a vein. I try to pull away, but his free hand holds me still. "How many can a person lose before they die?"

My mother doesn't respond.

"Forty percent, give or take," Pierce answers for her. He spreads his fingers to frame the vein he's found. With expert precision, he slides the needle into my skin. In a moment, black blood oozes into the tube and begins dripping toward the bag. Then he unties the tourniquet, and the blood flows free. "So it will take your child about an hour to die." He folds his hands between his knees. "I hope you don't mind waiting."

I thought that, reunited, nothing could scare me anymore. But my pounding heartbeat is quickening the blood flow because I am terrified.

I am a child again at my first bloodletting—and at my second, and at my hundredth. I'm in a dark room, and there's a Huntsman by my side, and I feel the steady draw of blood from my veins. But this blood isn't mine. It has never belonged to me: it's just a thing that keeps me going until the Huntsmen decide for me to stop.

"I haven't attended an exsanguination since Richard Mason's." Pierce shakes the coiled tube to ensure the blood flows unimpeded to the bag. "I typically find them dull, but the occasional exception must be made. We need blood for our experiment, don't we? It's more expeditious to take it from a single source, especially with all the fuss going on below."

My mother's breathing has turned to pants. Her eyes are wide, and she's looking everywhere, at everything. Looking for a way to escape her captors, a way to rescue me. But even if this room were as full of treasures as the *Blackblood*, there would be little she could do. Math and magic can't save us.

The minutes slip onward, and I begin to lose feeling in my arm. My head spins, and I close my eyes, trying to keep my breathing and pulse even. The only noise I hear is the steady drip of blood, which initially sounded like water striking plastic and now sounds like water striking water.

"She won't help you." I grit my teeth against the growing panic. "Armina."

Pierce shrugs. "Then I'll kill another mage. I'll keep draining them until she sees that her protests are pointless. That thing on her leg will kill her eventually, but if she refuses me, then I'll make sure her resistance kills every mage in Perishing first."

"Is this really about your enchantment?" *Plip, plip.* "Or is this about Averard?"

The sun is setting over Perishing, striking the walls with a golden light that is immediately absorbed by all the black.

"Not everything has to be about Averard," Pierce says.

Stars begin to prick the sky, and the first I notice is the eye of the now-familiar Skeletal Mare. It winks down at me, and I remember Armina saying that it was the goddess of death. I almost laugh, and my vision swims. "You people act like it does."

Pierce stands. He places one hand on either arm of my chair and looms over me. "One pint down."

He pushes away and crosses the room, and my fingers grip the chair's arms. *Enchant*, I beg the magic sluggishly flowing back into my limbs. But even as I try to summon power to my fingertips, it ebbs away in the direction of the blood bag. My head spins again.

Pierce grabs my mother by her elbow, and his Huntsmen guards drop her. She gasps in pain as he drags her upright.

"If you agree to these experiments, all this will stop. I will remove the needle and use another mage's blood for the spell."

My mother isn't an overtly emotional person—she has always taken things in her stride. She isn't even afraid of death; I'm not sure she knows how to be. But right now, tears prick in the corners of her eyes, making me wish I were already dead.

"You don't obey the Huntsmen anymore, Mother," I remind her.

Her mouth stops trembling.

Pierce lifts her higher, and her shoulder audibly pops. She gasps, her fingers grasping at the air as she tries to keep herself from crying out.

"Fine then," Pierce says. "I chose you for your knowledge of the Wanderer's magic, but I have thousands of mages capable of performing this experiment, many of whom would do anything for a little taste of freedom. You've just assured that your child's death will mean as little to the world as Averard's."

The room's door reverberates with a *crack*. It comes again, and the doorknob rattles.

Pierce whips around, brows furrowed, and gestures for his Huntsmen to investigate. They draw their swords, but before they can grab the knob, the door flies open. In a flurry of black blades, Armina leaps onto one of the Huntsmen, her boots hitting his torso and driving him to the ground as she buries a mageblade in his chest. Renn slices easily through the second guard's throat, and the pair stand above the corpses, chests heaving and faces freckled with red blood.

Armina's eyes sweep over the situation, and when she spots me, she lunges toward the chair.

Pierce, having presumably recovered from his initial shock, drops my mother and lurches toward Armina, but he has to fall away when she lashes out at him with her sword.

"Back off." She lifts the blade and shifts to stand between Pierce and me.

"Armina," he begins, but he jumps back when she swings again.

I hear the scrape of a sword being drawn, the ring of metal clashing, but it's all wiped from my vision when Renn appears before me.

I try to stay still as he rummages through the box at the side of the chair. He folds a square of gauze above the needle before pulling it from my vein. Relief floods my arm, circulation and magic slowly returning. Then Renn tapes the gauze to my skin and releases my bound hands.

"I'm sorry." He says it over and over as he undoes all the straps, to the point where I no longer know what he's apologizing for. The moment I'm free, I stand, then proceed to stumble. He catches me, and I lean my forehead against his chest. I try not to look at the swollen bag of blood still hooked to the chair.

"You should stay seated." Renn's hand steadies me by my elbow.

I glare at him. His lips quirk into a smile before he turns so we can both see the scene unfolding behind us. Armina and Pierce fight in periodic swings and sword thrusts—though Pierce lifts his sword only for the sake of blocking her clumsy attacks and otherwise stands his ground. Armina's shirtfront is coated in sweat, and she slams her sword once more against Pierce's.

He bats it away. "Stop this at once."

"I don't take orders from murderers." She tries to dart around Pierce to slice him in the side, but he follows her movement with ease.

"I can *save you*."

"No, you can't. All you've done is kill my only family, and now you're trying to kill . . ." She trails off, then jumps back, sword still raised. "Where is my mother, Pierce? Where is Kestrel?"

Pierce wipes the sweat off his forehead with his arm. "If I could reach her, do you really think I'd be wasting my time with you?"

Armina's shoulders tense. "Is she dead?"

"I don't know." Pierce's eyes flick to Renn. "She was present at the Community Richard Mason destroyed."

Renn takes a step away from me. I sway and grab the arm of the bloodletting chair to remain upright.

"My father didn't destroy that Community," he snarls.

"Well, someone did," Pierce says. "And Mason was certainly adamant that I never be allowed to see her. He's the one who stopped me from getting her help earlier. He's the reason for this." Pierce tugs open the top few buttons of his shirt, revealing the tarnished skin that runs from his collar and down, down his chest. "It used to be a handprint. Mason thought I wanted information on where Averard had disappeared to, that I had some revenge fantasy. Of course, I couldn't tell him the true reason I needed to see the Wanderer—an enchantment is a death sentence in the eyes of the Huntsmen."

"That isn't my father's fault."

"Your father *was* the Huntsmen. Of course it was his fault."

Renn lets out a growl of frustration and throws himself toward Pierce.

Alone again, the urge to crash back into the chair is staggering, but I stumble across the room toward my mother. I kneel beside her, and then her hands are upon me, on my shoulders and face and elbows.

"Canto," she breathes. "I didn't know what to do; I—"

"You did the right thing." I lean into her touch as her fingers tangle the strands of my hair and try to pet the pain away.

Pierce laughs as he turns out of Renn's strike and makes one of his own. "You're not half the swordsman your father was."

Renn blocks the blow. "I was good enough to kill Iverson."

The smirk plummets from Pierce's face. "If you killed Iverson, it wasn't due to your skill."

Armina tries to find her own opening into Renn and Pierce's battle, but Pierce manages to keep both within his sight. Renn darts in and snags Pierce's shirt with the edge of his blade, but Pierce recovers quickly enough to throw his arm back and catch Renn's jaw with the pommel of his sword. Renn staggers, spitting blood onto the floor, which leaves Armina to attack Pierce alone.

Pierce dodges her blows without lifting his own blade. "Armina." It almost sounds pleading. "This is a waste of energy that could be better spent on less trivial matters."

"Shut up." Armina's grip on her sword is so tight that it turns her knuckles a greenish white.

"Things could have been different if Averard had stayed. We could have cured our enchantments and created a new, better Order together—"

"*Excuse me*?" she demands. "Whatever you were to Averard before, it doesn't matter now. You could've abandoned Perishing with him, and I bet Averard would've welcomed you back with open arms. He would've done anything to help fix your enchantment. You stayed here because you *like* the power. Because you like being a monster."

Pierce opens his mouth to reply but is forced back when Renn's sword arcs through the air once more. Pierce throws up his own blade to block, but Renn follows through with blow after blow, his anger and weight behind each strike.

"You're *through*," he snarls as Pierce leaps away. "Everything you've done . . . I'm going to undo it. I'm going to make it right."

"You'll have to undo your father's legacy before you can even touch mine." Pierce sweeps his sword down to force Renn back, but Renn dodges and plows forward.

"I'm going to make it right," he repeats.

Renn's eyes are trained on Pierce's serious, stony face. He gets so, so close.

Then Pierce turns and, with a twist of his wrist, buries his sword in Renn's stomach.

Renn makes a choking noise as he falls.

It's like the world stops. The Skeletal Mare stares down at us from above, but now the full scope of her constellation has come into view. My mother's hand flies to her mouth. Pierce's chest heaves.

I lurch forward.

Pierce makes no move to prevent my approach. Instead, he lowers his sword and steps away, shoulders meeting the door beneath the stairs as he catches his breath. He wipes his wrist across his mouth.

I kneel beside Renn. He's patting the hole in his stomach with a look of utter bewilderment, and he turns to stare at me with incredulous eyes. Then he collapses on his side in a heap, red, red blood pooling around him. It spreads far enough to begin soaking into the knee of my pants before I gasp awake and grab him.

I ease his head onto my thighs, unsure how much it's okay to move him and what will make things worse. He convulses, and I grip his shirtfront. The jagged hole doesn't look like much, but its placement is bad, through the main section of his abdomen. It's impossible the blade didn't hit anything vital.

"Renn." My hands touch his stomach, and it spasms. "What do I do?"

He doesn't answer.

I look around, desperate for someone to tell me how to proceed. My mother has her fingers pressed over her lips and is staring at the hole in Renn's stomach, but Armina meets my eyes. With a roar of fury, she rushes Pierce once more.

She doesn't know how to wield a sword any better than I do. That was apparent before, and it's more obvious now. She swings her blade at Pierce's chest, and he moves smoothly out of the way. Then she swings again.

The world is quiet aside from Renn's shallow breathing and Armina's furious pants.

"Why're you doing this?" she snarls. "Why're you taking everything from me?"

"What are you talking about?" Pierce's voice has gone cold. "Renn Mason? A Huntsman who cares more about his papers than his people, the one I sent to *arrest* you? He can't possibly mean anything to you."

"You sent him to the *Blackblood*!" she shouts. "And I kept him, so he's a member of my crew now. I protect my crew!"

Armina shoves her way into Pierce's space, so close that he's pressed back against the door. Her blade meets his, flush against his chest, and he strains as he tries to keep her from pushing further. His chest expands with his staggered breathing.

"Are you going to kill me?" he demands.

In my arms, Renn is dying.

I feel an odd tugging sensation on my leg, and I glance over my shoulder while still trying to keep Renn in my sights. Behind me, my mother's hand pulls away from my boot.

She's clutching the key to Perishing between her fingers.

"Kill me, then," Pierce says.

My mother's hand tightens around the metal.

"You won't do it," he continues. "What good would I be to you dead?"

Black blood wells around her fingers. It overflows.

Armina's shoulders shake. "I never wanted any of this."

My mother presses her bleeding palm to the floor.

The black soaks into the moldering rug, into the grooves between the stones. It seeps deeper into all the black and magic stitching Perishing together.

Then the door behind Pierce flies open, and he and Armina tumble onto the rampart.

Or rather, what's left of it. In the gathering dark, I notice that part of the parapet has crumbled, leaving an open void that empties out a hundred feet above the ground. Pierce pitches partway over it, but he catches onto Armina's sleeve at the last second. His feet find purchase on the stone wall, but most of his weight is on Armina. Her body has wedged itself against what remains of the parapet, but with every inching second, Pierce drags her further and further over the edge.

A chorus of voices roar from below, and I imagine mages looking up, pointing at the dangling body of the Huntsmaster. I clutch Renn tighter, and he groans weakly in my arms. I don't know what to do. I'm afraid if I stop holding him, he'll stop breathing, even though I know somewhere in the back of my mind that doesn't make any sense. But I need to help Armina; I—

"Armina!" Pierce calls. There's a panicked edge to his voice that echoes the feeling in my gut. *Pull me up.*

Her muscles strain to keep her from plunging over the rampart with him. The leather of her sleeve is taut, but the seams don't tear beneath Pierce's weight. He tries to drag himself upward, but to no avail—the motion causes him to slip further, and a crack spiders down the section of parapet holding Armina steady.

At any moment, she could fall.

"Your Averard's daughter, aren't you?" Pierce demands. One of his boots slips, and Armina is pulled closer to the edge. "He would want you to save me. He would *tell* you it's the right thing to do."

The wind whips Armina's hair around her head, and her teeth clench. Her eyes meet the sky where the stars bear down.

"I am Averard's daughter," she says quietly. "But I'm not Averard. And maybe some people are better off dead."

She turns her body, makes herself small, and slips the coat off her shoulders.

Pierce goes tumbling with it into the dark.

The sound from the crowd below crescendos, then comes an agonizing silence.

I feel—distantly, like it's part of someone else's dream—a hand tug at my shirt. Renn gazes up at me, his lips pale, his eyes wide and searching. He pulls my sleeve harder, and I see his mouth moving, whispering something.

I lean in to listen.

"I'm sorry," he says. "About Georgian and Kateryna. And about the mage by the wall. And the mageblade. And . . . I'm sorry; I—" His entire body shudders.

"Why are you apologizing to me?" I ask, somewhat hysterically. "Apologize to *them*."

He shakes his head. "Going to die," he mumbles. "It's okay."

Death is inevitable. But death *now* is not. Not yet, not when I haven't figured out how to properly forgive him. Not when he showed so many signs of wanting to grow. People shouldn't be allowed to stop halfway. I won't allow it.

I roll him off my lap and stand. Armina limps back into the room, arms wrapped around her chest, but she's alive and safe and whole, and I will devote time to worrying about her later. I approach the chair where Pierce tried to kill me and rip the blood bag off its hook. Then I return to Renn's side and gather him up again.

He glares at me. "Won't you let a man die in peace?" These words appear to take considerably more effort than the last, and his shoulders seize once they're fully formed.

"What kind of Huntsman can't heal from a simple stab wound?" I rip a gash in the bag with my teeth.

He cracks a smile at that. "Most of us, when it tears through our stomachs."

I don't let him keep talking. I tug open his jaw and dump my blood into his mouth. He chokes, but I pour until the blood overflows his jaw, pour until I see him swallow, pour until inky blackness burbles from the wound in his stomach along with the red. Then I toss the bag aside and press my hands against him.

No mage would try this. Not even in a matter of life and death.

"Canto." Mother's hand falls on my shoulder. There's no time to look into her face, but I know the disapproval that must be written there. "Wait a moment. Don't you think he'd rather die than—"

"I don't *care* what he wants!" My hands press harder on Renn's chest even as all that blood slicks my palms. "This isn't about him!"

I lean my forehead against Renn's side. Concentrate; I have to concentrate. Just because no one does this doesn't mean it's impossible. Renn *can't* die. Not while I'm around.

Someone kneels beside me. I risk looking up and see Armina's face. Always present, always steady, even when everything is falling apart, even when she almost died. Her hands reach out to cover mine on Renn's stomach, and together, we hold in the blood.

I breathe. In. Out. Her breath matches mine, and although she cannot enchant, this does feel like a certain kind of magic. I close my eyes and begin.

29

ARMINA

I have a coat that fits now.

While I was helping the mages round up and treat the injured, Calliope pulled me aside. She had a square of black fabric folded in her hands and an uncertain smile on her face.

"I'm sorry, but in all the mess, I wasn't able to find Averard's coat." She held out her bundle toward me, pushed it into my hands. "I hope this is a suitable substitute. I enchanted it myself."

It's got a solid leather shell with a lining of soft wool. It's shorter than my last one—more a jacket than a coat, really—but it's been enchanted to always keep a comfortable temperature. Enchanted to be cut resistant, too. Not that I'm looking to get stabbed again.

There are no rips in it, no blood. When I pulled it onto my shoulders for the first time and realized I wouldn't need to roll up the sleeves to use my hands, I felt a strange swoop in my gut, sorta like vertigo.

It isn't the same. It's not Averard's.

But I think it suits me better.

It's been four days since the mages took Perishing, and I've barely gotten a lick of sleep. We've spent most of that time helping the mages find bodies and root out hiding Huntsmen. I think we've captured most of them now—the ones who weren't able to escape, at least—but Perishing's a big place, and a lot of the mages are too young to remember how to navigate it. If any Huntsmen are still tucked away in one of the numerous rooms, I suspect they'll be dragged to the prisons soon enough.

I'm sitting in the observatory, feet swinging above the abyss, waiting for the sun to set. The room's still a mess, but I've taken a little time each day to clear it. The chairs are gone, as are the molding carpet and the rotting books. No matter how much I sweep and scrub the stone, though, I can't seem to get the bloodstain at the center out.

The sun's golden aura has retreated beneath the mountain's treetops when I hear the door open. I don't need to look back to know who it is—the sound of their footsteps on the creaky stairs is familiar enough. When Canto folds themself beside me, I nudge them with my elbow. They nudge back.

For all I've been busy these past few days, Canto's had it worse. Calliope's taken charge of Perishing for now, and she's needed to sign off on every decision the city makes. Trials, communications, repairs—she appears to enjoy the work, but she's got this tendency to run off with an idea and not come around to a point. I think Canto's the only one who's kept her on target, but it's wearing them ragged.

Canto flops onto their back. They gesture to a constellation beginning to form above us. "That group there . . . is it half of the Twins? They're the highest gods, right?"

I squint at the sky. "Yeah, that's the Brother—see how his hand holds the end of the Magistrate's Branches?" I gesture to the webbed constellation that flows out from one point. "The Sister will be on his other side, but she doesn't appear until it's properly dark. And yes, they're the highest gods, so they preside over the realms of Everything and Nothing."

"That's a lot of responsibility."

I shrug and glance down at the ground. One hundred feet below, I can still see the *Blackblood's* tire tracks if I squint. "No more than the rest of us have."

Valaina's long gone by now, to Y'ashtria or the Tidal Wall or across the ocean on some new adventure. The *Blackblood's* long gone with her, and if I ever see it again, I know it won't be the same. Home has to be something new now. Family has to be something new. The things Averard left behind fell apart in his absence, and there are still holes in me that need mending. But as Canto and I watch the sky darken and flare to life with pinpricks of light, I think I might have the beginnings of something here. Something that could be wonderful. So I'll cultivate it for a while. See what grows.

Canto points out each of the shining pantheon as they come into view, and I tell them little stories—tales told to me by Averard that could've been Canto's, too, had things gone different. But I think the pair of us are tired of wishing for an alternate past, so tonight, we don't wallow. I point out the Resplendent Fox, and Canto asks about her instead.

When the door swings open again, neither of us acknowledge it. When the person walks up the stairs, sits at our side, and looks at the stars, we remain quiet. It's only when he reminds us he exists by speaking that we come down from the heavens and allow ourselves to remember.

"Anything good up there?" Renn asks.

He's looking kind of handsomely ruffled, like maybe he took a long bath and then went for a windswept walk to dry his hair. Every time he moves, he winces a bit, which I imagine is a consequence of the almost dying.

Another consequence is the blackened print over his stomach, shaped like Canto's hands.

Canto rolls onto their side and stares up at Renn, chin perched on their palm. "You're supposed to be resting," they say, "not climbing to the top of Perishing's tallest turret."

"I find this restful, actually. The mages working the medical bay don't like me anyway, even though I'm very nice and accommodating."

"I heard the mages here tend to be distrustful of Huntsmen. No idea why."

We settle into a silence I'd almost describe as companionable if it weren't for the fact that the pair of them are using me like a screen, keeping uncomfortable questions at bay.

When we brought Renn back from the brink of death, when we peeled away our hands and Canto saw that mark, they started sobbing. I almost did too—I could feel the horror of it sparking in my own blackened enchantment. Whatever Canto did was more than just healing, more than just closing up wounds and knitting together blood vessels. Canto had poured something else into Renn. Some stray feeling. Stray sentiment.

Problem is, Canto was in no fit state at the time to be conscious about it. They've literally no clue what they've done or how to fix it. They're trying to act normal, but when no one's looking, I'm sure they let themself fall to pieces.

Renn, however, seems none the worse for wear. He's cheerful, and he's been up and about enough to be infuriating. I don't know him all that well yet, but he acts about the same as he did before.

Still, those handprints remain.

I think Renn's pretending he doesn't notice the scarring. In fact, he's mostly been concentrating on *my* enchantment, which has grown well over my hip. We went to the library after things settled down, and while most of the shelves and books had been destroyed, the filing cabinets at least remained intact.

We didn't find a single shred of evidence that Kestrel ever existed.

There's a whole lot of future ahead of me that could be shaped into anything. Paths to follow, mages to free, moms to find. But I'm tired, and the sky is vast, and Canto and Renn are warm and present beside me. Maybe tonight, I don't have to worry about it. The three of us can lie back and enjoy how very small we are in the grand scheme of things.

"What's that one?" Renn asks.

"The Scarred Rabbit," I reply.

"And that?"

"That's just a bunch of stars. They're not all connected, you know."

Renn tucks his arms beneath his head and gets more comfortable. "But they could be."

Yeah, I think as my eyes follow the loose collection of spots he's pointed to. *I guess they could.*

ABOUT THE AUTHOR

Kree Sullivan is a YA author, passionate gamer, and monster lover. She grew up in New Jersey where she gained an appreciation for both the deep dark woods and the deep dark ocean. She holds a master's degree in creative writing from Johns Hopkins University.

She and her partner live in Northern Virginia with their two black cats: Jupiter and Hades.

ACKNOWLEDGEMENTS

First, thank you so much to everyone at Tiny Ghost Press, especially Joshua Dean Perry, for bringing *Blackblood* to life. From the moment I received that acceptance letter (after crying, screaming, and texting everyone I have ever met), I knew the book was in the best hands possible. Together, we made this story shine, and I couldn't be prouder of what we've accomplished. Thank you also to the team, including Reuben Davies-Hoare, Thomas Shah, Lewis Hughes, and Melody Jaikes. Without your hard work and insight, this book would still be a lonely manuscript searching for a home.

I'd like to thank Alexa Sharpe for their gorgeous cover. I have not stopped staring at it since the moment I laid eyes on it.

Thank you Mom and Kimmy, for being there for me during this wild ride. Thanks especially to Mom, who read this book, didn't get it, but loves it anyway. I also appreciate all the support of family and friends who have cheered me on since finding out about my writing journey.

Of course I have to thank the most wonderful ladies I know: Hope Anna Racine, A.M. Sutter, Kate Hyers, and J.C. Smith. I cannot believe how fortunate I was to find and work with you four in the greatest Wednesday critique group the world has ever known. I can't wait to see your books on shelves (especially my shelf, where they will have the highest place of honor).

Thank you to my fabulous beta readers and buddies Laura Eckenrode and Clay Cobb. Your comments and suggestions were fabulous and very, very necessary. I hope you can see your hard work in the pages. Of course thank you to the FFXIV raid group—of which these two are a part—who didn't do anything specific for this book but were a very welcome and loving distraction when needed.

Thank you to my beautiful partner, Gray Sullivan, who never once complained about me talking about this book, whining about this book, crying about this book, or rereading this book out loud. Anything remotely funny in these pages can be attributed to me telling them a joke and them immediately making a funnier one back. They're my rock, my angel, my devil, and the best parent our two silly cats could ask for.

Lastly, thank you to the readers. I appreciate each and every one of you, and I hope you found something to love in Armina, Canto, and Renn's story.

A ROMANCE TO HOWL HOME ABOUT

BOOKS ONE AND TWO IN THE BESTSELLING

THE ALPHA'S SON

SERIES ARE NOW AVAILABLE!

AVAILABLE IN PRINT, EBOOK, & AUDIOBOOK

WWW.TINYGHOSTPRESS.COM
@TINYGHOSTPRESS